Praise for *Shot*

In *Shot*, Jude Berman brings forth a powerful and haunting exploration of gun violence in America in a bold work of short stories that will captivate readers with its thematic unity and vivid prose, leaving readers to ponder what lies beyond the final moments.

—Jennifer Goldsmith, journalist and survivor of two mass shootings

In a poignant collection of twenty-six fictional stories, each victim of a mass shooting shares their final thoughts, dreams, and fears in the moments before tragedy strikes. Through vivid, heartbreaking snapshots, Jude Berman gracefully explores the human cost of gun violence, amplifying voices lost to an epidemic of shootings.

—Heidi Yewman, author of *Beyond the Bullet: Personal Stories of Gun Violence Aftermath*

Jude Berman presents well-crafted stories of individuals of various ages, occupations, and locations whose lives are abruptly impacted by gun violence. *Shot* captivates the reader with the details of each life and leaves us wishing the outcome had been different and knowing, in a different political climate, it could be.

—Marilyn J. Zimmerman, author of *In Defense of Good Women*

Shot delivers a poignant message about the US gun problem. Using fictional characters, Jude Berman does a brilliant job at putting faces and voices to the victims of gun violence. Anyone who cares about humanity and the thousands of firearm deaths annually will want to read this book.

—Julia Hatch, author of *The Very Best of Care*

"We become numb to gun violence because we can't cope with the reality that we or our child could be next. *Shot* helps readers process this helplessness in a human, nonpolitical way. Processing tragedy allows us to begin to protect ourselves. Highly recommended for teens—the generation to take action."

—Bridget Flynn Walker, PhD, author of *Anxiety Relief for Kids: On-the-Spot Strategies to Help Your Child Overcome Worry, Panic, and Avoidance*

"Jude Berman makes us fall in love with everyday people and then breaks our hearts every time by killing them off senselessly. This is how she makes her point, and what a point it is. *Shot* should be required reading for legislators."

—Lori B. Duff, author of *Devil's Defense*

SHOT

SHOT

A DICTIONARY OF THE LOST

Jude Berman

She Writes Press

Copyright © 2025, Jude Berman

All rights reserved. No part of this publication may be reproduced, distributed, or transmitted in any form or by any means, including photocopying, recording, digital scanning, or other electronic or mechanical methods, without the prior written permission of the publisher, except in the case of brief quotations embodied in critical reviews and certain other noncommercial uses permitted by copyright law. For permission requests, please address She Writes Press.

Published 2025
Printed in the United States of America
Print ISBN: 978-1-64742-928-7
E-ISBN: 978-1-64742-929-4
Library of Congress Control Number: 2025900949

For information, address:
She Writes Press
1569 Solano Ave #546
Berkeley, CA 94707

Interior Design by Kiran Spees

She Writes Press is a division of SparkPoint Studio, LLC.

Company and/or product names that are trade names, logos, trademarks, and/or registered trademarks of third parties are the property of their respective owners and are used in this book for purposes of identification and information only under the Fair Use Doctrine.

This is a work of fiction. Names, characters, places, and incidents either are the product of the author's imagination or are used fictitiously. Any resemblance to actual persons, living or dead, is entirely coincidental.

NO AI TRAINING: Without in any way limiting the author's [and publisher's] exclusive rights under copyright, any use of this publication to "train" generative artificial intelligence (AI) technologies to generate text is expressly prohibited. The author reserves all rights to license uses of this work for generative AI training and development of machine learning language models.

Contents

Anna. 1

Benjamin. .10

Chester. 22

Dixie. 30

Edith. 38

Fuji. 50

Ginger 59

Howard 72

Indigo. 80

Jon. 92

Kylor. 102

Li. 107

Moira 117

Nixon. 130

Owen 138

Prema. 152

Quinn 164

Rob 172

Sage. 180

Tex 188

Unity 192

Victor 199

Wanda 210

Xander 215

Yael 221

Zoe 230

Author's Note

I am not, technically speaking, the survivor of a mass shooting. However, due to the epidemic of gun violence in this country, I have come to believe all of us can—and perhaps should—consider ourselves survivors. Unless, of course, we are among those who have not survived.

The purpose of these stories is to give voice to those who did not survive.

On average, 316 people are shot in the United States every day; more than a million have been shot over the past decade. Sixty percent of American adults will experience gun violence (either themselves or through a loved one) in their lifetime. We should be ashamed.

And we should do more. More of us should do more.

Out of respect for the privacy of those who have died from or experienced the trauma of gun violence, these stories are fictional. Really, they're less about other people and more about *you*.

Please note that this book contains depictions of random acts of gun violence. Reader discretion is advised.

Anna

I am Anna and I am a statistic. I was twelve years old when I was shot. I lived with my family in a yellow house in Omaha, Nebraska. I was a straight-A student and wanted to be a scientist when I grew up. My pronouns were she/her. I am survived by my parents, two younger sisters, and our bulldog, Axel.

It's the beginning and it's the middle and it's the end. All at the same time. How could that be? Simple: Today is the last day of classes at the end of my first year in middle school. And of course it's also the beginning of summer, when I'll get to hang out with my friends and sleep in as late as I want.

Beginning, middle, and end coming together—that's the sort of deep-thinking stuff Ms. French wants us to write essays about. *Paradox*, I think she calls it. Or maybe *irony*. I can never keep those two straight. Like, for example, the fact that she teaches English classes for students like me who are headed for the pre-AP track and who everyone says have a bright future, but her name is Ms. French. That's kind of ironic, isn't it?

I'm pretty good at English. I write essays that are clever and essays that are funny. And some that are both clever and funny. Like the one I wrote about AI talking to animals. When I heard about how RoboBees talk to real bees, I thought it was awesome. It made me think I could use AI to talk to animals. Imagine learning to buzz! Or learning whale-speak or pig-speak or any other animal language. Human-speak works okay with Axel, but bulldog-speak would go so much further.

Of course if you aren't careful, it could get weird. Like if you accidentally used cat-speak with your dog. I know Axel would be insulted. I included that example in my essay. Ms. French kept me after class to say she thought it was so brilliant it could have been written by a first-year college student. I mean, wow!

But now, as I pick out clothes for this last day of school, my mind is more on science than English. The Young American Scientist award will be announced at this morning's assembly. I did a project for it, but I don't expect to win. Really, not a chance. Even with all the hype about STEM for girls, it's still tougher for us.

I put on my favorite pink shirt with the ruffled short sleeves and a clean pair of jeans. Then I pull my hair back with my purple dragon hairclip. As I'm checking my outfit in the mirror, making sure the colors match okay, I hear Mom call from the kitchen. Her voice is shrill, like when she wants to make me giddyap so I won't miss the bus.

I sling my backpack over one shoulder and step into my slip-on sneakers. But then I notice the hole in the fabric over the big toe on my left foot. Normally it doesn't bug me. It's actually pretty cool. What wouldn't be cool is if I have to get on stage for an award, and Mom sees a photo of me wearing shabby shoes. Because you know she will. So I exchange them for a pair of white Mary Janes I haven't worn since last summer. Except as soon as I squeeze one foot in, it's obvious they've gotten too tight. Wearing my high-tops isn't an option. Or my hiking boots. So back on go the sneakers. They'll have to do. And I'm out the door and down the stairs and into the kitchen.

Mom gives me her quick once-over, head to toe. Then frowns. In case I can't read her mind, she says, "Is *that* what you're wearing?"

I don't want to admit my dress-up shoes are too small. But if she makes me wear them all day, I know I'll get blisters. All for the sake of an award I'm not winning. "Mom," I object, "it's not like anyone will look at my feet."

She pushes a bowl of cereal and a carton of milk across the counter. "What's the matter with you?"

I pour the milk and start to eat. I'm in for a lecture, so I fix my eyes on the flakes.

It's nothing she hasn't said before: I'm intelligent . . . My experiment was super smart . . . It deserves an award . . . *I* deserve an award . . . I should stop doubting myself . . . Yada, yada, yada. But then she stops short of her usual "I know you can do this, Anna," and says, "*Why* do you always feel you're not good enough?"

It's one of those probing questions parents pull out when they're trying to gain their kid's trust. Except right now I just want to finish my cereal and get to school. We can do our mother-daughter bonding tonight when she's consoling me for not winning the science award. Even though I'll be perfectly fine not winning.

Of course originally I did want to win. Like, bad! I thought I could turn my essay on AI into a science experiment. I'd use AI to talk to Axel. But then I realized AI doesn't know dog-speak. At least not yet. So I settled on an experiment about climate change. That's more important anyway. I planned to compare a jar with a cellophane top and another jar without a top. I'd put both jars in the sun and measure their temperatures. The one with the cellophane would be hotter. It wasn't very creative, but it would demonstrate the greenhouse effect. I'd get extra credit, plus a decent shot at the Young American Scientist award.

But then I had a better idea. The biggest greenhouse gas is carbon dioxide. What if I could show that it was carbon dioxide that raised the temperature? The air wouldn't just be hotter because the jar had a top, it would be hotter because of the carbon dioxide. I just needed to make carbon dioxide.

I explained my idea to Mom and she help me research it. We learned that mixing baking soda with vinegar made carbon dioxide. She suggested I add extra jars with just baking soda and just vinegar so I could rule out that the rise in temperature was due to one of them alone. And she bought an infrared thermometer so I could measure the temperature. I did the experiment and, ta-da, I got the results I was hoping for.

That was when the trouble started.

I brought my project to school and entered it in the science fair, and for some reason, Freddie and his buddies decided it was the dumbest thing they'd ever seen. They started calling me Professor Woke. They made up a little jingle: "Dr. Annie Woke is a big joke." They whispered it whenever they walked by me in the hall. Then they put it online for the whole world to see. They knew how much I hate being called Annie. Suddenly I wasn't sure all the work I'd put into the project had been worth it.

I look up from my empty bowl of cereal, and Mom is waiting for an answer. "I don't know," I say. "I'm just not good enough. You need to get off my back about it."

She scowls. She doesn't say it, but I know she's thinking, *Don't you dare talk to me like that, young woman.* Which means she doesn't understand what I'm feeling. So I get explicit. Being explicit, according to Ms. French, is essential if you want to write a good essay.

"You think I'm smart," I say, "because I did an experiment about climate change, and you think that's important. But to some people, that's just plain dumb. To them, I'm just plain dumb. And when you're dumb, it's best to know it."

My mother looks at me and shakes her head. "Honey, I hate to hear you talk like that. It couldn't be further from the truth. You have to leave now, but we'll talk later, after you bring home your award. We'll celebrate, I promise."

I glare at her. "I'm not coming home with any award!"

"How can you be so sure?"

That stops me. How *do* I know? Despite what I'm telling Mom, I know I'm not dumb. It's just that sometimes all the bullying gets to me, and I start to believe I'm Annie Woke. When it comes down to it, though, all I have is the gut feeling I'm not coming home with an award. "I just know," I mumble.

"But how?" she presses.

She won't let it go. And I need her to let it go. I'm the one who has to go to school, face Freddie and the other kids. If I win, their bullying will be next-level. "Well," I say with exasperation, "if for some wild reason I do get that stupid award, you can keep it!"

I know I shouldn't be so rude to Mom, but the words just pop out. Probably I'm angry at Freddie and his friends, angry they're picking on me for caring about our Earth's climate, angry I let their taunts get to me. And angry I've had to work so hard these past months to keep Mom from finding out about all this. Being rude to her is easier than trying to deal with that whole mess.

Before she can respond, I grab my backpack and rush out the door. As it slams shut, I don't have to look back to know she's standing there, arms outstretched, waiting for her goodbye hug.

The school assembly is first thing in the morning. I meet up with my BFF Neveah and we join everyone filing through the metal detectors outside the doors to the large auditorium. Sixth graders sit on the left side, seventh graders on the right side, and eighth graders in the middle. As we take seats toward the left-side back of the hall, she babbles on about our plans for the summer: We'll go tubing on the Elkhorn River, earn pocket money mowing neighbors' lawns and walking their dogs, take goofy portrait photos of people and their pets, make homemade ice cream to sell in my front yard, create some awesome new flavors.

When she notices she's doing all the talking, she nudges me with her elbow and offers suggestions: "How about pizza ice cream? Licorice ice cream? Carmel cotton candy? Peanut butter and garlic?"

I'm totally into doing all of that with her, except my mind is still on the fight with Mom. I'm sorry not sorry—sorry I didn't hug her, because we always, always, always hug before I leave for school, but not sorry for pushing back against her heavy-duty expectations. Mostly, though, I'm just glad Nev and I are about to start enjoying summer.

This is my first time attending an end-of-year assembly in middle school, but it's easy to predict who the speakers will be and what they will say. First up is the principal, who highlights all the major events of the year, punctuated by the cheerleading squad with their hallmark "Give me an *O!*" No surprise there. I'd be bored if I wasn't having so much fun watching Nev doodle dancing ice cream cones on her phone. Other kids have their phones out too. Apparently the usual rules aren't being enforced today.

Next up are the academic awards, which are just the prelude to what students care most about: anything that has to do with sports, and of course the personality awards. I hope there's a biggest jerk award and Freddie wins it.

Eighth grade goes first. For each award—English, history, math, science, and wild card—the names of the three finalists are read out, then the winner is announced. That person comes up to receive their certificate, then stands in a line on the stage. After eighth grade, they move on to seventh. Same thing. I don't know many of the older kids but I clap for them, along with everyone else. A few of the more popular kids get synchronized applause that ends with loud cheers. I can't help wondering whether those kids feel more proud or more embarrassed.

By the time they get to sixth grade, ten winners are lined up on stage. Add five more from our class, run through the sports and personality awards, and we'll be done and out of here. I can't wait for this to be over.

The sixth-grade English winner is Logan, a tall, thin boy with shaggy hair. He wrote some pretty cool poems that he read aloud in class. Ms. French praised his creative use of metaphor. And paradox. The poem I remember best was about a squirrel in a cloud. All of us had different ideas about what it meant, and he said we were all wrong. Ms. French said no, we were all correct, because he had made us think more deeply, and that's what a poem should do. Next year I will write essays that make people think deeply. About super important stuff. Like climate change. And world peace. Logan had better watch out because I'm coming for that English award!

I'm so busy thinking about Logan that I miss the history and math winners. I tune back in just as they get to science. I should be listening carefully, at the edge of my seat, hoping to hear my name. But I'm not. I'm leaning over and silently giggling at Nev's cannoli ice cream cone with its long, thin, squiggly legs. Which makes it all the more stunning when the three finalists are named and I am one of them. There's a pause, and the winner is announced: Anna Solano.

In shock, I stand up.

I can feel Nev pushing me forward, cheering for me.

In a daze, I half walk, half stumble toward the stage as the whole school claps. For me. In a daze, I accept the certificate. In a daze, I walk to the end of the line of winners and stand there, the fourteenth student. Not just a finalist but the actual winner: sixth-grade Young American Scientist of the year.

I really didn't believe this would happen. But here I am, on stage before the whole school. I'm so surprised, I don't even have time to feel nervous or embarrassed.

I regret being so crappy to Mom. I can't wait to go home and apologize. Tell her she was right, I should have had more confidence in myself, believed I would win. It was a terrific science project. I'm going to think of more experiments to do over the summer. I'm excited to start seventh grade so I can take new classes, learn from new teachers. I'll be a star student in science *and* English. I stand here clutching my certificate, pulsing with excitement.

As I look down at the sixth graders in front of me, I see Freddie. He's in the first row, staring at me. When he sees that I'm looking back at him, he sticks out his tongue. Quick, so no teachers will catch him. Disgust and hatred are fighting for first place on his face. I know he'll taunt me later, with his friends as a backup chorus. But now that doesn't matter. This certificate shows me what the school and the teachers think of me. In their eyes, like in Mom's eyes, I'm smart. I'm a winner. With that conviction, I won't let Freddie get to me again.

Instead of looking away, I stare him down.

We're still staring at each other as the sixth-grade wild card winner takes her place next to me on the stage, and the whole school cheers for all the winners together.

As the applause dies down, there is some sort of commotion to my left.

Someone is trying to come out from behind the curtain. Probably a teacher. Probably with some special announcement. Or maybe someone who took a back entrance because they were late. I'm too intent on staring at Freddie to glance over to see who it is.

But then I see terror on his face. He's not looking at me anymore.

Now I'm not looking at him either. I'm looking at what everyone else is looking at: a young man wearing a bandanna that covers half his face, standing on the stairs at the far-left side of the stage. He is holding a large rifle and pointing it at all the winners, then quickly flashing it around the hall.

I want to believe it's some kind of skit, part of the assembly. But I know it's not.

Some kids beside me drop to the ground. Like we've been taught to do.

Others are screaming.

Some run toward the back doors.

A couple of teachers rush down the aisle. They have to get to the shooter before he pulls the trigger!

I'm frozen in place. As if I can be invisible and nothing will happen if I don't move. As if I'm not dizzy and about to faint. About to die.

Our last active shooter drill felt nothing like this. It's all happening so fast, but it feels like slow motion.

I drop to the ground.

But not before a volley of shots has gone off.

I hear my voice crying, as if from far away: "Mom! Mom! Mommy!"

I don't hear her answer.

Now I don't even hear my own voice.

There is no sound.

There is no beginning, no middle. Only the end.

Benjamin

I am Ben and I am a statistic. I was seventy-four when I was shot. I was living with my wife of half a century, Betty, in Cleveland, Ohio, in a condo on the shores of Lake Erie. My pronouns were he/him. I am survived by Betty, our daughter Samantha, my brother Bill, and our two grandchildren.

I never had the slightest interest in genealogy. But then Betty bought us both DNA test kits for Christmas the year I retired. She was on the hunt for ways to keep me busy and also expand my horizons—something more stimulating than the jigsaw puzzles of tropical scenes with which I'd been whiling away the hours, and less pricey than going on cruises. Cost consciousness aside, she knew being crammed on a ship with three thousand people had never been my idea of a fun pastime. I'd much rather be out in nature, enjoying it with Betty.

We did talk about investing in a camper and touring the national parks. We're still talking about it. The main reason we haven't done it yet is that our daughter, Samantha, had twins the year after I retired. Recognizing how stretched to the max Sammy and her husband, both trial lawyers, would feel even if they hired a capable nanny, Betty and I made the snap decision to sell our home in the hills overlooking San Francisco Bay and move to Cleveland.

The twins are almost four now. We spend most of our afternoons babysitting for them when they get home from preschool, and thinking up the next alluring activity to introduce them to. Like making guitars out of painted tissue boxes and rubber bands. Or baking alphabet cookies that spell out their names: Leo and Cleo. Only four letters between the two of them. Honestly, I haven't had an ounce of extra energy to put into buying a camper and fitting it out. Not to mention how much we'd lose out on if we were on the road, away from our grandkids for long stretches.

I was brimming with energy, however, that last Christmas in California as I anticipated the results of our DNA tests.

Because the truth was I knew next to nothing about my ancestry. Neither of my parents had ever talked much about their families. My dad said his folks came over from Europe, but when I pried for details, he was vague. The stories he did share centered on the hardships of growing up in New York City during the Great Depression—how he stood in breadlines on frigid mornings, collected junk to sell instead of going to school, hoped they wouldn't be kicked out of their apartment and wind up in Hooverville. How his overalls were patched hand-me-downs from his sister.

My mother didn't have any such colorful stories. Whenever I asked about her family, we somehow ended up talking about Dad's family instead. Or she retold the story of meeting him at a college sock hop and the thrill when he kissed her at the end of the evening as they rummaged around for their shoes in a dimly lit hallway.

Growing up, I could have been more curious, I suppose. I could have asked my father why he'd lost contact with his parents after he moved to California, asked my mother why I'd never seen a photo of her as a child. But I took my cues from them: If my parents preferred to relegate the past to the past, so would I.

As the years went on, I had no reason to do otherwise. It was natural to look to the future when I worked in Silicon Valley; everything we did was focused on the future. I liked to remind my colleagues whenever we found ourselves in crisis mode that we couldn't change the past, we could only change the future. That was my motto. It's also how Betty and I raised our daughter, and probably why Sammy isn't one to hold onto the past either.

Another mindset that stuck with me—and with my brother, Bill—was our parents' lack of interest in all things religion. Like most families in the neighborhood, we celebrated Christmas and Easter. But unlike our neighbors, we never set foot in a church. Since religious affiliation tends to be inherited, this felt like the logical extension of our close-to-nonexistent ancestry.

I did of course quiz my parents about their beliefs.

"I don't believe in anything," my father said.

"So you're an *atheist*?"

"Jeez, Ben, it's not a dirty word," he said, as if I were the one swearing.

"But you don't believe in God?"

"No."

"Mom doesn't either?"

"In this screwed-up world," he countered, "how could anyone believe in God?"

Although my parents had sworn off sanctity of any shape or sort, they expected my brother and me to make our own choices when we were old enough. I appreciated their faith—if you can call it that—in us. Even so, by the time I found myself caught up in the day-to-day maelstrom of software engineering, the larger existential questions had slipped into the far reaches of my brain. I pretty much followed in my parents' footsteps by default.

When I met Betty, she'd been flirting with Buddhism. Her practice of mindfulness didn't require a belief in God, so we were more or less on the same page. And we built our family on that page. I was relieved—even thankful—our daughter had not taken any interest in religion either.

All that imploded the instant I read my DNA results.

There it was in black and white: 100 percent Ashkenazi Jewish. I wouldn't have been surprised at, say, 20 percent. But 100 percent? That could only be taken to mean one thing: Both my parents had deliberately hidden their Jewish heritage.

I turned to Betty, who was with me, checking her own results on her laptop. "Did you suspect this?" I asked, sticking my screen under her nose. "Is this why you got us DNA tests?"

She said not at all. She'd assumed she was mostly Scandinavian and I was some combination of German and Eastern European and maybe English. We'd have fun tracking down our ancestors, see if we could trace our roots all the way back to Charlemagne. It would be a great party game.

"What on earth were they thinking?" I said.

"Who?"

"My parents. How could they have seen being Jewish as such a terrible thing you have to hide it from your kids?"

I didn't waste any time calling Bill with the news. He said he wasn't surprised. He'd always felt there was a gap in our family story. Yes, our parents didn't claim a religion, but it was reasonable to suspect that, having immigrated from Europe in the early twentieth century, they were Jewish. It might as well show up big in our DNA. He said he'd often joked as a psychotherapist about himself as being, in Freud's words, a "godless Jew." Intellectually and culturally, it resonated.

As we talked more, I could see his point. The clues had been there all along. Like, for instance, the mere handful of family photos from before my birth. My mother once said they had no photos of their wedding because it was a civil service, with only a small gathering afterward. But she never explained the absence of extended family on holidays as we were growing up—unlike our friends, who were all surrounded by wide circles of relatives. And then there was Mom's trip to Israel. She said she went to attend a conference on permaculture, but it sounded like an intensely emotional experience.

None of that, however, explained withholding the truth from us.

Since my father had died when I was in college and my mother ten years ago, I couldn't turn to them for answers. My only hope was to undertake some genealogical digging. Which Betty fully supported.

I didn't have to search long. Starting on my father's side, I located the record of my newlywed grandparents passing through Ellis Island in 1922, having traveled from Hamburg, Germany. They settled in the Lower East Side, where they promptly changed their name from Horowitz to Horn. With the flip of a single letter and the deletion of four more, an entire heritage was erased for generations to come. Records showed that they started a family, only to fall into hard times after my grandfather's textile business went belly-up during the Depression. All that jibed with my father's stories.

My next discovery was that my grandfather had eight siblings and my grandmother six. All fourteen born and raised in Germany. At least some likely wanted to follow them to the States, but none made it here. Every last one died in a concentration camp. It took months of research, but I pulled together the details: Buchenwald, 1942. Auschwitz, 1944, 1945. Theresienstadt, 1943, Treblinka II, 1945. I had names and places and birth dates, and in some cases photos. These people were real. They suffered horrible deaths. Deaths so inhumane that merely reading about them left me physically shaken. Yet the more I learned, the more I needed to know.

As I read their stories, I asked myself why it had taken me so long to look into all this. The only answer, really, was privilege. My life had been easy. Since people assumed I was Christian—by default at least—nobody had placed obstacles in my path, threatened my security, let alone endangered my life itself. I had sashayed into success with a cadre of engineers during the dot-com boom, then managed to dodge major damage when the bubble burst. I only retired because everyone else in our company at that point was my daughter's age. If not younger. And I had the money to retire comfortably. Those cruises would have been easily affordable had I wanted to go on them.

It wasn't hard to understand why my paternal grandparents had been unwilling to admit to being Jewish in America. They wanted to avoid being attacked on the streets. They didn't want to be falsely accused and ostracized, to have made it all the way to this country only to be economically and socially sidelined. They hoped to make enough money to move uptown. I imagine another reason was guilt. The weight of being the only ones among their siblings to survive must have been crushing.

I wondered if my grandparents had corresponded with their siblings before their murders, but I wasn't able to uncover any letters. I also wondered if they had kept their secret from my father. It was hard to imagine he lived his entire life without knowing. Even if he had learned the basics, I could see how he might have carried on the secret nonetheless—much as I had unquestioningly carried on his beliefs.

I printed out the photos I'd found online, put them in frames, and lined them up on the mantle. In one, a girl—her black hair secured with an enormous taffeta bow, a rolling hoop and stick in one hand—stares at me with haunting dark eyes every time I walk into the room. The grandmother I never knew. Now I'm doing what my father failed to do: honor her and my other ancestors.

Before I looked into Mom's family, I took a breather from genealogy. I wasn't ready to handle more trauma.

But when I got back into it, after we had settled into our condo here in Cleveland, what I found was even worse. Both her parents had perished in concentration camps. The details were sparse, but from what I could piece together, they'd been able to put her, at age twelve, on a Kindertransport that took her from Austria to England, where she was cared for in a series of foster homes. After the war, she traveled to America, having received a scholarship to study at New York University. She never saw her parents after they put her on that train. Nor did she ever speak about them.

I searched for books and articles about Holocaust survivors, read as much as I could. The trauma had been so overwhelming for some that it was decades before they could speak about it, even to their children and loved ones. For my mother, it had been the entire rest of her life.

After I explained this to Betty, she took me in her arms as I wept.

Her seemingly simple Christmas present had turned out to be anything but simple. It was the most momentous gift I'd ever received. I'd been given answers to questions I didn't even know I had. I'd found my identity, my people. As I wept, my tears were because I felt it had come too late. There was nothing I could do.

Yet there was more to do. It was time to bring in Sammy. I'd been holding off on talking to her while I engaged in the research, but this discovery affected her too. Again, Betty was in full support.

Sammy came over one evening after work, while her husband took care of the twins. I poured her a glass of chardonnay and showed her my DNA results.

"You know what this means," I said.

"What?"

"You're fifty percent Ashkenazi."

"Right."

I waited for her to say more.

"I mean I don't have a problem with it," she said when she realized I was still in listening mode.

"You shouldn't."

She shrugged it off. "Honestly, Dad, I don't care."

"Wait a minute," I said. "You don't care about what?"

She backtracked, saying she meant she wasn't raised with a religious identity and doesn't consider herself Jewish. She's indifferent to my DNA results because they don't change anything for her.

I bristled at that. "Sounds like you want to deny—"

She cut me off. "It's not like you cared about any of this when I was growing up. I'm almost forty, and this is the first time you're telling me I'm Jewish."

She had a point there. Given my history, I wasn't in a position to judge her.

Still, our conversation didn't sit well with me. I hadn't expected her to make major life changes, but I was hoping for greater resonance, for some sense she'd been touched by this revelation. That she had gained something. As I saw it, what was lost had miraculously been found. I didn't want to believe that meant nothing to her.

In the end, her lack of interest spurred me to check out a synagogue. Although my ancestors had been murdered for being Jewish, they hadn't necessarily been religious. So I hadn't initially considered the religious side of being Jewish. But realizing my daughter was unlikely to carry that forward in any way made me feel a certain duty toward my ancestors. Yes, it had taken seventy-plus years to discover who I was, but now that I knew, I wanted to explore every part of my identity. I didn't know what I would find or how I would feel about it. All I could do was approach it with an open mind.

I located a Reform synagogue a few miles from our condo and told Betty I wanted to attend a service.

She offered to accompany me.

That Friday evening, we walked past the security guards and through the lobby, and took seats in a pew at the back. I looked around surreptitiously as the service began. The artifacts, the language, the sitting and standing were all unfamiliar, and I wasn't sure I was ready to become a student again at my age. But one thing grabbed me: the music. The first time I heard the refrain of "L'cha Dodi," tears welled up. It was as though that song had been sleeping within me since before I could remember, and was finally awakening.

It awoke anew each day after that, filling me with hope and joy. Even before I learned the words or understood it was a love song—and why it was part of the service—I was humming the tune in the shower. I hummed it for the twins when I put them down for a nap.

Betty and I have continued to attend services every Friday evening. In some inexplicable way, the songs and rituals of Judaism have forged a connection with my ancestors and eased the existential sense of exclusion I'd suffered from, even if I never understood it for what it was. I've also been meeting people with stories similar to mine, Jews who are children or grandchildren of immigrants and who lost relatives in the Holocaust. I even met several who didn't learn until well into adulthood that they're Jewish.

None of this means I've ceased to be an atheist. But that hasn't been a problem. I feel welcomed at the temple.

We only attend services when the twins are with their parents, so bringing them with us has never been a consideration. Besides, they've been too young to sit through a service. Now, it turns out, our temple is holding a special morning service on Rosh Hashanah, designed for families. We've been encouraged to bring children, even as young as age two.

Immediately I want to bring Cleo and Leo. This is a chance to introduce them to their heritage, to make sure they never feel their grandad hid something so important from them. Of course I wouldn't do any of this without their mother's consent.

When I ask Sammy, she hesitates.

"What's the matter?" I ask. "They'll love it."

When she doesn't elaborate, I push harder: "Are you afraid I'll force a belief system on them you don't approve of? Is that it?"

"Of course not," she says. "I know you're into the whole religious thing. I just don't see why you have to involve them."

I explain that I want them to have what I missed as a child. I want to enrich their lives. I'm not forcing anything; they will make their own decisions when they grow up. Just as I let her do. When she's still noncommittal, I say, "Here's a solution. The service is on Saturday, so why don't you come? Then you'll be familiar with everything. You might even like what you see."

That's not the solution she has in mind. "Saturday is my only free day. I don't want to put anything on the calendar." She pauses, then adds, "Go ahead and take them. I'm sure it'll be fine."

To ease her concerns, I remind her this is the Jewish New Year; I won't ask to take them every week. And she'll always have the final say in what experiences her children are exposed to.

Of course, all this is automatic for most families: As a child, you go to whatever church or temple or mosque your family attends; as grandparents, your grandchildren go with you. And if your family doesn't follow any religion, you don't go. Either way, most people don't think twice about it. Yet here I am, a man whose life was turned upside down during his seventh decade, who longs to see his progeny carry on traditions that were lost to his family. I want them to grow up with a connection to their roots, a sense of belonging. Yes, ultimately they will make their own choices, but they won't require a DNA test to know what choices are theirs to make. I also want them to know they'll never have to live in fear because of their religious identity or see it as something to hide, even from their own kin.

Sammy drops the twins off at the condo first thing Saturday morning, on her way to the gym. They look adorable—Leo in his pressed shirt and slacks, Cleo in a pleated plaid skirt and wool cardigan.

"You both look sparkling new for the New Year!" I tell them.

That elicits a grin from Leo but puts a frown on Cleo's face.

She points to her outfit. "This isn't new."

I forgot that kids their age can take things literally.

Betty helps me out. "Let's find you something new," she says. "Something pretty."

Cleo follows Betty to the bedroom, and when they return a few minutes later, her black hair has been pulled up and back with a big bow, fashioned out of a brand-new cream-colored satin ribbon. My eye goes straight to the photo on the mantle—to that head of black hair, that old-fashioned bow, those haunting dark eyes. I don't want to say anything now; there will be time tonight to ask Betty if she also sees the resemblance to my grandmother, if that was what gave her the idea for the bow.

Walking past the guards and into the temple, we find a festive atmosphere. Many families have come with children, but there are also older adults and university students. When the kids see me put on a kippah—a custom I described to them as we drove here—they both want one too. Since this is a Reform synagogue, I don't have to tell Cleo it's only for men and boys. They pick matching blue kippahs out of the box and giggle as they put them on. By the way they fuss to adjust them so they won't slide off, I can tell they feel proud.

Plastic shofroth have been placed on the pews. Parents are trying—with little success—to convince their youngsters to wait for the right moment to blow them.

Because so many people have come today, we sit close together: Leo on the aisle, then me, then Cleo wedged between Betty and me. Some of the smaller children sit on their parents' laps to save space.

When everyone is settled, the rabbi explains that we will have a brief service to learn more about the holiday. Together we will sing some songs. She will let everyone know when to blow their shofroth, and how many times to blow. Then the children will go outside with their parents for some activities, after which we will all share a special snack.

A musician joins the rabbi and begins to strum a guitar.

Cleo grasps my hand and whispers, "I know *that*!"

"You do," I whisper back, pleased she recognizes "L'Shanah Tovah." I've been humming it lately at nap time; as soon as they hear its joyful but soothing melody, they nod off. Never fails.

"Can we sing now?" she says.

I'm about to tell her that yes, we will all sing it together, when an overpowering blast rocks the building. Sounds like an explosion and gunfire and glass shattering—all at once. And right outside.

I catch Betty's eye as we both spin around to see what's happening.

Two men with AR-15s rush the doorway, having shot or bombed their way past the guards. They run up the central aisle, toward the rabbi. A third and fourth are close behind.

This is an organized attack.

Shots ring out.

My mind stops. I don't quite know where I am anymore. What was a synagogue is now a war zone.

But there's no time to think. No time to reach out to Betty. No time.

I do the only thing that's instinctive: I grab Cleo and Leo and with one motion pull them to the ground and cover their bodies with mine.

I feel them quivering beneath me. Hear their whimpers. I'm doing everything humanly possible to make sure they survive.

In the next instant, I've been shot.

The pain is excruciating. I can't move a muscle. I hear Leo scream. Feel Cleo struggling to free herself. I know I've been fatally wounded, but I'm certain the bullet didn't reach either of my little ones.

I can't see Betty. All I can do is pray she is alive.

I have barely enough breath, enough strength, to bury my nose in Cleo's satin bow and whisper, "I love . . . you . . ."

Chester

I am Chester and I am a statistic. I was sixteen when I was shot. I was living in Buffalo, New York, and I was in eleventh grade. My pronouns were he/him. I am survived by my dad and my sister. And by a collection of rap poems no one will ever know I wrote.

It was a Thursday. I was at basketball practice after school, doing my knee-hug warm-ups, when the coach ran over to me. I figured he wanted me to pick up the pace. Get those knees higher. Then I saw his face all pinched. Like he didn't want to say what he was about to say. He told me my dad had sent an urgent text. I had to go home. Immediately.

As soon as I saw Dad slumped at the kitchen table, head in his hands, I knew what had happened. He'd rushed straight home from the hospital so he could talk to me, man to man. Even before he lifted his head, wiped his eyes, and motioned for me to sit down, I knew Mom had died.

I was in eighth grade when she found out about the cancer. At first, I thought she'd be okay. A couple of my friends' moms had also had breast cancer, and they all survived. The chemo was tough, but she handled it. She was strong. She was our rock. And she did seem to be getting better. But then it came back. And it spread.

That was when I started to really worry.

My whole ninth-grade year is a blur. I was in a fog of fear about Mom. My grades took a hit. Some nights I couldn't fall asleep; other days I couldn't wake up and was late for school. I got out of condition, missed easy layups in games. When I asked Mom why she hadn't gotten better like my friends' moms, she said something about her genes. And that she'd skipped screening tests she should have gotten. But honestly, who could blame her for that when she was so busy with her job, on top of taking care of us?

Her death blasted through our lives like a sledgehammer. All that was left was rubble. At least, that's what it felt like. We were all hurting, but I think it hit my dad the hardest. In addition to his sixty-hour workweek, he suddenly had three kids on his hands. He drove a school bus during the day and was a bouncer at a bar and grill in the evening. How was he supposed to be a full-time parent?

Of course I did everything I could to help out. My brother Tyre is ten, my sister Jasmine nine. Both much too young to lose a parent. Not that I'm old enough. They'd always naturally looked up to me, so I tried to become the best second parent I could be. Mainly it's the little stuff. Like making sure they have lunch money. That Jasmine doesn't have her cell phone hidden under her panda pillow when it's time for lights out. That Tyre isn't trying to snitch her phone again because he let his phone die.

I also make sure they get dinner when Dad's not home. Which is most nights. I've been low-key leveling up my food game. I started with simple things, like heating up a can of soup. But the other day I made chicken wings. I'm not talking about the frozen kind you nuke in a microwave. Legit chicken wings. I did my best to recall what Mom did and then—you could say—I just winged it from there. The kids' smiles when I handed them their plates told me all I needed to know.

Dad was definitely not feeling it when I told him I had quit basketball. He praised my athleticism and basketball IQ and said I was making a mistake if I didn't stick with it.

"No way," I said. I mean, family comes first. Mom taught me that.

I don't regret my decision. I've always stepped up—babysat for the kids, tied their shoes, played catch with them, taught them things. But now they really need me.

I'm doing this parenting thing, but I make time for myself too. After the kids go to bed, I stay up late and do what I want to do. Like watch TV. Or write poetry. I don't mean as a homework assignment. I mean rap poems.

I started writing after Mom died. It was a way to get out my feelings about losing her. Then I kept going. Now I have almost a hundred poems. No one has seen any of them. Not yet. I know I'm not the next Drake or Eminem or anything like that. But one of these days, I'm going to put it out there.

Often I'm still awake when Dad gets home, and we have our special time, just the two of us. I tell him whatever he needs to know about the kids, and he asks how my day went. Or we'll hang out, no words needed. It's special just knowing I have a parent.

Like tonight.

I'm half asleep on the couch when Dad comes in shortly after midnight. He grabs cold pizza from the kitchen and sits down beside me. He's halfway through his first slice when he gestures toward the TV, which is still on. "You're watching the news?"

I tell him I was watching basketball and didn't bother to turn the TV off when the game ended. I hunt for the remote in the depths of the couch and flick it off.

As we sit in silence, I weigh sharing the rap poem I worked on earlier: "In the soul of the city / where our lobs meet the skies / we lace up our sneakers / try for new highs." I think he'd be touched to know basketball is still playing in my mind these days. Except to do it right, I'd want to do it with music, and that would wake the kids. Plus I feel shy, never having read aloud to anyone. I promise myself to do it soon. Very soon.

"I hear there's major snow coming in off the lake," Dad says, breaking the silence.

"Tomorrow?"

He nods. "I might get off work early."

"Maybe they'll let us out of school," I say, trying not to sound too stoked.

"Possibly. If it's bad enough."

I tell him I'll make sure the kids get home safe. We'll be waiting here for him. If the power goes out, we will have beans. No one's going hungry on my watch. We can all have dinner together. The kids would love that.

When I wake up the next morning, it's cold and cloudy but not snowing. So we all head for school. The kids walk to their elementary school, and I catch a bus downtown to the high school.

There are little snow squalls off and on during the day, but nothing that amounts to more than a dusting on the ground. All of us keep glancing out the windows during class, which annoys the teachers but doesn't result in school closing early. I figure Dad won't get off early either.

As school lets out for the day, the storm amps up. Now the wind is blowing and snow is coming down thick and fast. Seems like they could have predicted this and let us out.

I text Jasmine and Tyre that I'm on my way home. Tell them to leave right away and meet me there.

The bus is slow due to the slick roads, so it takes me longer than usual to get home. When I walk up the steps and into the house, Tyre is waiting by the front window, watching the snow pile up. I take off my jacket, hat, and gloves and head to the kitchen to get us a snack.

He follows.

I grab three snack-size bags of chips from the cabinet and hand him one. "Where's your sister?"

"Don't know."

"She wasn't with you?"

"We didn't walk home together," he says. "She left before I did." He looks at me sideways, knowing I'll need a good reason for why they didn't stay together. Like I told them to. "I kinda got into a fight," he says. Before I can come down on him, he adds, "Just snowballs!"

I'm annoyed anyway. If Jasmine left first, like he's saying, she should be here.

I text her to find out where she is.

When she doesn't respond, I try calling.

The call doesn't go through, and I realize my phone isn't working. It's gone into SOS mode. Since it's getting dark, I flick on the light switch. Nothing. The power is out too.

I walk over to the living room window. It's snowing so hard I can't see beyond the edge of the front porch. In the few minutes since I got home, this has turned into a hell of a storm.

Tyre looks scared.

I push aside my annoyance. It's on me to make sure he feels safe. I don't want him to realize I'm also worried. I want to tell him everything will be fine, we'll wait it out, and sooner or later Jasmine will get home. Except what if she doesn't?

"Did she say where she was going?" I ask.

"She was with Alicia."

"Yeah. She usually stops at Alicia's on her way home," I say, thinking out loud. If she doesn't have a lot of homework, they hang out and listen to music. "But I told you both to come straight home. She got my text, right?"

He nods. "Maybe Alicia's mom told her to wait out the storm?"

"Maybe."

As we eat our chips, I stare out into the whiteness. This feels like the biggest decision I've ever had to make. And I don't know what to do. Dad is probably still on his bus route, which must be hard if the plows aren't keeping up with the snow. He doesn't need the extra worry about Jasmine. No, I'm the one who needs to take care of that. I'll fill him in when he gets home.

And so the decision is made: I will go and get her.

I've only been to Alicia's house a few times. It's one block off Ferry Street, a brown house with a large front porch. Not far from here. Shouldn't be hard to find. Of course I can't leave Tyre alone.

"Come on, bro," I say. "Put on your jacket. We're going to pick up Jazzy."

A strong wind is howling and the snow is drifting, but even so, it shouldn't take long to walk over and get Jasmine. The main problem is that the power is out. No streetlamps. No lights in windows. Just darkness. And everywhere the whiteness of snow.

I feel I made a smart decision. Dad will be proud when he finds out I didn't wait for Jasmine but braved the storm to get her. And I'm glad Tyre is with me. To show him, I shape a snowball and toss it at him. Bull's-eye.

He startles. Then he realizes I'm playing. He picks up some snow and tosses one back.

We run down the middle of the street, slipping and sliding, throwing snowballs at each other. White bullets hitting their targets. Or missing if we duck fast enough.

When we tire of the game, we walk in silence.

It's still dark and the snow is coming down, but I'm not worried anymore. I'm into this moment, out on the street with my brother. A poem pops into my mind: "Yo, it's a cold winter's night / whole world's turning white." I like that.

And another line: "I'm a snowstorm poet on a rapper's spree. / In the heart of the storm, I'll find my decree."

I repeat the lines to myself so I can write them down later.

When we reach the middle of the block where Alicia lives, I climb over a snowbank and step into knee-deep snow where the sidewalk should be.

Tyre stops in the street. "That isn't her house."

I turn back to him. "It's not?"

He shakes his head.

I look around as best I can in the dark. He could be right. This house is bigger than how I remember Alicia's. The other houses seem bigger too, and farther apart. Or it could just seem that way because it's dark. I stand here, unsure what to do. "You're positive it's not her house?"

"No."

"We could have turned the wrong way on Ferry," I say. I didn't notice because of the storm. And because we were having fun. But going home without Jasmine isn't an option. I reason that we haven't walked that far. This is still our neighborhood. We can't be lost in our own neighborhood.

Tyre wants to turn around and figure out where we went wrong.

The problem is we can't easily retrace our steps in the dark, in the snow.

"Let's ask these folks." I turn and start walking toward the house. "It can't hurt to ask."

"Are you sure?" Tyre follows but stops short of the front steps.

"I'm sure."

I climb onto the porch and ring the doorbell. Then I wonder if it will work without power. So I knock. As I wait for someone to come, I hop up and down, trying to warm my feet. A soft light is shining through one window, probably a candle someone lit.

When no one answers, I knock again.

It's a really nice house. There are white pillars and a hanging swing at one corner of the porch. I can imagine the owners sitting here in the summer, having cocktails on a warm evening. But this is hardly summer, and no one is coming to the door. I heave a sigh of frustration and turn away.

I join Tyre at the bottom of the steps. "Come on," I say. "Let's try to retrace how we got here. Like you said."

Then I hear a noise behind us. Someone has come out after all.

I turn my head, expecting to ask for directions.

A heavyset older man is framed in the doorway. With a shotgun.

Without hesitation, he aims and fires.

Pop! Pop! Pop!

Tyre's body flies backward, lands in the snow.

I want to lunge toward him, protect him, get us out of here. Get us home. But my own body is crumpling.

Into the snow.

Into whiteness.

Dixie

I am Dixie and I am a statistic. I was twenty-six when I was shot. I was living in Abilene, Texas, and I was eight months and one week pregnant with my second child. My pronouns were none of your business. I am survived by my husband, Mason, and my son, Skeeter.

I'm reclining on my zero-gravity chair, just chilling, when Skeeter pops up from his nap. He was asleep on the pillow by the TV where he always conks out after lunch, his mouth wide open. I should ask his pediatrician about that. If he grows up breathing through his mouth all the time, girls aren't gonna like it. But now he's up and running around the room like the normal active toddler he is.

I'm the opposite of active. The third trimester will do that to you.

In less than a month, Skeets will have a little sister. I've been wondering how he'll treat her. Will he push her around like he does his trucks and other toys, or will he know to be gentle? Right now, he's ramming his trucks around in the space beneath my chair like it's a frigging sideshow in a parking garage.

"*Froom! Froom!*"

"Hey, kiddo," I say, "you've got a lot of trucks down there."

"*My* trucks!" he chirps.

"Got your best truck?"

He jumps out from under the chair so he can display his green camouflage military fighter truck. It's a real beaut. Fifty-dollar value, but Mason picked it up on sale for less than half that. Had it tucked away in our closet for a year, waiting for Skeeter's third birthday. It's been his favorite ever since. He sleeps with it most nights.

"Watch!" he says, pushing a button on the rear bumper. He squeals as the front lights flash and the truck cycles through all its honks and beeps and shooting sounds. "*Pow! Pow!*" he echoes as he drives the truck around my feet, along the edge of my legs, and up into the air. He crash-lands it on the floor, then scuttles back under the chair with it.

I tell him he's the world's greatest driver, fighter, pilot. Superhero. Not everyone can make a military all-terrain vehicle fly. "Good job!" I say.

"I'm the good guys!" he counters.

"Yes, you are," I say. "You're a good guy! You're my good guy!"

To punctuate my point, I reach under the chair and slap his little rump. It's a blind swat, but somehow my hand manages to connect, without the chair toppling over and causing disaster for me and the baby.

He shrieks and swats back.

But my arm is already safely out of range. It's back on the chair, cradling my belly, stroking the little one curled up within me.

I've always enjoyed playing with Skeets. He's so imaginative, creates such amazing make-believe worlds with his trucks and other toys. Now that I'm on parental leave, we'll have more time to hang out and play. Having his mom around is important for his development. After he was born, I went back to work as a receptionist at the real estate agency almost immediately. I regret that now. I want my kids to have at least one parent with them at all times while they're small. I'm going to talk to Mason about staying home full time after our daughter is born.

Not that Mason isn't a loving and attentive father. Every weekend he takes Skeets with him to the shooting range. He used to go with his buddies, but after Skeets turned three a few months ago, he decided that's old enough. Now on Saturday afternoons, Skeets puts on his big-boy jeans, Mason lifts him into the car seat in his pickup truck, and off they go. He meets up with his buddies, and they spend the whole afternoon there.

To be honest, I think he dispenses with the car seat when he's on the open road. I think he holds Skeets on his lap. I've never actually seen him do that, but it's the only thing that made sense to me after I heard Skeets talk about how he and his dad steer the truck together. I haven't questioned Mason about it. What matters is seeing our boy getting so close with his daddy, seeing him so happy, high-spirited, and rambunctious.

"So," I say now with a chuckle, "the good guys are winning?"

"Yep!"

"You'll get all those bad guys?"

"Yep!"

He's such a cutie! I can hear him pushing one of his trucks—I'm pretty sure I know which one—across the room behind me. *Froom-froom* all the way. He must have figured out that the bad guys are hiding in the hallway, and he's going there to track them down and attack. This kid is never going to be a pushover, that's for sure.

The sounds of his play fade into the distance as I drift in the direction of sleep. I'm so comfy in this chair that I've slept here instead of the bedroom a few times during this pregnancy. Mason encouraged me to do whatever relieves my lower back pain and insomnia.

These days, my daydreams are about our little girl. Her nursery is ready and waiting. I insisted we do it in pink. I know some people don't like that anymore. They think girls should look like boys, and boys should look like girls. A load of crap, if you ask me. I'm glad I live in a community that supports my values.

I was always a girly girl, and I don't see why my daughter shouldn't be one too. I guess if she's a bit of a tomboy, that wouldn't be terrible. But at least I can make sure she starts out in a pretty pink-and-white nursery with frilly fuchsia curtains, pink bows on the four corners of her bassinet, and pink ballet shoe–patterned wallpaper. I can't wait to slip her into the soft polyester rosebud onesie I bought online.

Of course, I want her to have a successful life. Maybe she can go into real estate, become an actual agent, instead of just a receptionist like me. Or if she aims big, maybe she'll want to go to college and become a teacher. I like to picture her as a teacher in a pink—yes, pink!—dress, standing in front of a class of first graders. She'll have kids of her own, but she'll be like a mom to her students.

I've been talking about all this to her in the womb. "You go, girl," I say. "You're blessed. You can do anything you set your heart and mind to. I will make sure you have a great and fantastic life. Count on it."

I float out of my daydream when I hear Skeets roar back into the room. He scoots under my chair again, banging around.

"Hey, kiddo," I say. "Get those bad guys?"

I feel him pounding on the underside of my chair with his little fist.

"What's my good boy up to?"

"Getting the bad guys!"

Really, he's such a darling. "Who are the bad guys?" I tease.

He stops pounding for a minute. Like he's thinking.

So I ask again: "Who are the bad guys?"

"Mommy," he exclaims. "Mommy, *you're* the bad guy!"

I play along. "Yeah, I'm a bad guy. See if you can get me!"

Now he's pounding on the chair not with his fist but with something harder. It hurts a bit, but nothing I can't take. For the sake of the game. "What are you gonna do to the bad guys?"

"Shoot 'em!" he exclaims.

"Yeah, Skeets," I say. "Shoot those bad guys!"

There is a pause.

Then a deafening *bang*.

It feels like something has pierced the middle of my lower back. My spine. My baby . . . *My baby?* I almost pass out, but somehow I hold on.

"Skeets?" I whisper.

He crawls out from under the chair. With one hand, he's rubbing his ear. It must hurt from the bang. His other hand is holding Mason's pistol.

He stands beside me, staring at me.

I stare back at him.

Confusion is smeared all over his face.

"What did you do?" I ask.

He looks scared. Terrified.

But I don't want him to feel bad. I need him to know he didn't do anything wrong. That pistol was in the drawer of our nightstand. We always keep it there. Every family should have a firearm for protection. Mason has at least a dozen. Loaded, of course. That's the whole point. Skeets must have gone into the bedroom while I was napping and taken one. Maybe he didn't know it was loaded and could hurt someone. Like it was a toy. He doesn't look so sure about any of that now.

"Skeets, baby," I whisper, "it's okay."

He drops the gun on the floor, leans against my legs, and looks up at me. "Mommy?"

"Mommy's right here," I say, keeping my voice calm to reassure him I'll be fine. And I'm positive I'll be fine. *I. Will. Be. Fine.*

It's the baby I'm worried about. She needs medical attention. Now. I reach for my phone. My hand is shaking so badly, it's good I have Mason on speed dial.

He picks up on the first ring. "Dixie?"

"I've been . . . shot."

"Shot?!"

"Yes."

"Oh fuck! You had an intruder? Is he still there?"

"No."

"Are you okay?"

"I'm okay." It's a lie, but I don't want to upset him. "I'll explain when you get here."

"Did you call 911?"

"No. Can you?"

"Of course," he says. "Hang tight. I'll be there as soon as I can."

When I get off the phone, I look at Skeets.

He's whimpering now. Backing away from me.

"Don't worry," I say. "Mommy's okay."

I want to pick him up, cuddle him. But I'm weak and light-headed. Afraid that if I move it will harm the baby. Not even sure I can move.

After what feels like an hour but is probably only a few minutes, I hear sirens. Then banging at the front door. People rush into the room. Officers with guns pointed at me. It's so chaotic, so overwhelming, that I pass out.

When I come to, I am lying on a gurney.

A young paramedic is leaning in, close to my face. As soon as he sees me looking at him, he flashes a light in my eyes. "That's better," he says, then turns to someone behind him. "She's back."

"We gotta move fast," a voice says.

I look around for Mason. I don't see him, but one of the officers is holding Skeets in her arms. He's crying.

I reach out for him, but pain seizes me. "I want my baby!" I manage to say.

As the paramedics move the gurney toward the door, an officer explains that they're taking me to the hospital. I will get all the care I need. "Your son is in good hands," he says.

I want to protest that my son needs his mother, that I need him with me, but I lose consciousness again.

This time when I wake up, I'm in an ambulance, hooked up to all kinds of monitors, breathing through an oxygen mask. I hear the siren, feel us speeding through the streets.

I look for Mason. He should be here by now.

But I don't see him.

The young paramedic is close to me on one side, an officer on the other.

"Stay with me," the medic says. "Can you do that?"

I nod.

"Do you know who did this to you?" the officer says when it's clear I am staying conscious.

I get the sense he only expects a nod or a shake of my head, but my mind is surprisingly clear now. They must've given me something super strong. "It was an accident," I say. "Total accident."

He looks like he wants me to elaborate, but he and the medic exchange glances, and instead he says, "You don't have to say anything now. We'll get your statement at the hospital."

"I'm going to be okay, right?"

"Just hold on there," the medic says.

Off to one side, I see another EMT adjust whatever is flowing into my arm through an IV line.

I start to relax. The pain I felt on the gurney has faded. Now it's hardly noticeable. I know I'll get through this okay.

The little one in my womb will be okay too.

To make sure of that, I whisper a prayer: "Dear Lord, watch over my little girl. Keep her safe from harm. Thank You for watching over our lives. In the name of Jesus, amen."

I'm starting to feel more clearheaded and in control. I know with certainty what's going to happen. We'll be at the hospital in a few minutes. The doctors and nurses will have me and my baby fixed up in no time. Yes, there will be some discomfort, but it won't last. They'll probably do a C-section. That shouldn't be a problem since this pregnancy is so far along. Heck, I might have needed one anyway. And of course a bit of surgery to repair any damage from the bullet. But I'll be fine. I know I'll be fine.

It's just a gunshot wound. People don't die from one bullet. Not when it was shot by accident. Not when your own kid shot you. Not when you're a young, healthy, strong adult. Like me.

When this is all over, I'll have to talk to Mason about putting a child safety latch on the nightstand. He didn't think that was important, but now that we have two kids, we can't risk any more accidents.

Mason must already be at the hospital. I can't wait to see him, to tell him there wasn't any intruder, that it was just an accident and the baby and I will be fine.

As I relax more, I start to drift off.

It's a foggy, sweet feeling. I see Mason's face up close, like he's right here. Smiling at me, like he does when he wants to make love.

Suddenly, as if coming from some distant planet, a high-pitched alarm is going off, steady and unrelenting.

Eeeeeeeeeeeeeeeeeeeeeeeeeeeeeeeeeeeeeeeeeeeeeeeeeeeeee . . .

But, really, I couldn't be less interested.

Edith

I am Edith and I am a statistic. I was eighty when I was shot. I was a retired librarian and I was living in a condo in Des Moines, Iowa, with my beloved teacup terrier, Terry. My pronouns were she/they. I am survived by my three children, nine grandchildren, and one great-grandchild. And by the memory of my dogs.

I have had four dogs in my life.

Four. My daughter, who pays attention to such things, says four signifies stability and strength. I suppose that could be said to apply to all four-leggeds. However, I'm not someone who pays attention to such things.

What I can tell you is that my first dog was Max, a loving and loyal and very large German shepherd. He is right there in my first childhood memory of this lifetime, lying on the braided rug by my playpen. I'm raising myself up with the help of the wooden bars and reaching out between them to touch his wet nose. Actually, I was too young when that happened to remember it now. If someone claims to have memories from under two years of age, take it with a grain of salt. They're probably just recalling a photo they saw. Like the coffee-stained black and white of me in my playpen and Max on the rug, which I recently digitized so I could share it in an online group for dog lovers.

In those days, no one I knew had a little dog. Any dog smaller than a cat wasn't considered a real dog. It was an embarrassment to the canine species, and by extension to the dog's owner. And positively a point of ridicule to felines and their owners.

Until I was ten, Max weighed more than I did. That didn't bother either of us. I chased him around the backyard, climbed all over him. When my sister and I got into a fight, which was frequently, I lured Max into my bedroom with biscuits and let him sprawl on my bed while I sobbed to him about how mean she was. About how unfair life was. I hiked with him when our family went camping in the Adirondacks, made sure he slept alongside my sleeping bag in the tent. Somehow, I believed he'd be my dog forever. But he left just as I was hitting puberty.

Even so, Max showed up in my dreams. I'd find myself in a meadow, and he'd be sitting under a tree, chewing his mangled octopus fleece ball, wagging his tail to greet me. The second I realized we were in doggy heaven, the air would become dense, as if the oxygen levels had plummeted. The dream would turn into a nightmare as I struggled to wake up and bring Max with me. He never made it.

Those dreams fed my longing to have another dog at some point.

When Toby and I got married, I told him I wanted three kids and three dogs. He was good with the three kids but not more than one dog. Because of his career in the military, we moved constantly during our early years. Bringing three kids into the world was enough to manage, without adding a pet. Only after we landed in Des Moines, where Toby took a civilian job as an engineer and I went back to school to study library science, did I finally see my opening.

Toby and the kids—all school age by then—were on board.

Izzy was a long-haired setter, plus a smorgasbord of Heinz 57 we could only guess at but never confirm. Her full name, spelled out in silver script on her water bowl, was Isabelita. Those syllables were too much for our lazy mouths, so Izzy she became. Setters are known for being gentle, good-natured family dogs, but one of the fifty-seven must have overridden that, because Izzy was high-strung and demanding. Things always went wrong around her. Like when she knocked over Toby's water bottle, causing me to slip on the wet floor and fracture my wrist. Or the time she ran away from home just as we were leaving for a Puerto Vallarta vacation. She turned up at the kids' school—empty for the summer—but not before we'd canceled the trip so we could launch a citywide search for her.

Not that the kids didn't love Izzy. They loved her and all the chaos she caused. I think they appreciated having a dog who was more trouble than they were, who made them look well-behaved in comparison. Not to mention she provided them with a ready-made excuse when they needed one.

With hindsight, I can see that Izzy might have been an omen for the trouble brewing in my marriage. At the time, I told myself love evolves. That the increasing isolation I felt was the sign, unfortunate but expected, of a maturing relationship. Couples grow apart. You don't complain about that; you adapt. And I adapted. After the kids left for college and Izzy for doggy heaven, I spent longer hours at the library, started cooking less and relying more on takeout. Toby wasn't around most evenings, so I invited my friend Marge over and we stayed up late watching movies.

Then—on my sixty-fifth birthday no less—Toby made a surprise announcement. He'd had enough of marriage. He wanted to retire and travel the world. Oh, and he intended to do it with someone he'd met recently, a woman half my age. A woman who didn't have a dog or anything else to tie her down. Who, I later learned from my kids, didn't even like dogs.

I was in terrible shape the first year. Toby and I sold the house, and I moved into a condo in Des Moines's East Village, down the block from Marge. It should have felt like a fresh start, but the hard truth is that nothing had prepared me to live on my own—totally on my own, without children or pets, without even an aloof partner to keep the bed warm on winter nights. Everything I'd done to adapt had fallen far short. I sank into depression.

Marge, who'd been happily single since breaking up with her long-term girlfriend, swore by online dating sites, which were just becoming popular. Though I had a decade on her, she thought I wasn't too old to try. "Do one for golden agers," she said. "You don't have to look for a new mate. Just meet some people—men, or women if you want. It'll get you out of the dumps, boost your self-esteem."

Eventually I signed up. It couldn't hurt, right?

I went on one date.

The man had long flowing hair, like that of an Afghan hound, only pure white. I guess some would call him attractive. But I was clueless about vetting new friends. Creating my dating profile was hard enough. When I got to the question asking if I had pets, tears burned in my eyes. It was merely part of a formula to assess compatibility, but I was unnerved nonetheless.

I was even more unnerved over coffee with Mr. Afghan hound. As he fired questions at me about my hobbies, the movies I'd seen, how much a cardio workout raised my heart rate, whether I was a cat person, I crumbled. I wasn't up for being vetted.

I went home and deleted my profile.

"I'm done!" I said to Marge. "If I have to be single for the rest of my life, so be it."

That's when she suggested a dog.

I didn't warm to the idea right away. It had been so long since Izzy died, and I wasn't sure if having a dog now, without a husband or kids to share the responsibilities, would tie me down. But then I thought, *Tie me down from what?* Being tied down might be exactly what I needed.

A toy poodle named Fifi was dog number three.

I had never liked little dogs. I didn't see them as an embarrassment to the canine species or anything like that, but I hated their yap-yap-yapping. And Fifi did yap. But for some reason, her yapping didn't bother me. Whenever someone came to the door, I told her to keep quiet. But she never did. I guess she knew even if yapping might bother them, it didn't bother me. And I was the one she cared about.

She didn't want to let me out of her sight. Ever. And I was happy to have her companionship. She walked with me to the park, accompanied me to the grocery store, traveled with me whenever I visited one of my kids. She was a purse dog, so there wasn't anywhere she couldn't go. She even refrained from more than one or two stifled yaps when I took her to the library in a comfy dog purse. Soon I had a whole collection of purses of different colors and patterns that she loved crawling into.

And she had me cooking special meals. Just for her. After she tasted my chicken livers, she refused anything from a can. Definitely no dry kibble. With all the spoiling, her weight increased so much that her dog purses became a tight fit. The vet advised a strict diet. I'm afraid to say that had no more effect than the same advice I received for myself from my internist.

Toy poodles have a relatively long lifespan for small dogs. Believing Fifi would outlive me, I included elaborate arrangements for her care in my will. I couldn't leave her my inheritance—my lawyer said one piece of property can't own another piece of property—so I set up a trust, with Marge as her guardian. But then I discovered the breed is prone to canine diabetes. That's what happened to poor Fifi.

So here I am, at age eighty, without my little girl.

I'm alone. Again.

Alone and heartbroken.

Never mind that eighty is an obvious multiple of four, I feel anything but strong, stable, and secure. When my kids call from California, Maine, France, or wherever they happen to be, I worry aloud that I may never see them again. Maybe never even speak to them again. Who's to say I won't fall asleep some night and not wake up?

My son is trying to talk me into moving to an in-law unit on his property in Maine. Aside from the fact that the unit hasn't been built yet, I'm not interested. Iowa is home.

Of course Marge will come immediately if I need her. We've timed it: She can get here from her condo in under five minutes. But honestly, it's not the inevitable end of my life that has me down; it's all the lonely and uncertain moments between now and then. All the moments of mortality taunting me with reminders of how fragile life is, of how much I have already lost.

Marge knows better than to promote online dating again. If I had a partner, what would we do? Sip martinis and debate who will die first? And if she suggests another dog, that too is out of the question. At the very least, it wouldn't be fair to the dog.

As I wallow in my depression, I get a call.

It's Marge.

"Edith," she says, "I have someone I want you to meet. Can you come over?"

"Don't start with the dating nonsense again," I say.

"Trust me," she says with a chuckle. "This isn't another Mr. Afghan hound."

So I go.

When I walk into her condo, I see only Marge. "Okay," I say. "You got me. When will they be here?"

She lifts a finger to signal *wait a sec*, then ducks into her bedroom. A minute later, she returns carrying a small bundle, which she thrusts toward me. "Meet my Kerry!"

As I take the rolled-up fleece from her, I feel something squirm. A few more wriggles, and a tiny gold-and-black head pushes its way out. I squeal in delight as the blanket falls away and I hold three pounds of teacup terrier fluff in the palm of my hand.

I raise my eyes to gape at Marge. What a one-eighty! I mean that literally, no pun intended. She's never had a dog or even expressed the slightest interest in one. She tolerated Fifi, yes, but that was about it. I'm not sure what has changed.

Of course the first words out of my mouth are "I want one too!"

It doesn't take a lot of convincing. When I mention my worry about orphaning a dog, Marge tells me not to be concerned. If, God forbid, anything happens to me, she will take care of my dog, just as she would have done for Fifi. Besides, how could I resist? It's already clear I can't.

Soon we are the proud owners of two teacup terriers: Kerry and Terry, both full grown and—most important—fully housebroken.

They say the third time is the charm. But for me, I have to say, dog number four is the charm. To be clear, I'm not saying Terry is more charming than Fifi was or I love one more than the other. I wouldn't do that any more than I'd compare my children or grandchildren. Or my soon-to-be great-grandchild. No, I mean Terry is a good-luck charm with the power to dispel my depression and bring me back to the land of the living. To slash my biological age so it no longer advances in step with my chronological age. Eighty suddenly feels like a mere number.

I'm single and I'm happy. No more of that romance business for me, thank you.

I do all the paperwork to update my will so Terry's future will be secure. Then Marge and I get busy shopping for collars, bows and barrettes, and tiny sweaters. She says zippered rain-and-snow boots are a must, as are rubber-soled sandals to protect against hot pavement. We can dispense with indoor socks since our condos have wall-to-wall carpeting. She is, however, eager to splurge on windproof anti-fog doggy sunglasses. This isn't just a fashion statement—though it is that—we want to protect their eyes.

After our pooches are outfitted, we experiment with shampoos and hair products to see which produce the best results. And there is the matter of hairstyle. Having always kept Fifi clipped, I lean toward a short cut for Terry too. Teddy bear cuts make a dog look extra cuddly.

Marge has other ideas for Kerry. She wants to grow her hair to floor length. When I ask if all the brushing won't be too much work, she says, "It's the best look for dog shows."

This is the first I've heard about showing our dogs.

"It'll be fun," Marge says.

Then it dawns on me: She would do anything to save me from the clutches of depression, even if it means turning her own life upside down with a dog.

But when I put it to her, she scoffs. "Baloney!" she says. "I'm entering Kerry in a show whether you do it with me or not."

So of course I have to do it with her.

There is a bit of a setback when we discover that official dog shows accept miniature dogs but not teacups. A little extra research turns up some mixed-breed shows that allow all sizes. I find one scheduled for early summer and register us. Kerry's hair should be sweeping the floor by then.

As we discuss the training our pups will need, what comes to my mind is their limited social life. The two are besties, even share each other's food without umbrage, but they've had little contact with other dogs, especially not large ones. I worry they won't do well in the exhibition setting. Faced with an overload of sensory stimulation, they could get spooked.

When I mention this, Marge suggests a trial run at an off-leash dog park. There's a nice one over at Riverwalk. We'll just need to get entry passes.

"Let's make it a double date," I say. "Edith and Terry, Marge and Kerry!"

So, bright and early on the first sunny day in March, after most of the snow has melted, we dress our dogs in their boots and best outfits. Kerry's purple sweater says TINY BUT SASSY across her back. Terry's sweater is black, with pink letters that say Pawsitively Woofing for You. We pop them into our faux-leather and mesh sling carriers, and off we go.

It's quiet when we arrive at Riverwalk. Along the far-side fence, a schnauzer is chasing balls tossed by a man with a plastic thrower. We take Kerry and Terry out of their carriers and set them on the ground.

They run in circles, sniffing then scratching at the damp soil as they pick up the scent of other dogs. More people arrive with their pets. A cocker spaniel tears past us, frantic to chase after the schnauzer's ball. He has zero interest in Kerry and Terry. Other dogs are similarly disinterested, except for the obligatory sniff and greet. Which our two graciously reciprocate. Like they've done it their whole lives.

I'm about to pronounce our date a success when I see a Rottweiler bounding in our direction. A woman in a chartreuse puffer jacket trails behind.

I grab Marge's arm. "Maybe we should leave."

Her eyes bulge at the sight of the oncoming dog, but she doesn't want to abort our mission. We came here to provide exposure to other dogs, to make sure ours are ready for exhibition. It's been going well, and we need to see it through.

I feel my blood pressure skyrocket. I'm practically gasping for breath.

But when the huge dog reaches us, it doesn't even notice our little ones. It stops a few feet away, waiting for its owner to catch up. Minding its own business.

Kerry and Terry seem equally oblivious.

Honestly, it's a relief to see that dogs of diverse sizes can coexist peacefully. If only humans could do the same.

Just as I am breathing freely again, I see Terry freeze. It's as if his brain has only now parsed all the information: This massive form is in fact a living critter of the *Canis familiaris* species. A critter he doesn't want in his and Kerry's universe. He emits a long, low growl—a sound I didn't realize his vocal cords could produce—then charges at the Rottweiler, yapping fiercely and nipping at its long legs. Kerry follows.

Marge and I rush to scoop them up before they can do damage. Or be damaged.

The owner casts a look of disdain at Marge and me.

We make apologies as we shove our dogs into their carriers and hurry away.

"Gosh," I say when we are safely in our car, headed home, "that could've been a disaster."

No matter that Terry was the aggressor, the Rottweiler could have mauled him, squish-squashed him. Three pounds versus a hundred and twenty-five? Are you kidding? Clearly Terry has no conception of himself as a small dog. All he has is instinct. Though you would expect instinct to align with self-preservation, his brain must not have factored that in. No, we should never have gone to the park.

When I suggest it might be wise to back out of the dog show, Marge says no, what just happened is the motivation we need to up our game. Terry and Kerry must get proper training. We should have realized that before, not just relied on their cuteness. But there's still time. She will hire a professional handler.

Over the next few months, our dogs go through a complete behavioral overhaul. They learn to sit, to stay, to come, to heel, to be quiet. To follow our commands. Marge and I learn too: hand commands, voice commands, when to give rewards, how to build their confidence. Instead of scooping them up as we've always done, we learn to use the up command to let them know we intend to pick them up. This shows them respect as well as builds esteem.

Eventually the handler suggests another trip to the park.

This time we go to one with a section for small dogs, and it's a success: no chasing, no nipping, no barking. Well, maybe one or two happy yaps.

By early summer, Kerry and Terry have earned their certificates and are all set for the dog show. As anticipated, Kerry's hair is sweeping the floor. Marge and I are ready as well, with our new beige skirt suits and matching flats.

The event is being held on the outskirts of the city, at a fairgrounds bordered by cornfields. We park in the lot, stand in line at the gate to receive our registration packets, then head to a tent where we can do our final grooming. Marge brushes Kerry down, then fusses over the double-looped pink chiffon bow that won't sit straight on her topknot. I have to rush Marge so we don't miss the start of the exhibition.

We are among the last to enter the ring.

The bleachers are packed with friends, families, fanciers, and dog lovers of all kinds. A stage with the announcer's podium has been set up at one end of the ring. A booth for judges is on one side of the stage, and a press booth on the other side. Dogs are grouped by size around the perimeter.

We are ushered to the section for small dogs, adjacent to the judges' booth.

I shoot Marge a wide grin.

She knows what I'm smiling about: All the work to get here was worth it. Our dogs look as gorgeous as this Iowa summer day. They will be as well-behaved and orderly as the rows of corn outside the venue. At eighty, I may be the oldest handler but I stand with pride beside Terry, eager to walk him through his paces and lead him to the pedestal. I'm confident he will hold all his poses with equanimity. And without yapping.

The announcer explains the rules and the order of events. The smallest male dogs will be called into the ring first, followed by the smallest females. The other groups will wait in their respective sections.

I bend over to give Terry's teddy bear cut a final fluffing. As I whisper a pep talk and tell him his big moment has arrived, I don't notice the masked man emerge from beneath the bleachers and enter the ring. With an AR-15.

I look up as he starts to spray the crowd with bullets.

People are shrieking, running every which way, falling.

It's total mayhem.

Dogs large and small are breaking free of unsuspecting handlers.

Terry jumps in terror, slips his leash, and charges—all four feet airborne—into the ring.

Marge has dropped to the ground, clutching Kerry. She pulls on my skirt, yells at me to get down.

All I can see is Terry. In the ring. Circling the gunman.

My poor doggy darling!

No way do I let my baby be slaughtered.

Suddenly my own life feels immaterial.

Kicking off my flats, I run after him, as fast as my body will move, into the ring, into the gunfire.

I catch him and scoop him up in my arms. No up command. Just hold him close, close, close.

As we go down together.

Fuji

I am Fuji and I am a statistic. I was fourteen when I was shot. I was living in Torrance, California, and attending ninth grade. My pronouns were he/him. I am survived by my parents and grandparents.

I'm a quiet kid. Really, really quiet. I don't mean I never talk. I just don't talk to a lot of people. I've got one best buddy, Omar, and we talk every day. We're in a lot of the same classes, so it's easy. Plus we text all the time. The slightest thing, and we'll shoot each other a text. Even in class, when our phones are supposed to be off. Or when something cool happens.

Like now, while waiting for the school bus that will take me home, I text him my new highest score on the Freaks video game. Challenge him to beat it.

I could calculate the odds on how many games he will have to play to do that. Except if I'm right about how many, he'll get on me for being a know-it-all.

I may be mad good at math, but I don't want anyone to say I'm a know-it-all.

You'd think I'd be good at languages since I grew up in a bilingual family. My grandparents speak mostly Japanese. I can understand them, but that's about it. I always answer in English. If I'm not going to talk much, I might as well say what I do say in one language.

I'll stick with numbers.

When I was little, I realized I could figure out all kinds of number problems most people couldn't begin to do without a computer. I didn't need a computer, because my brain worked as fast as one. Like in first grade, when our teacher, Ms. Blais, told the class we celebrate the birth of our country on the Fourth of July.

I already knew that. And I had known it for some time, because it is my birthday too. Without bothering to raise my hand—I wasn't as quiet back then—I called out: "My birthday's July Fourth!"

She wheeled around and grinned at me. "What a great birthday, Fuji!" Then she started to laugh like someone was tickling her ribs and she couldn't catch her breath. "But I bet you weren't born in 1776!"

The other kids roared with her.

They were laughing at me, like I was an idiot. I wanted to die on the spot. "N-n-n-o," I stammered. "But, but, but I was born on a *Thursday*. And July 4, 1776, was a Thursday too."

I wasn't showing off; I was just standing up for what I knew. And for being born an American. I didn't get why Ms. Blais stopped short and gave me a funny look. Like whoever had been tickling her had just pinched her nose with a clothespin instead.

A few more incidents made it clear most people's brains were slower than mine. I could have gotten a lot of attention by showing off my brain's speed. Maybe I should have appreciated that, but I didn't. I hated it. I especially hated that the counselor made me take a bunch of tests none of the other kids had to take. My parents were called in for a special meeting about it. They didn't tell me, but Ms. Blais let it slip.

After that, I just shut up and didn't speak much. Even when I knew the answer to a question, I kept quiet. I only spoke if the teacher called on me and forced me to say something.

Most days after school, Omar and I ride the bus together. We stop off at his house, because his mother works late and no one is around to tell us we can't play any video games until we've finished our homework. After we've played a bunch of games, I hightail it home so I can finish my homework before my parents can complain that I haven't started it yet.

Sometimes one of us has something else to do after school. Like today. Omar texted me that a wire on his braces came loose. His mom is picking him up and driving him to the orthodontist.

Which means I'm riding the bus by myself.

I take a seat toward the front and start another Freaks game. I want to beat my new best score before Omar does. Besides, anyone who sits next to me will see I'm too busy to talk to them.

Just as the door is closing, a student jumps on the bus. He's a big kid and he plops down on the seat beside me. Doesn't even check if there are other empty seats.

I know him. He's TJ. He's in my math class, but he's a lot bigger than me because he has repeated two grades.

I keep my eyes on my screen and ignore him.

He drums his fingers on his algebra textbook, keeping beat with whatever is in his earbuds. Making sure his rhythm jostles our seat enough to cut my concentration and slow my gaming speed by a few milliseconds. Every millisecond counts. I suspect he knows that.

I edge closer to the window. Hope he won't notice I want to get as far away from him as possible.

But he does notice. "Hey, *Apple*," he snickers. "You're real smart, aren't you?"

It's not the kind of comment you can respond to. If I say, "Yeah, I'm smart," he'll say I'm a smart-ass. Or that everyone knows I'm really a dumb fuck. And I can't say I'm not smart, because he'll have a comeback for that as well.

If I say something like "You're smart too, TJ," he'll think I'm being fake. Which would be true. But it would piss him off. Really, I can't win.

What I want to do most is tell him my name isn't Apple. I want to ask if anyone has ever called him a slur word, and how he felt about it. Tell him to stop being a bully.

Except I'm smart enough to know you can't reason with a bully. So

I just endure the rest of the ride. It's only ten minutes, but it feels like a very long ten minutes.

When we get to my stop—which is also his stop—he leaps up, elbows past everyone, and dashes off the bus.

I move slowly, trying to put some distance between us. As I start up the sidewalk, he's already two houses ahead. He lives a block farther than I do, yet he'll probably get home before me. I'm fine with that.

Then I see something TJ is totally unaware of. A slip of paper falls out of the algebra book he's carrying. It catches the breeze, goes airborne for a few seconds, then sails toward some low-growing plants at the edge of the sidewalk.

I hurry to catch it as it lands on a bush.

Normally when someone drops something, I pick it up, then run after them and hand it to them. No second thoughts. And they thank me. TJ isn't the kind of guy you can do that with. I stare at the piece of lined yellow paper, which has been folded into a rectangle about the size of a packet of mustard, then stuff it into the zippered pocket on my backpack and head home.

A plate of Mom's freshly baked *melonpan* is waiting for me on the kitchen table, along with a note explaining she's on a conference call in her office. I sit down and play video games on my phone while I eat two buns. I reach for a third, but I know she'll be disappointed in me if I eat more. She'll say she was testing me to see if I could resist temptation. If my grandma comes over, she'll for sure say something about *enryo suru*.

So I push the plate away. Then I gather up my phone and backpack and head to my room.

I don't think about TJ's paper until I'm ready to start my homework. I reach for a stick of gum, and there it is—in the pocket of my backpack. Examining it more closely, I see the edge is ragged, like it was torn off a pad. There are red ink marks on one side, not legible though. Because it was folded multiple times, even when I turn it over in my hand, I can't see what's inside. I assume there is something written inside.

Yet I'm not sure I want to know. I'm not interested in getting into TJ's business. Like I wouldn't stick my toe in mud just so I can say it's mucky. Really, I shouldn't have picked the frigging paper out of the bushes in the first place. So I toss it toward my wastebasket, on the other side of the room.

Only I miss.

Which means I have to stand up, retrieve it, and put it in the basket. That extra effort makes me more curious. Instead of trashing it, I take the paper back to my desk, unfold it, and smooth it out.

Three words have been scrawled with a red Sharpie on a diagonal across the page: KILL YOU MFs.

I quickly refold it and stick it back in my pack. Like I didn't read it.

Except I did.

And I know what it means. I know what *MF* stands for. And I know a threat when I see one. My brain doesn't have to function like a supercomputer storing every pixel of an image for me to remember those three words from now until forever. I can't unsee them.

So I focus on my homework. Try to pretend this didn't just happen.

Omar texts me. Says his tooth hurts. Says he took the aspirin his mom gave him, so he should be okay in the morning. He asks me what's up.

I want to tell him about TJ's note. But this isn't the kind of thing you can put in a text, so I just type, "nothing c u tmw." And go back to trying to forget what I've seen. To convincing myself TJ's threat can't be real.

If it were real, I'd have to tell my parents. Or somebody. I'd have to speak up.

But it can't be real. TJ may be a bully, but he isn't a killer.

If I talk to my parents, they could overreact. They could decide it's not safe for me to take the bus, go to Omar's house, do all the stuff I normally do. Even if the note is just a dumb joke, I could lose my freedom.

Honestly, I wish I had never picked up that stupid paper. I consider going back and sticking it in the bush. But it's not like I can do that either. It's got my fingerprints all over it now. Almost like I wrote the note.

I could tear it into little pieces and throw them away.

Or burn them.

But none of that will make me forget what it says.

If there is any chance TJ's threat is real, destroying his note won't stop him from carrying it out.

When I finally get to bed—after eating dinner with my parents, finishing my homework, playing several more video games, falling just short of a new high score—I still can't get the note out of my mind. I don't want to wait till tomorrow to talk to Omar. So I text him to see if he's still up. But his phone is offline. He probably went to sleep early because of his tooth.

Since I can't sleep, I lie in bed and run through all the possible scenarios in my mind.

The first is to take the note to the principal's office. Tell them who wrote it and where I found it. Tell them I was worried he might do something for real. Let them take it from there. I'm pretty sure that's what my parents would expect me to do.

Then I imagine talking this over with Omar.

He'd probably say, "Dude, what if TJ finds out you ratted on him?"

That's a good question. What if he does?

I don't think the principal would reveal I was the one who turned in the note. She'd just call TJ's parents and say a note was found. But it would be clear she knew who found it.

And then, when he hears about all this, who is the first person TJ will think of? Me. Of course. He'll know he still had the note on the bus. He'll realize he lost it between the bus and his house. And he knows I was following him. He won't need advanced math to put two and two together.

So how do I get the note to the principal without it being tied to me in any way?

I could put it in an envelope and slide it under the door to the principal's office. That could work.

But then I realize they'll bring it to the security team, to the police even. When the police investigate, they'll focus on the forensic evidence. They'll find my fingerprints. Which would be a disaster if they pick up my prints and not TJ's. And think I wrote it. They'd be at our front door in no time. I quickly nix that option.

Maybe it would be better to call the police hotline. Or a mental health hotline. Instead of saying I found a note, I could say I overheard TJ saying those words. But what if he never said them to anyone? What if he only wrote that note? It would all still come back to TJ realizing someone knows about his note, and that someone must be me.

My mind is going in circles.

If only he didn't sit next to me on the bus. If only the wire on Omar's braces hadn't broken. If only, if only . . .

By now it's the middle of the night. I decide to change the question I'm asking myself. Suppose there's no way to report TJ's note without him tracing it back to me. Suppose I go ahead and report him anyway. Would that be so bad?

He'd have more pressing problems than me at that point. Unless . . . that makes me his most pressing problem. He could end up seeing me as the biggest MF on his list. He could make my life hell.

I can't risk that. I mean, I'd risk it if turning him in could stop him from doing something terrible. But I'd have to trust that the principal or the authorities could stop him before he does whatever he wants to do to me. Or to anyone else. I'm not sure I can count on that.

It's almost dawn when I reach the end of these thoughts. All the scenarios I've played out are based on what happens if I report TJ. I haven't considered what happens if I don't do or say anything.

So I think about that.

The worst-case scenario is I don't say anything and he does something crazy. Really crazy. Obviously it's a chance no one would want to take.

But what kind of odds are we talking about?

I recall hearing that twelve kids die from gun violence every day. It's one of those stats you don't ever want to think about. *How*, I wonder, *would it translate into the odds of a student who wrote the kind of scary note TJ wrote actually killing someone?*

I want to calculate those odds, but I don't have enough information—like for starters, how many kids write these notes or even think these thoughts—for my computer brain to be able to run numbers. I want to say it's low odds. It's not zero, though. Which doesn't make me feel much better. Still, it's all I've got for now.

I get out of bed, take a shower, and put on my school clothes. In the light of day, the thoughts that have crowded my mind all night have lost some of their power. There are lots of bullies at school. A lot of kids say or write things they don't mean. Right? I've probably been blowing all this out of proportion. Jeez, I'm worse than my own parents.

I realize I don't have to make a decision now. I can talk to Omar after school today and get his ideas.

I put the note in an envelope and stash it at the bottom of my backpack. Just in case I see things differently later.

Omar has saved me a seat on the bus.

"You okay?" I ask as I sit down beside him.

He flashes a metallic, toothy smile. "Yep!"

I don't bother to look around and check if TJ is on the bus. Instead

I focus on making sure Omar didn't beat my top score on the Freaks game. He didn't.

I expect to see TJ in our first-period math class. I tell myself I'm going to walk past him and ignore him like he's a big fat zero.

But when I get there, I notice the seat in the corner by the door where he usually sits is empty.

As the teacher announces that we'll be doing quadratic equations today, the door opens and TJ slips into his seat.

I know I said I'd ignore him, but I feel I should keep an eye on him. I don't want him to realize I'm watching him. But I feel like someone needs to.

He is fumbling with his textbook under his desk. Then I see it's not about his textbook. He's using the book to hide something else.

All the other kids are facing forward, watching the teacher write an equation on the board. I'm the only one who has noticed that TJ is holding a gun on his lap.

Cold blood rushes through me.

My mind spins. I should have gone to the principal. Immediately. What was I thinking? Whatever happens now is on me. It's all my fault.

As I watch, he raises his gun, aims at the teacher.

I do the only thing that's left to do: take the bullet myself.

I spring from my seat and dive at him.

As I land on him and the gun goes off, the last thing I see is TJ's eyes. Filled with fear.

Ginger

I am Ginger and I am a statistic. I was thirty-five when I was shot. I was living in Boulder, Colorado, a single mom juggling three part-time jobs: preschool aide, ski instructor, and online customer service agent for a travel company. My pronouns were she/her. I am survived by my parents and my daughter, Kayla.

"Count me in. I'll be there!" That's what I texted back to Ashley yesterday—the same words I used when she invited me a year ago to join her climate activist group.

She knew I'd been wanting to get more involved ever since my daughter's first serious asthma attack, brought on by smoke from the Rocky Mountain wildfires. As Kayla and I left the ER and I got her inhaler prescription filled and ordered air purifiers for our home, I wondered if we should relocate. Go somewhere fresh air and water would be guaranteed. The only problem was . . . where?

Ashley's kids don't have immediate health issues, but she sees the big picture. She stresses over the future for our kids and grandkids, as she rides her e-cargo bike around town and tracks the damage caused by her carbon footprint daily on more than one app. Knowing that signing petitions, making donations, and recycling everything that can be recycled and not buying anything that can't be is not sufficient, she organized a core group of eight, with others to be added on an as-needed basis for specific activities. I signed on as one of the core.

We call ourselves the Climate Corp 8, or CC8 for short.

It's a diverse group, yet each of us is connected to Ashley in some way. I know her because our kids attend the same school. Veena and Ron are colleagues of hers at the university, where they work in the administration. Mark is Ashley's cousin. Juanita has been her friend since college. Leigh is her next-door neighbor. Ming-Tao is a mentor of hers and probably knows more than the rest of us combined about climate justice. Ashley didn't include her husband in the group, though he's also an activist. She said it was precautionary, much as some parents of young children consider it prudent to fly in separate airplanes.

We've accomplished a lot this past year. We started by organizing events to raise money: a plant sale, an upcycling workshop, a used-book fair, a concert, several house parties. We also traveled to protests led by national groups. Later we compiled what we'd learned and created a climate info packet. We gave it to some teachers, who used it in their classrooms and then spread the word; soon it was being picked up in schools around the country.

This evening, while most people are at home eating dinner, the eight of us are in Ashley's downstairs rec room, seated around a table with an assortment of chips, crackers, cheese, dips, and sodas. I peel the beeswax wrap off the focaccia with bruschetta I made last night and cut the bread into a dozen pieces so folks can help themselves.

We've all silenced our phones. Mine is on vibrate in case Kayla tries to reach me. That's what you do when you're a single parent with a thirteen-year-old who's home alone for a couple hours.

"Okay," Ashley says when it's clear we have settled in. She reaches for some crackers with hummus, then says, "We've been talking about going bigger. I think it's time."

"You mean take action on the university's investment in fossil fuels?" Ron says.

She nods. "They still have several hundred million in old energy systems."

"Which undermines their commitment to their own R&D and

educational efforts to create more sustainable energy solutions," Ming-Tao adds. "I don't understand how they justify it."

"So hypocritical," Leigh says.

"We should challenge them," Veena says.

There is a murmur of agreement.

Ron points out that students have staged protests, but the university isn't budging. They haven't shown a genuine willingness to listen to the community.

Juanita turns to Ashley. "What do you propose?"

"To be clear," she says, "this isn't about me proposing anything. Everything we do, as always, must be endorsed by the whole group."

"To be equally clear," Ron says, "some of us are university employees. We can't protest in any official capacity. We'll be there, like everyone else, as members of the community at large. Members of the Earth community."

"Even if our activism puts our jobs in jeopardy," Veena adds.

There is a moment of silence as the gravity of that sinks in.

"I'm willing to pay the price," Ashley says. "If it comes to that."

After those of us who don't work at the university have commended this level of sacrifice, we brainstorm options. We could do a sit-in on university property. Perhaps a die-in on a campus lawn. Or a blockade of the entrance to the administration building. We could chain ourselves to each other. We could print and distribute flyers, talk to students about a classroom walkout. For all these actions, we will want to include members of our extended group.

"Whatever we do," Ashley says, "we will adhere to the principles of nonviolent civil disobedience. Our actions may break a law and we may risk arrest, but we will not damage or cause harm to property or people."

"Right," Ming-Tao adds, "our purpose will be to call attention to the issue at hand: Investing in fossil fuels contributes to climate change, which disproportionately affects vulnerable and marginalized communities. These investments contradict the stated values and goals of the university. We want to invite publicity and create a broader platform for our message, without engaging in actions that could alienate those whose support we want to gain."

Everyone is in agreement.

After a wide-ranging discussion, we narrow it down to a sit-in either on the steps of Regent Administrative Center or on the steps of Norlin Library.

Ron says the administration building makes more sense because their policies are our target.

Veena lobbies for the library, saying more students will be in the vicinity, and we want to get students involved.

Ron counters that the library is better suited for large protests, where the speakers stand on the steps and a crowd rallies on the lawn. Our sit-in would be dwarfed in that space.

It's starting to look like we're deadlocked. But then Mark has an idea. "Here's something out of the box," he says. "What if we hold the protest at Pearl Street Mall?"

"Off campus?" I say.

"Yes. We're protesting university investments, but fossil fuels affect the entire community."

"I like it," Ming-Tao says.

Once we've made the pivot to off campus and decided to focus on speaking with people rather than staging a sit-in, we quickly settle on the Boulder County Courthouse. It's in an area where folks shop or hang out, so it has high visibility. At the same time, it represents government, policymaking, accountability. The space near the fountain is perfect for our group.

The next question is when.

Ashley points out we can gather legally on the weekend because our presence won't block the entrance or interfere with courthouse business. And we won't have to skip work. A two-hour event, give or take, should give us the level of community exposure we're looking for.

We agree to meet the following Saturday at eleven. Over the next few days, we will reach out to our extended group. More people will amplify our impact.

Leigh is wiping crumbs off the table and into a napkin, and the others are standing up, turning on their phones, readying themselves to leave, when Ming-Tao signals for our attention. "Before you go," he says, "there is one thing we haven't considered."

"What's that?" we ask in chorus.

"Who might come after us if we do this."

Ashley looks deflated. "Say more."

The others silence their phones, sit down again.

"In the past year," he says, "our info packets generated a lot of buzz, enough for schools around the country to seek us out. We've also seen more people following us on social media, donating to causes we support."

"When I mention the CC8, many people have heard of us," Mark says.

"That's a good thing, isn't it?" I say.

"Of course," Ming-Tao says. "But we need to appreciate that attracting attention means we've also been noticed by groups that oppose our work. It's a catch-22. Now that we've been successful, we're also on the radar of some repugnant entities. We know for a fact that extremist groups in this area are watching us."

"Like the Red Boiz," Ashley says.

Ming-Tao nods. "As long as they thought we were only educational do-gooders, they were willing to look the other way. But once they saw us getting traction, they started to push back. You all saw their veiled threats on social media. Now they're waiting for us to make a move."

"Like this protest," Ron says.

"Exactly."

"But we won't publicize it," Ashley objects. "Are you suggesting they'll know what we're planning anyway? Like they're listening in on our chats or hacking into our computers?"

Ming-Tao hesitates, as if he's considering how likely that is. "Not at this point. At least I doubt it. Like I said, we're on their radar. If we receive live media coverage on Saturday, they could very well show up."

"And stage a counterprotest?" I ask.

"Something like that."

Ashley is following his train of thought, putting the pieces together. "They could rush down to the mall and set themselves up nearby."

"That's a possibility."

"It could get ugly."

"Yes."

"There could be violence."

He nods. "They're associated with a national group that does this kind of thing. It's what they're known for: intimidating social justice and climate justice groups. By any means necessary."

There is a pause as we take this in. Maybe we should have thought of it before, but we didn't. The truth is, except for Ming-Tao, we don't have much experience as activists. I know I have a lot to learn.

"Well," says Ashley finally, "those scumbags may be intimidating, but we won't be intimidated."

"No, we won't," Mark echoes.

"There's a reliable security presence at the mall, isn't there?" Ron adds.

No one disputes that.

Ming-Tao clarifies he doesn't mean we should abandon our plan. We should simply be aware of all the possible factors.

"Point taken," Ashley says. Given this new information about the level of risk involved, she thinks we should all confirm we're still on board.

It doesn't take long to go around the room. Everyone says they're in.

She gets to me last. "Ginger?"

All eyes turn in my direction.

I know what they assume I'll say, but suddenly I'm not so certain. "Can I have a minute?" I ask.

"Of course," Ashley says. "And if you need more time, you can email us between now and Saturday and let us know what you've decided."

That confuses me. "I thought you said we won't take any actions that aren't endorsed by the whole group."

Ashley clarifies that she sees a difference between making sure every action is backed by the whole group and requiring all of us to participate in every action we agree as a group to undertake. In other words, I don't have to attend the protest, but I do have the power to veto it. In the latter case, we'd have to discuss how to modify the plan so everyone can get on board, even if I or anyone else is uncomfortable attending. Clearly we won't have time to do that tonight.

"I'll decide now," I say. "Give me five?"

No one objects, so I walk over to the Ping-Pong table on the far side of the room. Kayla has played many games with Ashley's kids on this table over the years. I pick up a ball and pour it back and forth between my hands as I consider what might happen if the CC8 goes through with the protest as planned.

I picture us at the courthouse. Eight of us are there, plus a dozen friends and supporters, in the area by the fountain in front of the building. It's a warm, sunny Saturday, and the tulips are in full bloom along the mall. All fifteen thousand of them. People are approaching us, eager to discuss how they can get involved in the climate movement. Members of the press are taking pictures and posting them on social media. We're pumped to get all the coverage. Things are going as planned. If anything, better than planned.

Then the Red Boiz show up. Only three of them, but they're loud. They position themselves across the street and heckle us.

We don't respond.

They want us to react, so they escalate. They taunt. They threaten. One tosses a bottle that lands in the fountain.

We don't take the bait. We came to protest peacefully, and that is what we do. Despite the knots tightening in our stomachs, we stand our ground.

Mall security station themselves farther down the block and monitor the situation, which provides some reassurance.

But then what? Do the Boiz walk away after they get tired of shouting at us? Do they just say, "Oh well, have your little protest," and then leave?

I don't think so.

One way or another, they will assert their dominance.

In my imagination, I see an SUV pull up in front of the courthouse, and the three Boiz who have been heckling us pile in. Before we can breathe a sigh of relief, their passenger-side windows crack open. The barrels of three AR-15s poke through. As they speed away, they fire a volley of bullets, killing as many of us as they can. Mall security is powerless to stop the attack.

All that flashes through my mind in a matter of seconds. And I know that visualizing a worst-case scenario doesn't mean it is likely to happen. It isn't a reason for me to veto our group's plans. Ashley and the others are taking real risks with their jobs. I tell myself I need to dig deep and muster at least as much courage.

As I try to do that, I feel my phone vibrating.

It's a text from Kayla: "when will u b home?"

This meeting wasn't supposed to last so long. Now I'm keeping everyone waiting. Including her. I quickly text: "half hour max"

She replies with the folded hands emoji.

"sorry," I text. "want me to call?"

She sends the arms-crossed emoji. That usually means, "Nope, not doing that." But now as I read between the lines, so to speak, I understand that she's saying, "Don't you dare phone me while you're in your meeting; that would be so embarrassing."

Confident I've deciphered teenage code, I reply with a heart emoji.

Now another scene is playing in my mind as I stare out the window behind the Ping-Pong table. The sky over the mountains may be flaming orange as the sun sets, but I'm thinking about Saturday morning.

Kayla is at home alone. No, actually she's at her soccer match, which is scheduled for the same time as the protest. I imagine her running down the field, her long carrot-red ponytail flying behind her, trying to score a goal. Just as she scores, news comes through on her coach's phone: There's been a terrorist attack at the courthouse, a few blocks away, and protesters were shot. They halt the game, go into shelter-in-place mode. Kayla knows I went to the protest. She's beside herself with worry. Then she gets confirmation: I am dead. I see her collapsing, crying, wailing, hysterical. Inconsolable.

I can't bear to imagine more.

I turn around and cross the room to the others.

Since I've taken extra time to consider the risks, they assume I've gotten to yes.

But I haven't. I look at one and then the other, full circle around the room. "I can't do it," I say. "I'm sorry."

Ashley puts her arm around my shoulder. "It's okay," she says. "We understand."

I'm relieved she isn't making me explain. I'm not sure what I would say. If I said my daughter has only one parent, so I have to protect myself in order to be able to protect her, they might feel my decision is warranted. But I'm not the only single parent in our group.

More importantly, if it came down to it, all our kids would suffer in a scenario like the one I just envisioned.

"I want you to know," I say, "this isn't a veto. I support all of you doing the protest. It's so important. And I promise I'll find other ways to contribute to the cause we all believe in."

It's Saturday and I'm sitting in the stands, on the top row, watching Kayla's soccer match. The score is 0–0, but it doesn't matter. Everyone is having fun and I'm grateful to be here.

At the same time, I would be lying if I said I wasn't worried about the CC8. And a bit guilty that I'm having a relaxing morning while they're putting their lives on the line. Literally. I'll feel a lot better when the protest is over and everyone is home safe and sound.

In the meantime, I text Ashley for updates.

She texts back that things are going well. They're seeing lots of community support. Everyone, she says, loves the colorful signs Kayla painted. As proof, she sends photos. I smile when I see Veena with the sign saying DON'T BE A FOSSIL FOOL! I wish I were there, holding it myself. I forward it to Kayla so it will be the first thing she sees when she turns on her phone after the game.

Then I notice Ashley's husband in the photo, his face partially obscured by the sign. I zoom in, and it's definitely him. What happened to their separate airplane strategy? If there was ever a time for precautions, this would be it. Anxiously I scan through the other photos, searching for evidence of anyone looking even remotely suspicious. But all I see are animated, engaged, fired-up faces. I'm not even sure what I'm looking for. Which of course is the problem in a nutshell.

Ashley texts a little while later to say staff from the *Daily Camera* and the *Boulder Weekly* have come by. Word is getting out. Everything is going as planned.

I send back a string of celebratory emojis.

But in truth, my anxiety is rising. What if everything is going great ... until it isn't? Part of me wants to slip out—Kayla will understand when I explain later—so I can go downtown and be the eyes and ears I'm afraid my friends are failing to use for themselves. Of course that means taking precisely the risk I've come here to avoid.

So I focus on my daughter. She's been running the field like a champ but missed several goals and couldn't convert on a penalty kick. That doesn't stop me from cheering at the top of my lungs, "Go, Kay, go!" Even if she can't hear me, putting all my energy into the cheer eases my anxiety.

At halftime, the score is still 0–0. As I pick up my phone to search social media for updates on the protest, a message from Leigh comes through: Ashley was interviewed by Denver7. The protest will be covered on the TV nightly news. She also says that having met and exceeded all expectations, they're about to conclude the event so everyone can grab lunch.

Again I send celebratory emojis. But this time I'm not caught by an undertow of anxiety. I'm starting to believe that the unthinkable I was so worried might happen won't happen. The CC8 staged a climate protest, and no extremists showed up. When we get home, Kayla and I will watch the news and she'll see her signs. Her friends will see them. We'll all be proud of her.

To make sure I'm not floating on a false sense of success, I text Ashley: "all ok?"

She texts back, "couldn't be better!"

As much as I'm pleased to hear things went so well, I feel a pang of regret. I can see now that my fears were overblown. Yes, there was a risk we could have been massacred by extremists, but it was far from inevitable. In reality, I would have been fine at the protest, along with everyone else. Kayla would not have been traumatized, as I feared.

I text Ashley to apologize, to let her know I'm sorry I didn't come.

She texts back: "no worries, you'll be here next time"

I feel my body relax. She's right. There will be plenty of opportunities to get more involved. I won't let fear drive me anymore. I text back: "count me in, i'll be there." I smile, realizing those are the words I used before. I mean them now more than ever.

When I look up from my phone, the second half of the match is underway.

Kayla is advancing down the field, in full control of the ball. She passes it to a teammate, who receives it and deftly fends off a defender, then delivers it back to my daughter with a perfectly timed pass. In a split second, Kayla gauges the proximity of the opposing players and the angle between the ball and net, then lifts her foot.

The fans are standing, jumping up and down, rocking the bleachers.

I stand and cheer with them: "Go, Kayla!"

She takes her shot.

The goalie dives and misses.

She scores!

Her teammates surround her, lift her up. They've taken the lead.

Any regret I had about being here vanishes. This is where I am supposed to be—cheering on my daughter as she makes a winning play. What a star!

As the game resumes, I hear shouts off to my right. These aren't cheers, though. They're angry voices.

I turn to see some scruffy-looking young men locked in a heated argument. It could be about the game, but I get the sense none of them are friends of the players. I'm not sure who they are or why they're here.

One reaches out and slugs another.

He returns the punch.

Several others join in.

Although the soccer match is continuing, everyone in the bleachers has turned to watch the brawl. A couple of bystanders step in to keep things from escalating further.

Two young men shove them aside and pull out guns.

They start shooting.

People around me duck. On their bellies, squeezed between seats.

But that seems too unsafe, so I jump up, as do some others, and try to scramble down off the bleachers.

The game stops, and the players stare up at us in horror. Security officers rush toward the stands, guns drawn.

I vault over one row, then another, moving as fast as I can. Just one more row and I'll be on the field.

Suddenly it's as if I've been punched hard from behind.

My body pitches forward. I feel it double over, tumble across the bottom row, fall headfirst onto the ground.

The hard cement is up against my face.

I can't tell if my eyes are open or closed.

A blurry form a few inches away coalesces into a child's dirty sneaker. Beyond it, a discarded newspaper. And a wet substance spreading out around my body in all directions. An unmistakable pool of dark red liquid.

Already Kayla is light-years away.

Howard

I am Howard and I am a statistic. I was sixty-seven when I was shot. I was retired from a career in urban planning and was living with my wife, Ella, in Dorchester, Massachusetts, in the two-story Colonial we bought when our kids were little. My pronouns were he/him. I am survived by my two sons and five grandchildren.

Ella and I have had a few decades to create our bedtime story. Or I should say, stories. Plural. We see ourselves as creative artists of the night, with a full repertoire of rituals for every mood and moment. The fact that we've weathered so many storms and learned to read each other well helps. We also like to mix it up, to surprise each other with a little bit of this and a little bit of that. It would be boring to do exactly the same thing night after night. Lately, massage has been our go-to ritual.

Bedtime starts when one of us goes upstairs, turns down the bed, puts on soothing music, takes out the oils, dims the lights. Makes sure everything is perfect in every way. Last night I gave the first massage, which means it's my turn to receive one first tonight.

Ella leaves the living room earlier than usual. Thinking she must have something extra special planned, I skim to the end of the article I've been reading in today's paper, detailing the latest proposal to restore affordable housing programs in Boston. I had a long career in urban planning and was a zoning administrator in several local jurisdictions, and I like to keep up with news in the field. Then I put the paper down, turn off the lights, and head upstairs. Two steps at a time. That's my mood tonight.

The sultry voice of Nina Simone greets me as I enter the candlelit room. Ella is perched on the edge of our bed, wearing her shimmering blue satin robe. Even in the low light, I see the cute way she bites her bottom lip as she welcomes me to lie down beside her.

I step out of my shoes and drop my clothes on the armchair by the window, then join her on the bed. She has sprinkled dried rose petals on the pillows. That's my wife. She thinks of everything.

Her hands are warm and velvety as her effleurage strokes glide up my back and across my shoulders. My body melts into the mattress as I inhale the ylang-ylang she has added to the massage oil. It's my favorite, and she knows that.

Usually she builds up to a firm, deep touch that allows her to seek out and knead the areas where I hold tension, but now she simply runs her fingers lightly over my skin. Not that I'm complaining. My body is buzzing. Like a living, vibrating honeycomb for bees. I wonder if—no, I hope—she has lovemaking on her mind.

After a while, when the buzz has reached a steady pitch, she motions for me to flip onto my back, then lays her hands motionless on my chest, signaling the end of my massage. Time to switch places.

I pull myself off the bed—always the hardest part of this ritual—and help her out of her robe. My body has enough internal heat that I'm fine staying in the buff. While she relaxes onto her stomach, I drip oil onto my hands and rub them together. "Okay, hun," I whisper as I place a knee on either side of her. "I'm gonna take you there."

"Mm-hmm," she whispers back, as if we're already more than halfway there.

The playlist is now on the Isley Brothers, making it easy to match Ella's mood of slow and tender. Starting at the top of her head, I move my fingers in small circles through her gray curls, gently stimulating her scalp. Stopping at her ears, my thumb and forefinger linger on the lobes. When I get to her neck, I trace the sides of her vertebrae as my hands travel toward her thoracic spine. Still keeping it tender, still keeping the mood.

As I go lower, I notice a change in her breathing. "Hun?" I say.

When there is no response, I bend over to check more closely.

She has fallen asleep.

I won't deny my first reaction is to feel some kind of way. I mean, I thought we were on board the love train. This old body of mine certainly was!

But I stifle my disappointment. Because I sense we may have a bigger problem: This isn't the first time lately she's been overtired. The truth is, I'm worried. Especially since we had a laid-back Saturday, didn't do anything strenuous, turned in earlier than usual. I'm pretty sure she didn't intend to cut our lovemaking short.

We'll have to discuss this over breakfast.

I get up quietly, cover her with the quilt so she won't catch a chill, then go into the bathroom and rinse the excess oil off my hands. I put on my pajamas and crawl back into bed beside her.

Not tired myself, I listen to a Coltrane instrumental track as I reflect on what to say to Ella in the morning that won't put her on defense. She still works four days a week as a dental hygienist and has no plans to retire. I get that she wants to stay active, but those hours are taking a toll. And I'm not just thinking about our sex life. I'm thinking about all aspects of her physical and emotional well-being. I retired at the earliest date possible so I could do volunteer work that excites me. Ella says I'm working as hard now as I did for the city. I tell her there's a huge difference.

One thing about my wife, though: She's always been set on doing things her way. I love that about her. It also means it's pointless to preplan what to say to her about her exhaustion. I decide to wing it in the morning and trust whatever comes out of my mouth to be the words she needs to hear.

When the playlist ends, I put one arm around her and burrow my nose in her hair, careful not to wake her. The sweet, pungent scent of oil lures me toward sleep.

As I drift off, I remember Ella on our first anniversary, when we drove up to Revere Beach for the afternoon, followed by an elegant dinner out. She was eight months pregnant and looked amazing in her maternity swimsuit. I see us at the water's edge, tossing a multicolored inflatable beach ball between us. That ball made so many trips to the beach with the kids over the years. But on that day, one of my tosses went a bit too far. Ella took a dive for it and lost her footing. Suddenly she was clutching her stomach as she struggled to get up and out of the waves. The waves were only knee-high, but I panicked: *Oh my god, the baby!*

By the time I reached her—a matter of seconds—she was on her feet and laughing. Everything was fine. We held hands as we waded farther into the water to retrieve the ball.

Now, I let myself float into a dream. Warm, gentle waves lap against my thighs as my wife's lips meet mine in an endless kiss.

I'm deep in sleep, not even dreaming, when I feel something touch my elbow. I'm about to shrug it off, roll over, and go back to sleep when I realize Ella is sitting up beside me, tugging on my arm.

I drag myself into an upright position. "Hun," I say, "what's the matter?"

I expect her to say it's one of those cramps she gets in her calves. Or she had a bad dream. I'll give her a hug or rub her leg or fetch her an aspirin, and we'll go back to sleep.

But it's quickly apparent she's having trouble even getting words out. When I extend both hands to steady her, to hold her, I feel her whole body shaking.

"Something . . . wrong," she manages to say.

"Can you describe it?"

Again she hesitates. I wonder if she really can't speak or just doesn't want to scare me. She has to know I'm already scared.

I reach for the dimmer switch and turn on the light, careful not to make it too bright. I can see she's in pain. "Maybe a little water?" I say as I pick up the glass she always keeps on the nightstand and hand it to her.

After a few metered sips, she is able to talk coherently. She describes an electric-like chest pain that woke her. She still feels it, though not as strongly, under her breast and between her shoulder blades. It's making her lightheaded.

"Okay," I say. "This sounds serious." I know she's thinking heart attack, even if she doesn't want to say so. I grab my phone from the nightstand and turn it on.

"What are you doing?" she asks.

"Calling an ambulance."

"No!" she says. "Don't."

"Why not?"

Ella doesn't have a clear answer, so I remind her of the typical and atypical signs of a heart attack, the importance of seeking care, and when. She told me all this years ago, when she studied it as part of her medical training. We've never had to apply it in a real-life moment.

As we talk, she is no longer shaking, and her voice regains its usual strength. She's able to get herself to the bathroom without my help.

Still, she's adamant about not calling an ambulance. She also begs me not to contact either of our sons. She doesn't want them to worry unnecessarily.

I know if I push harder, she'll only push back more. I ask how we can get her the medical attention she needs.

We settle on a compromise: I will drive her to the emergency room. It's not what I would prefer, but I don't want to waste more time debating it. Hopefully we won't encounter much traffic at this hour.

As soon as we walk into the ER, it's clear this is a busy night in Boston. It's 2:00 a.m., and almost every seat is taken. After the admitting clerk has gathered all of Ella's information, we take the only two adjacent chairs.

I scoot closer to her so she can close her eyes and lean against my shoulder. Across from us, a mother is trying to soothe an agitated baby while a toddler clings to her leg. An older woman with her arm in a makeshift sling is arguing with her companion. A young man sits in as close to a prone position as is humanly possible without slipping off his chair, while his partner bends over her phone. I suspect all these folks have been here for some time.

I take Ella's hand in mine and stroke her palm with my thumb, gently probing the fascia, then rub and caress each finger—the massage she didn't receive earlier. She murmurs her thanks, then gives me her other hand. If we were at home, I'd move on to her feet and toes. And from there, well . . .

Suddenly the main entrance doors burst open. Two EMTs rush a gurney into the waiting room, past us and through the swinging doors into the triage area. Seconds later, another gurney follows, at equal speed.

Everyone is startled. Even the fellow in the almost-prone position lurches upright.

Ella and I exchange glances.

"I know what you're thinking," she says.

"Yeah. Our wait just got longer."

I recall a headline in yesterday's newspaper, something about "rival gangs face off in Boston." I have to assume we're seeing the evidence now. It doesn't matter that our state has one of the lowest rates of gun deaths in the nation; we have to do better.

"Maybe we should go home," she says.

I tell her that doesn't make sense. We've come all the way here. We already agreed on the need for her to be seen.

She considers for a minute. "When do you think they'll call my name?"

I can only guess. "An hour?"

She says she doesn't know if she can make it that long.

"Are you feeling worse?" I ask.

"No," she says. "I feel better. The pain in my chest is gone. I'm simply exhausted. What I need is sleep."

"I get it," I say. "But that's what gets people in trouble: They think their symptoms are better, and when the pain comes back worse the next time, it's too late." I remind her I know this because she taught me.

"I'm not suggesting we ignore my symptoms. But *they*"—she gestures toward the reception desk—"didn't see any urgency. If they had, they would have rushed me back there. Like the guys on the gurneys."

"The person at the desk isn't a doctor," I object.

She counters that she might just have a bad case of heartburn or indigestion. If we go home, she can call for an appointment tomorrow.

"Tomorrow is Sunday," I say. "I mean *today* is."

"I know that," she says, in a tone that suggests she has moved into the frame of mind in which she needs things to be done her way.

I wish I knew more about cardiovascular issues and whether she could be in danger if she waits a couple days for medical attention. "I'm not okay with this," I say. "What if something happens between now and Monday? We don't want to have to rush back here. It makes more sense to stay. Don't you think?"

Her silence indicates she doesn't disagree. Either that or she doesn't have the energy to debate me.

She pulls out her phone and scrolls through some screens. I take that as a sign she's feeling more like herself.

Hopefully they'll start calling more names soon. Everyone who's been waiting has to be seen at some point.

I check my own phone. It's almost 4:00 a.m. Really, all we can do is settle in, wait it out.

As I gear up to do that, there's a loud noise outside the main door.

My first thought is another gurney is being brought in.

Instead, a young man crashes through the metal detector, setting it off.

He stops in the middle of the room, wobbly on his feet, looking around, dazed and frantic, as if someone is after him. Or he's after someone.

A thick stream of blood is running down one side of his face. Dripping on the floor.

I assume he's another victim of a brutal Saturday night. Of course he needs urgent care. Even if that bumps us further back in the queue.

Before he can take another step, two security guards rush in. Guns raised.

He pulls out a gun. Like he wants to shoot them before they shoot him.

That's not what happens.

He fires randomly into the room. Not aiming, just shooting at close range. He hits the woman with the baby. Then the woman with the sling.

The guards are firing too.

It's all happening so fast. There is nowhere to hide, nothing to do. Except cling to Ella as tightly as she's clinging to me.

I don't know which of us is hit first.

We collapse together as one body.

Indigo

I am Indigo and I am a statistic. I was fifteen when I was shot. I was living with my mom in Tampa, Florida. My pronouns were ze/zir. I am survived by my mom. And—separately—by my dad. My dreams for a better world died with me.

It's a late-evening flight and I'm on my way home to Tampa after visiting my dad in Salt Lake City over spring break. This was the first time Mom didn't pay the extra fee for me to fly as an unaccompanied minor. I'm glad—not just because it saved money but because I like knowing she respects my maturity. Plus I can really do without some well-intentioned flight attendant bugging me as I process my crazy week with Dad.

When craziness happens, I handle it by journaling. As soon as I've stuffed my duffel bag under the seat in front of me and buckled up, I start writing up a storm on my tablet. I'm on my third page even before the plane has taken off. I don't stop till we hit turbulence, and then it's only briefly, to make sure I don't get nauseated.

That's when I notice the guy in the seat next to me. Or rather, he notices me. No, let's get that straight: He lets me know that he's noticed what I'm all about.

He says, "I hope you're planning to be a famous writer."

Obviously he's joking, but I take it as a compliment. Though I don't normally talk to strange guys on planes, I kind of warm up to him. Most guys around my age try to grab you with their eyes. Smile in a creepy way that makes you want to jump in a shower to rinse their creepiness off. He's got none of that going on.

And he's not into small talk either. He's interested in my writing. In *me*. We skip over all the boring bullshit and get to the real shit. And fast.

Tan—that's his name, and I was wrong about his age; he's ten years older than me—gets me from the start. He intuits that I lack role models, mentors, and guides, and steps up to offer a bit of that by sharing what he went through when he was my age. There's no mincing words as he describes how his parents rejected his queerness. Really, we've gone from no bullshit to absolutely zero bullshit.

Right here, sitting in our window and aisle seats, with an empty seat between us, he carves out a space in which I feel safe talking about how my dad tried to strong-arm me into being the daughter he expects me to be.

He started the day I arrived, and he didn't let up. The first thing he said was I should grow out my super-short hair. He didn't ask; he demanded I do it.

I said, "Why?"

He said, "You look androgynous."

I said, "Like that's a bad thing?"

His only answer was to twist his face in disgust.

I told him I like my hair, and Mom is fine with it too. And she's fine with the tiny turtle tattoo on the nape of my neck, which is one reason for super-short hair. She's also fine with what I choose to wear.

That got him started on my clothes, and he kept at it all week. Too baggy. Too drab. Too dowdy. Too shabby. Too garish. Too clownish. Even when he contradicted himself, nothing about me was right.

He thought he could convert me. And I don't mean just dictate what I wear. He thought he could mold me into his image of me. When he saw his efforts were going nowhere, he resorted to threats. Like he could force me to see queer as pathetic or gross, to reject myself. Like I'm some kind of chameleon or puppet on a string, with no identity of my own.

Tan understands all this even before I've fully spilled my guts.

He also gets that being strong and standing up to my dad all week doesn't mean I'm not hurting inside. He's still my dad. I only see him once a year, but it's not like I can upgrade to a better model father. Of course I still want him to respect me. To love me. It's painful that I would have to become someone I'm not just to get him to care.

Mom sometimes tells me I'm too thin and should gain weight. I'm okay with that. She's nothing like the kids who call me "boy-girl" in the schoolyard and say I'm so skinny I could wipe my ass with floss. No, Mom has on her nutritionist hat when she's talking to me, and I know she means well.

Tan understands, without my saying, that I'm somewhere on the aro/ace spectrum. I guess because he is too. In truth, I don't know where I fall. I'm more clear about what I don't want to do touch-wise with other humans than what I might want to do with them at some point. I've never kissed anyone. Not like *that*. I'm not interested. Of course I'll have plenty of time to figure it all out. Mom said she didn't know she was bi until after she left my dad. She wouldn't tell me how she figured it out, but I can sort of imagine.

By the time we land, I'm feeling better about myself. Talking with Tan was at least as valuable as journaling. As we prepare to deplane, he hands me his phone number, says that since we live in the same area, hopefully we can meet again. He adds that I don't have to give him my number if I'm uncomfortable. But I want to. Like I said, something about him feels safe.

I've been home for a month, and though I thought about Tan for the first few days, I didn't expect him to call. You hear people say they met a stranger on a plane and felt a deep connection but never saw them again. It's not something to be disappointed about.

But now I look down at my phone, and there it is: a text from Tan.

He wants to know if I'll meet him for a soda. He has a project he wants to tell me about.

It's Saturday and I don't have any plans, so I text back that I'll meet him at Starbucks in an hour. We'll be downtown, in a public area, so I can walk away if anything gets weird. Not that I expect anything weird. Not with Tan.

When I get there, he's waiting outside. He looks up from his phone and gives me an air five. I appreciate that he remembers excessive touch isn't my thing. Maybe a minor point to most people, but it's big for me.

I get a raspberry Italian soda and he gets a coffee, and we take our drinks to a bench down the street, where we can sit in the shade of a palm tree and look out at the bay.

He starts by describing a group of teens he is facilitating at a community center not far from here. They want to put on a drag story time for kids at the local library. The library is on board, and a schedule has been worked out for the summer. They'll start rehearsing soon. He asks if I'd like to join the group.

"Me dress up?" I tell him that's not my style. Plus I'd be a terrible performer.

He smiles. "That's how I thought you'd feel. Most true writers don't like to take the stage. I was thinking you'd be great at picking the books. And maybe helping with logistics." He explains that he wants the events to be run entirely by teens.

I tell him I've never done anything like that.

"But you'll consider it?"

I don't need more than a split second of consideration to get to yes.

He air fives me again and explains I'll be working with a bunch of cool teens. As our producer/director, he will work behind the scenes, offer support, answer any questions. He's smiling broadly as he describes who will do what. Then he gets serious. "We'll keep everything purely PG. No adult content. No sexualizing of the stories. Just a celebration of diversity and authenticity. We've assured the library all the kids and everyone else will be safe." He pauses. "I want to make sure you're also comfortable with our vision."

I tell him I am. It sounds like something I could be proud of.

"Awesome," he says. "And of course we'll need your mother's permission."

I assure him that won't be a problem.

And it isn't. When I describe the project to Mom, she has no objections. Her only caveat is "I suggest you don't tell your dad about this."

Which of course I wasn't planning to do.

I'd be lying if I said I didn't freak out even a little before my first meeting with the group. *What was I thinking?* It's not like I normally go out of my way to be in a room full of people I don't know.

But I do know Tan, and when I get to the community center, it doesn't take long to realize he was right: It is a cool group of kids. I don't know any of them, beyond having seen a few in the school hallways. Most are a grade or two ahead of me and seem to know each other well. But my nerves fade quickly as we start discussing which story to present first. Tan has introduced me as a talented writer, so they turn to me for ideas.

My first suggestion is a classic: "The Princess and the Pea."

"I like it," Tan says. "It speaks to how we often unfairly judge people. And how we need to value sensitivity instead of seeing it as a weakness."

"Like how we want to teach kids to be," says Chris.

As we continue planning, I see Chris is a natural leader. He has a presence that is large but mellow, and a goofy sense of humor. He seems comfortable in his own skin, confident he can go through life being exactly who he is. Everyone wants him to be the narrator for our first story. He says he'll dress up as the princess and carry a bejeweled wand. From what he says, I gather he's been into drag since middle school, but this is his first time being out about it.

Ryan wants to be the prince. She's thinking colorful face paint and sparkling crystal crowns for everyone.

"Wait," Matt says, "shouldn't the prince narrate the story?"

"Why?" Chris counters. "It's not like the male always has to be the focal point."

This leads to a discussion about what it means to be a narrator, and who among us should dress up, and as which characters.

After a while, Tan steps in to say there is no right or wrong here. We can have the princess read the story, while the prince flits around the room looking for her. He reminds us there is a queen in the story too. Then he asks a question that stops everyone: "Who wants to be the pea?"

"Dress up as a pea?" Ryan echoes. "For real?"

Tan shrugs. "No one has to. I just thought it might be fun for the kids."

I could almost see myself doing that. But then I realize I'll have enough to do managing the volume of the music, dimming the lights when the princess goes to sleep, making sure kids who come late have a place to sit. Besides, I'd rather be inconspicuous in black jeans and a black shirt than stand out as a pea.

In any case, River wants to papier-mâché a beach ball and paint it green to wear as the pea.

It's Friday afternoon in the first week of summer vacation, and we've finished our final dress rehearsal—an extra one Tan suggested for good measure. We're ready to perform tomorrow. Our costumes and makeup and wigs and crowns and other accessories are all set. We even did a dry run at the library.

Several of us are sitting around the picnic table behind the community center, hanging out. We told Tan before he left that we're not nervous, not at all. We're jazzed. Psyched for tomorrow. But if you stop to feel the vibe, you'll see most of us are faking it.

Chris calls our bluff. "Bet none of you gets much sleep tonight."

We reply with a chorus of "Says who?" And "We're chill, dude!"

He laughs. "Look how jittery you all are!"

We try to deny it. But we're hopping and bouncing around like we all just shot up a cocktail of adrenaline.

"If you say so," he says as he gets up to leave. I mean, his cool is real. He shoulders his pack and adjusts the princess crown he's still wearing. Without the rainbow wig that's part of his princess costume, the crown sits lower on his head. He starts to walk away, then turns back and says, "If y'all can't sleep, stop by the Flaming Flamingo. There's a great drag show."

"You're going to a *nightclub*?" River registers our collective astonishment.

"Yup."

"How?" Ryan says. "You're not eighteen."

Chris sits back down and explains that his older sister is friends with the club's owner, Meg. When he went with his sister one time, Meg looked the other way and he realized the club is lax about carding people. Since then, he's gone many times and nobody's said anything. He repeats his invitation: We're welcome to join him tonight.

"Why are we only hearing about this now?" Matt wants to know.

Chris says that's because it's been on the down-low. But tonight is our time to break out.

Of course everyone wants to go.

Ryan and a couple others say they can't risk it with their parents. River already has a date. That leaves Matt and Jean-Luc and me.

Matt and Jean-Luc just want the deets on how to get in.

Chris explains that Meg leaves a back door open. They should meet in the farthest back section of the parking lot on the north side of the Flamingo at eight o'clock. No costumes, just everyday clothes. And no backpacks. He'll show them which door is unlocked.

Matt and Jean-Luc confirm they'll be there.

Chris turns to me. "What about you, Indigo?"

"I'm not sure . . ."

"I know you want to go," he says.

He's right. I've wanted to see a real drag show for as long as I can remember. Of course I've seen drag online. But that was on my phone, nothing like being there in person. I tell him I'll have to think about it.

"Whatever you decide is fine," he says.

On the bus home, I pull out my tablet and start furiously journaling.

I write about how much I want to be part of this community—creative people, loving people, people open to different gender identities. As Chris said, it's about breaking out. It's also about learning. I have so much to learn. That's a big part of being fifteen. I mean, you shouldn't have to reach some legally defined age before you can figure out your own sexuality.

There's only one problem. I know what Mom will say if I tell her I want to go to a drag show: "Wait till you're eighteen. You can do anything you want after that!" I've never lied to her, never snuck out of the house, never disobeyed her—at least not in any major way. And I'm not about to start.

Or am I?

Then I think about what Dad would say. Actually, I don't want to give that even a moment's thought. I just want to thumb my nose at him and go. Show him I can do what I want, whether he likes it or not.

Tan isn't a parent, but he might share Mom's views. Or maybe not. He might think it wouldn't be such a bad thing to go, especially if it's just one time. For a second, I consider asking him. I could text him. But I don't want to bring him in, make him responsible in any way.

By the time the bus reaches my stop and I close my journal, I know what I'm going to do. I'm going to the Flamingo. I can't pass up this opportunity. But it will be just this once. I won't make a habit of lying to Mom. All that remains is to get out of the house this evening without alerting or worrying her.

As luck would have it, before I reach home, she texts to say she has to work late, tells me to pick up some Chinese takeout for myself.

I text back that I'm thinking of going to a movie—a double feature. It's Friday night, so she can't object.

And she doesn't. She tells me to be home before midnight and she'll see me in the morning.

I exhale my guilt as best I can. Tell myself the lie I just told hurts me more than it will ever hurt Mom. Then I turn around and catch a bus back into town.

My favorite take-out restaurant, an Asia fusion café, is a convenient two blocks from the Flamingo. When I get there, I order a sushi burrito and take it to the parking lot where Chris told us to meet. I sit on the curb by a dumpster belonging to one of the apartment buildings. The burrito, with just the right amount of honey-sriracha aioli, is elite. As always.

I still have an hour before the others will be here, so I grab my tablet and pick up where I left off earlier. Journaling works best when you write whatever comes to mind, no censoring of thoughts. What comes up now is the fear I won't be safe at the club. Someone could try to hit on me. Doesn't matter if it's a man or woman, boy or girl. I'm afraid that when I don't respond, they'll turn on me. They'll out me for being underage, threaten to call my parents. Even if I don't engage and just walk away, it will be humiliating. I'll feel totally destroyed.

I write two pages about everything that scares me, then abruptly stop. Really, giving energy to this is dragging me down even more. So I delete all of it.

And start over.

I imagine walking into the club and finding . . . Tan. He's sitting by himself at the bar. Of course he's surprised to see me. But he's cool with it. Like he's been cool with me from the moment we met on the plane. I write an entire conversation between us in which we talk about the club and the show we're watching together—the music, the lights, the talents of the various drag queens. About how we each view friendship. And sexuality.

I'm nowhere near finished when Chris shows up. He's still wearing his princess crown. Looks like he didn't expect to find me here.

"What?" I say, closing my tablet and stashing it in the small bag I brought. "You thought I wouldn't come?"

He doesn't deny it. "Just glad you did."

The others arrive a few minutes later.

Their timing is perfect, as the deepening dusk will make it easier to sneak into the club. Chris points out the door we'll enter at the rear of the building, on the second floor, up a short fire escape. Once inside, we'll go down a dark corridor, past some closed doors, then turn right and take a narrow flight of stairs down to the back room of the club, where the drag show is.

"If I'm not back in a few minutes," he says, "assume I got in okay." He directs us to follow one at a time. Says he told Meg he's bringing a few friends tonight, and she was fine with it.

"All good?" he says, as he turns to leave.

"What about your crown?" I ask.

He gives me a split-second *huh*, then takes it off and stares at it. I don't think he remembered it was still on his head. He's probably thinking, *How could something so harmless pose any sort of problem?*

We debate whether he should stash it by the dumpster, carry it in discretely, or just take his chances wearing it. In the end, he pops it back on his head.

The three of us watch the glint of his crown cross the darkened lot and disappear into the building. When it's evident he's not coming back, Matt takes off.

After Matt seems to have made it, Jean-Luc suggests I go next. He doesn't want me waiting alone in the dark.

"Okay," I say. "See you inside."

I scurry across the lot and up the fire escape. The doorknob doesn't turn, and I worry someone has locked me out. But it opens with an extra tug. Everything inside is exactly as Chris described. I find him and Matt at a table near the stairs, in front of the DJ booth. They've saved chairs for Jean-Luc and me. And Chris has ordered a round of non-alcoholic drinks.

As soon as I sit down, I find myself scanning the room for Tan. There's no reason to believe he'd be here. And of course he isn't. Even so, I'm disappointed. I wish we could share this moment, like I wrote about in my journal. It's almost like I have a little crush.

I've never crushed on anyone before. Not that I want to touch Tan or anything. Which means it's probably not a real crush. And probably better he's not here. At least that's what I tell myself.

By the time I've resolved all this in my mind, Jean-Luc has slid into the seat beside me and the show is starting.

From the very first beat, I'm riveted. The music is throbbing, the strobe lights pulsating, as the joyous world of drag explodes around us. If I were someone who jumped up and danced in public, I'd be doing that now. Like Chris and Matt are. I'm in awe of the confidence they feel to be exactly who they choose to be. I want that in my life.

I'm so glad I came. Though I'm not sure about limiting myself to just this one time. I won't be eighteen for almost three more years. That's a long wait. I'll have to find a way to get Mom on board. Maybe after she's seen our drag story time—I know she'll be super impressed—and met my new friends, she'll relax a bit.

As the DJ shifts to a reggae vibe, I catch Chris's eye. His hips are swaying to "Love Like This" as he winks at me. I signal back that I'm going to the restroom, so he doesn't think I'm slinking out. There's still plenty of time to make it home before my midnight curfew.

The easiest route between tables takes me alongside the stage. It's the perfect moment to tip the performer. I pull a bill from my pocket and hold out my arm, as I've seen others do.

The queen, glistening in iridescent purple organza, spots me, sashays to the edge of the stage, bends over, and graciously accepts the bill.

For a second our eyes meet.

I'm in awe. Smitten.

In that instant, there is a loud blast.

Thinking it must be the sound system, all heads pivot toward the DJ booth, near our table. Turning, I see a man who looks like Tan standing beside Chris. Before I can tell if it's really him, a masked man rushes down the stairs and into the room, gun raised.

He shoots the DJ. Shoots Chris. Shoots into the crowd.

People are pushing, shoving. Screaming.

Bodies are falling.

As much as I want to go to Chris, I know I need to get to the front door. To escape.

Except I'm wedged in. Trapped.

Helpless.

Suddenly my head explodes. I can't tell if it's because of the press of people and the deafening noise or if I've been shot.

My life splinters.

Beneath all the screams, "Love Like This" is still playing.

Jon

I am Jon and I am a statistic. My best friend and husband, Jrue, and I had just celebrated our fiftieth birthdays and our silver anniversary when I was shot. We were living in Jrue's father's Italianate house in Portland, Maine. My pronouns were he/they. I am survived by the best friend anyone ever had and by his father.

I poke my head into Jrue's office, where he retreated as soon as we'd finished dinner. As per usual. "Asiago or Gruyère?"

"For what?" he asks without glancing up from his screen.

I hold out the shopping list I've scribbled on the back of an old envelope.

He looks up and registers surprise. "You're going to the market?"

The true answer would be no, I'm not. Or at least that's not how I want to spend my evening. My idea is to catch up on personal emails because, procrastinator that I am, I've let far too many pile up. Jrue and I both love to cook. We both love to eat. And we love our wines. But truth be told, neither of us loves to shop. Especially not in the evening. So now what I'm looking for is his support to stay home and cozy up with my emails. Even so, when you've been with a partner as long as the two of us have been together, you know the best path to get them to do what you want them to do doesn't always run on a straight line. A circuitous route can be more harmonious. More efficacious. So instead of a no, I counter with, "Or maybe a sharp cheddar?"

He takes the list, confirms no cheeses are on it, and hands it back to me. "You know I won't eat it," he says. "Or that fake stuff they call cheese."

"I do know. I was the one who suggested you might have a lactose problem."

"You were right," he says. "So why are you bringing this up?"

"Your dad," I say. "I'm thinking of your dad." I explain that since the doctor encouraged us to help Pops gain weight, I've been reviewing his diet. It's something I do as a matter of course for clients in my telehealth practice. I think he'll respond well if we add some cheese at lunch. As long as we keep an eye on his cholesterol. I've researched calories, and aged Asiago is high on the list.

I say all this, but the truth is I'm not trying to get Jrue to select a cheese. Or approve a revised diet plan. I'm simply appealing to his desire to make life better for his dad, which I know is a huge priority of his. My plan is to inspire him to drop what he's doing—despite all inclinations to the contrary—and make a run to Hannaford. Like detours that force you north as the only way to go south. Or recipes that tempt you with a hint of tartness in a sugary dish.

It seems to work.

He thanks me for caring about Pops, like he's my dad as well. Agrees we should fortify his diet.

"So you'll go?" I say.

"To the market?"

"Yes."

He glances at the image lighting up his screen and frowns. "Okay, I'll go . . . Just not now. I have to finish this ad for a campaign that goes live at midnight. That's a stretch as it is."

I return the frown. For a second, I thought my plan was working. He almost volunteered. Almost. But he didn't. Now I see that I'll have to switch to a direct, these-are-the-facts strategy—the one I was avoiding because I feared I'd end up caving and agreeing to go myself.

"Okay," I say. "The shopping can wait. But Pops's prescription can't."

He stares at me with the mix of surprise and anxiety I've come to recognize as his *backed-into-a-corner* look. He didn't see this coming, but he knows he messed up. He's let me down. He owes me. And he doesn't have any way to make it right. All of which I was trying to avoid.

"God damn," he says. "We're out of his heart meds again, aren't we?"

There's a long pause.

This is such a classic couple's dilemma. We both know how it breaks down: I bought our groceries last time, so it's his turn. Plus it's his dad's meds. Simple fairness. The fifty-fifty rule. Sure, we can bargain and negotiate and be flexible, but in moments like this, it's hard to ignore the fact that ultimately Pops is Jrue's father. This is Jrue's responsibility. None of which means he'll agree to go.

Earlier this year, we returned from our home in Hawaii to Portland so Jrue could take care of his dad. At a frail eighty-nine, his transition into nursing care was only a matter of time, but we wanted to forestall it as long as possible. Maybe we should have anticipated this before we moved so far from the East Coast, but we were finally living our dream. Five days a week, we got up early and logged on to our respective jobs. Because all they saw was my virtual background, clients had no inkling of my physical body's latitude and longitude. During the winter, I cranked up the AC and put on a jacket to keep up the pretense.

Our workday over by noon, we headed to the beach for a snorkel. We were living the life! And we deserved it. We'd worked our butts off for nearly three decades, mostly while crammed into a one-bedroom apartment in Manchester, New Hampshire. Sure, we'd indulged in fancy dinners at Stages in Dover and sometimes at Mooo in Boston, and taken our fair share of vacations in the Caribbean, so it was far from a miserable existence. We just figured we'd wait to get our dream home until we retired, so we could fully enjoy it.

Except, along came the pandemic. Cooped up for too long and getting crankier by the hour, we went online one frosty evening in search of a warm spot that could be our permanent getaway. And we found it: a three-bedroom aqua-blue house with an open floor plan, white deck, and panoramic views of Kaneohe Bay. Even a functioning aquaponics system. We were certain this was where we wanted to drop the bulk of our hard-earned nest egg. Sight unseen. Our jobs were already remote; all we had to do was terminate our lease—easy, with so many New Yorkers seeking their own escape—pack up our apartment, and fly to Hawaii.

Less than a year later, after his father took a bad fall on the stairs, Jrue was on a plane back to Portland. It was touch and go for a while, but Pops pulled through. There were no long-term cognitive effects from the concussion, but his fractured hip meant he needed twenty-four seven care with bathing and other activities he used to handle on his own. I stayed in Hawaii, hoping Jrue would return. But he wasn't about to dump Pops in a nursing facility. So I faced a choice: stay in paradise alone or follow Jrue to Portland. Not much of a choice, really.

We've been renting out the Kaneohe house on a month-to-month basis, trying not to feel demoralized every time we get another update from the occupants saying how much they're savoring our tilapia and veggies. The idea is to go back as soon as we can. It's not something we talk about, though. It's not like you can actively discuss what you're going to do after your dad dies. That could happen any day, but somehow talking about it would feel like we were quickening the inevitable.

Jrue and I can talk about certain things, others not so much. Like the discussion we're stuck in right now, as I wait to see how he'll manage to wriggle out of the run to Hannaford.

He starts by telling me he's really sorry about screwing up. He knows it's his turn to go. It's his dad's meds. He's sure I have other things I'd rather do. Then he hangs his head and asks if I'll go. He doesn't promise to make it up to me; he simply puts it out there: "It would really help if you could do this."

I feel a sharp twinge of annoyance. I'm always the one relenting, the one going the extra mile. The one going north when I want to go south. The one who's more flexible. Like coming back to Portland: That was me being so flexible it skewed our fifty-fifty way out of balance. I'm not sure we can get it back. I may always feel he owes me.

Then I feel another twinge—a twinge of guilt. I'm being selfish and unreasonable. Jrue can't help that his father is a widower, any more than I can help that my parents are blissfully ensconced in a Florida retirement community. As far as the shopping goes, Jrue has a valid reason: He's on a deadline. I, on the other hand, can work on my emails equally well tomorrow. What we're struggling over isn't exactly a crisis. It isn't a matter of life and death. It's one trip to the market.

So I say okay.

Of course, he then feels his own pang of guilt. "Are you sure?" he says. "I could do a run for the meds and go back tomorrow for the shopping. It'll be tight, but I should still be able to post the ad by midnight."

Really, we are experts at out-guilting each other.

However, having failed on my circuitous route, I tell him he doesn't need to do that. I said I'd go, and I will.

He gives me a hug, says how appreciative he is. Even promises to make it up to me.

We spend a few minutes going over the list so I'll be able to pick up the prescription, then grab everything, run it through the self-checkout, and get home as quickly as possible. We cross off a few nonessentials, including the cheese. Jrue wants to first assess the risk to his dad's cholesterol levels.

I go downstairs to the mudroom, where I put on my parka, ski cap, lambswool tartan scarf, and pac boots. This isn't a fashion statement; it's what I need to face the cold. These clear, star-filled November nights are nothing like the balmy nights in Kaneohe. But I'm still reluctant to leave. For no good reason, really.

So I pop into my office for a quick check of my work emails. I don't do late shifts, but I like to stay on top of things. Sometimes multiple checks in an evening. Probably why I've let my personal emails slide.

Like Jrue, I have an office of my own in Pops's Italianate house, with its five bedrooms and three and a half baths. Mine was originally a guest bedroom, with high ceilings, damask rose wallpaper, and windows overlooking the garden—arguably a spiffier workspace than the dining nook off the kitchen I repurposed in Hawaii. Its quiet location is ideal for telehealth calls, and I haven't needed to use a virtual background since I had the king-size canopy bed taken out. Even so, I wish I was back on the island, looking out over the turquoise ocean instead of at a scraggly, now-bare maple tree.

One email is marked urgent. I log into my portal and scan the notes left by the after-hours operator. The client is a young woman with an eating disorder whose case I've been managing. I thought she was doing well and am surprised to learn she was admitted to the hospital. The notes are vague, but it sounds like some kind of poisoning, possibly intentional. I move a few things around on my schedule so I can make follow-up calls first thing in the morning. It looks to be a full day ahead.

Which reminds me to check the time.

Thirty minutes till the pharmacy closes.

Even so, I linger long enough to peek into Pops's room so I can say goodnight in case he goes to sleep before I get home.

But he's already asleep in his recliner by the TV, feet propped up on the ottoman.

I tiptoe in and switch off the TV, then stop by once more at Jrue's office.

"Jonny boy!" he says. "I thought you left."

I tell him about the emergency email and that I'll have to get up early. Then I tell him Pops is asleep in his recliner. "Maybe we should move him," I say. "I can help you get him into bed."

He shakes his head. "If you don't leave now, the pharmacy will be closed. I'll keep an eye on him. Hopefully he'll wake up and we can give him his meds when you get home."

"I'll be home before you know it." I plant a kiss on the bald spot high on his head. This time I'm really going.

"Bring back a little something," he calls after me.

This is a game we used to play. Haven't done it recently, so it feels fresh and enticing. "Like what?"

"I don't know," he says. "Surprise me."

As I drive down Route 9, I consider what might please Jrue but is different from the treats I've typically gotten him: honey glazed nuts, choco-nut ice cream, nocino, hazelnut liquor. Basically, anything with nuts. I'm up for the challenge.

The annoyance and guilt I was feeling are gone. Wiped away by the bond of trust built over decades of living with my best friend. We may struggle to be fifty-fifty, but in reality we've always been and will always be a hundred-hundred.

Of course, Jrue knows that. He jokes that even our till-death-do-us-part vows are too limiting. Too finite. If I die before he does, he won't stop loving me. His plan, he says, is to die by my side, whenever that time comes, so we can explore the vast beyond together.

I say he'll have to convince me there *is* a vast beyond before I can sign on to any such plans.

Fortunately the traffic is light and I get to Hannaford before the pharmacy has closed. I pick up Pops's refill, then snag a shopping cart and head for the veggie aisle.

First thing into the cart is a bag of McIntosh apples, a variety I missed in Hawaii. Next are some broccoli crowns. Spinach, it turns out, is either out of season or just out of stock this late in the day. I choose Swiss chard instead. Then a bag of carrots. And a bunch of bananas. At the far end of the veggies, I spot a display of leftover Halloween bargains. There might be something for Jrue, so I inspect the candy corn, marshmallow monsters, and jack-o'-lantern candy buckets. Nothing appeals. Certainly nothing on par with, for example, the platypus Beanie Baby he surprised me with when I was down with pneumonia in grad school. Wonder if he remembers that? I'll have to ask when I get home.

I'm about to walk away when a lone pack of peanut butter zombie eyeballs catches my eye—literally. They're cute, staring up at me with their bursting blood vessels. Maybe not platypus cute, but hey, they contain nuts. I place them in the flip-up child seat of my cart, careful not to smoosh the little corneas or break any more blood vessels.

As I do this, a text comes through from Jrue: "coffee?"

In fact, I forgot to put it on the list. Probably because I never notice when we're running low, since I don't drink it. I text back: "consider it done"

On my way to the beverage aisle, as I'm passing the cheese counter, I catch a whiff of Roquefort. A few samples are still waiting for late-evening takers. I lift a morsel out of its little cup, put it on one of the slightly stale gluten-free crackers, top with a dab of fig jam, then shove the works into my mouth. Not bad! Considering their impending fate, I indulge in a few more.

And I have a little epiphany: Jrue and Pops may have dietary restrictions, but that shouldn't limit me. If I want Roquefort with my salad at lunch, I can have it. Or maybe some crumbly Greek feta. Either way, without a serving of guilt.

We have to stop with the guilt. As they say, life's too short.

As I'm standing here, picturing us at lunch tomorrow—me with my cheese, Jrue with his zombie eyeballs, and Pops loving it all—I hear a voice call out, "Hi, Jon?"

It's Clarita. We work remotely for the same agency and have only met once in person. She explains that she likes shopping late because it's quiet. Easy in and out. Except for some reason, there are a lot of people here tonight. As she's speculating on what might have brought them out on a nippy evening, her glance takes in the zombie eyeballs. I expect her to ask what I'm doing with old Halloween candy, but instead she gestures toward the cheese counter and says, "What do you recommend?"

"Depends on your taste."

"Not mine," she says. "My kids are tweens and all they eat is string cheese. I'm trying to broaden their horizons."

I've never raised a child, and when I was one myself, the only cheese in our house was American. "Gouda?" I say, scanning the case for options. "Maybe smoked Gouda?"

But she isn't listening. She selects a slab at random and reads the label: "Asiago. How's this?"

"Sure," I say. "Why not?"

She shrugs and drops it in her cart. "If they don't eat it, I will."

I tell her to let me know how it goes.

As she whizzes off to the frozen food aisle, I turn back to my own choice: Roquefort or Greek feta? But there's no need to choose. I place both in my cart—as I said, why not, right? Then I review my list to see what I might have missed. Just English muffins. I'll pick them up, then head to the front of the store and check out.

As I'm turning my cart around, deafening cracks shake the store. Like thunder.

But there is no storm. And it's not thunder. I've never heard anything like it, yet I instantly know what it is.

Then another volley of shots. Louder. If that's possible. Closer.

My body is shaking uncontrollably. My knees are buckling.

At the end of the cheese counter I see a red sign: EXIT.
It might as well be a mile away.
My body is sliding to the floor.
In my hand, my phone.
Will Jrue know I tried to call him?

Kylor

I am Kylor and I am a statistic. I was forty-two when I was shot. I was living in Lewistown, Montana. My pronouns were he/him, obviously. I am survived by my mother and stepfather, my younger twin brothers, and several girlfriends.

The Lucky Draw gun show in Great Falls is the event of the year around here. Sometimes I go to acquire a firearm, sometimes just to browse. But I always go. And I always meet up with one or more of my guys. We have fun comparing notes and exercising our Second Amendment rights. Always ready to sling some lead.

People say the Lucky Draw sounds like a place for gambling, and I think they have tables in the back area, or at least some slot machines. But I go for the guns.

This year I have my eye on an MCX Spear.

I've been reading everything I can find about it online. Salivating over its hotness. Who could resist a civilian version of the XM7? How could you do any better than that? I'm already safe and protected with the guns I own, but now I'll be even safer.

My buddy Bill has agreed to come along to help me make the smartest choice. He owns more guns than I do. But I'm telling you, that's about to change. I'm making good money in life insurance sales, so I can afford anything I want. And what I want is more firepower. Mega more.

Saturday morning, Bill pulls up in front of my house bright and early in his refurbished Hummer H3.

"Hop in, Kill!" he says, gesturing for me to reach through the passenger-side window to unlock the door.

We call ourselves the 'ill bros. For Bill and Kill. He's not the only one who calls me Kill. Killer's been my nickname since grade school, when a friend thought Kylor sounded like Killer. That same kid gave Wesley the nickname Wee-Wee. He wasn't exactly wrong in either case. I do love guns, but I like to think people see me as more of a teddy bear type than a killer.

As we drive toward Great Falls, we discuss bump stocks. And hellfire triggers. Most people couldn't talk about that shit for a full two hours, but the two of us could go on all day.

My ex bitched at me whenever she heard me talk about anything gun related. She owned a gun herself, and our first date was at a shooting range, so I don't know what the hell bugged her. It was like she was always trying to shut me up. Like she wanted to mess with my First Amendment rights.

Which is why I got me my current girlfriend. She doesn't poke her nose in my convos with buddies. That's my business, and she knows it's my business. Besides, she knows that if she ticks me off, I'll be calling on girlfriend #2. And girlfriend #3 is also waiting in the wings.

I didn't invite my girl to come today. But I did promise to take her out for dinner if we get back in time. I bet she'll be blown away when I show her my new Spear. Funny thing is, even though she's never owned a gun, she's way more dialed in than my ex ever was.

At the show, Bill and I check the floor plan, then head to the aisle where I expect to make my big purchase.

I inspect all the Spears on display. I run my finger over their sexy bronze barrels, raise them and take sight. Tickle the trigger. Only thing I don't do is look at the sticker price. Then I select the model with the highest magnification capability and close the deal. Thank goodness it doesn't involve messing with permits, background checks, or any of that bureaucratic bullshit.

"I want to go home now," I say with a grin. "Take this baby out of her box!"

Bill reminds me we planned to spend the day here and says he's not ready to leave.

Of course he's right. And the truth is, I'm nowhere near ready to leave either. I'll have to lug this box around with me. Not that it's heavy, just bulky. I suggest we start by finding us some eats. The only thing in my stomach is a cup of dead eye.

Bill agrees. We can pick up sandwiches, then bum around.

Turns out other folks are thinking the same. As we wait in line at the concession stand, we chat about our gun collections. I got my first Glock for security, for protection against home invasion. Protection in any situation, really. I'm carrying it right now. No one better fuck with me when I'm strapped.

Lately I've been buying guns for protection on a broader scale too. With immigrants and liberal wackos threatening our basic freedoms, we need to look out for the community. Bill and I have talked a lot about this. But talk's cheap, as they say. We've been stockpiling ammo in a location I'm not about to disclose.

As we reach the head of the line and grab ourselves some pulled pork sandwiches, I tell him that, having made my big purchase of the day, I want to focus on fun stuff. Maybe check out some antique pieces. I've been thinking about starting a collection.

He likes the idea but says he wants to catch the live-fire demo at the range adjacent to the hall. It's scheduled for the top of the hour. He suggests we eat our sandwiches as we walk over there, maybe shoot a few rounds after the demo if the range isn't too crowded, then come back and browse.

"Sounds like a plan," I say, raising my arm so I can use my short sleeve to wipe away the barbecue sauce dripping from my chin. "Let's go."

The range is just beyond a low hill on the north side of the building. Because we are still working on our sandwiches, we walk slowly, winding between tall grass and thistle, stopping briefly to debate whether the ability to shoot through body armor is a deal-breaker when purchasing a weapon.

I argue that's one reason I got the Spear. It pretty much renders body armor obsolete.

"Sick," he says. "But if I had to choose, I'd prioritize the ability to be a thousand-yard sniper. Imagine, you could take some guy out from a mile away. Dickwad would never see it coming."

"Nope, sure wouldn't," I say.

As we near the top of the hill, shots ring out.

"Damn," he says. "They started early."

"We're almost there," I mumble as I stuff in a final mouthful of pork.

Then another round of shots.

Doesn't sound like a demo. Too disorganized. Too many people shooting at once. And people screaming. Not cheering—this is screaming.

Bill stares at me as he chokes down his last bite of sandwich. "Something's off."

"Yeah. Sounds weird."

"Could it be an active shooter?"

"You mean somebody shooting to kill?" I say. "At a gun show?"

"Sure sounds like it." He's shouting to be heard over the noise.

"No way!" I laugh. "A gun show is the safest place on earth!"

But he's not laughing. His finger slides to the trigger of his pistol. There's no time to discuss what comes next.

"Let's go," he calls over his shoulder as he dashes toward the range.

If only my Spear were loaded and ready. But it's not. I can't leave the box here, risk someone taking it. Hell, it cost a small fortune.

Balancing the box under one arm, I reach with the other to pull my Glock out of its ankle holster, then sprint after Bill.

Cresting the hill, I see people running in every direction, aiming guns. Firing. Bodies on the ground.

Some dude has gone crazy. But who?

In the chaos, it's impossible to tell.

I know what I have to do. And it doesn't matter that I've never shot a living person. This is what I've trained for. This is why I have a gun. I scan the scene and notice one guy who looks different. Don't ask me how. Just somehow different. It's a snap decision. As they say, trust your gut.

I take aim at him.

In the split second before I pull the trigger, I see someone else, off to the side, aiming at me.

Suddenly I don't know . . .

Don't know which one to shoot.

Or who is shooting me. Or why.

Don't know how I got here.

Don't know where I went wrong.

Don't know why I have to die.

Li

I am Li and I am a statistic. I was eleven when I was shot. I was living with my family in Atlanta, Georgia, near an awesome mall. And an awesome skate park. Mom promised I could get a cat if her new allergy meds kicked in. I'd just started sixth grade. My pronouns were she/her. I am survived by my mom and dad and my older brother.

Everybody's got a bestie. I'm lucky because I have four. We agreed last year to all be besties, and we stayed besties over the summer. Now that we're in sixth grade, we are tighter than ever.

We hang out every day after school. And every weekend. Some kids make fun of us for being so close. Like, one boy said our parents must have wanted to save money on a single GPS tracker for us. Another said we'd be good recruits for a chain gang. But I think most of those kids are just jealous.

We all like reading. After downloading the same book on our phones so we can read it at the same time, we meet up at the food court in the mall and sit around and talk about it. Usually over milkshakes. We all like creating funny memes and posting them on social media so we can rack up views and likes. My favorites are anything with cats. We all like glitter on our nail polish. And we all like skateboarding. The reason we became friends in the first place was that we were the only girls in our grade to join the skateboard club.

We have so much in common, but we're also unique. Like the five memes I made for us: cool cat, sleepy cat, fluffy cat, ninja cat, grumpy cat.

Scarlett wants to be a TikTok influencer. She's definitely the cool cat. She got an account and has been posting videos. I'm pretty sure her parents don't know about that. They certainly wouldn't approve. Even though she's only eleven, her account isn't set to private. I'm not sure how she managed that.

Paisley wants to be an author. She's been writing stories and poems, and I don't mean just for school. She gets new ideas all the time and dictates them into her phone. Then she fills out the details on her laptop. She stays up late, but her parents never tell her she has to go to sleep. Which makes her the sleepy cat. Her parents approve of her writing, though I doubt they'd approve of all her stories. She shares all of them with us. And we love it.

Tia wants to become a stylist. She's the fluffy cat because she's always brushing out her hair. Even during class. She was the first to turn us on to sparkly nails. She found some polish with glitter that doesn't peel right off or look like kid stuff. Plus it's vegan, so our moms can't object.

Riley used to want to be a doctor, but she doesn't talk about that anymore. Now she mainly talks about yoga. Her mom teaches yoga classes, and Riley goes with her on Saturday mornings. She taught us how to do a cat pose on our knees. It was okay, but—sorry, cats—I liked the dog pose better. Obvi, Riley's the ninja cat. Also known as the flying cat.

I'm not really sure what I want to do with my life. I can get grumpy about that. Like in the grumpy cat. But with such awesome besties, I know I'll have plenty of time to figure it all out.

Last night we had a sleepover at Tia's house. We put on our sweats and did each other's nails. With glitter polish, of course. I did mine to look like French tips. Scarlett said her sister saw some cool press-on fingernails at the beauty supply shop. So we decided to go to the mall as soon as possible and check them out.

The other thing we talked about last night was boys. Which is another reason we go to the mall: to check out boys.

We each have a boy we like. I don't mean we actually talk to these boys. We talk about them, though. A lot. We discuss what we like about them. And which girls they like. If any. We talk about their quirks and about things they did but don't think anyone noticed. Like stashing chewing gum behind their ear. Riley swears she saw Dirk do that in math class. She even still likes him.

Scarlett likes Josh. He's the nerdy kid who plays video games on his watch during math class but still gets top scores on all the tests.

Tia likes Zachariah. I think just because he's super cute.

Paisley likes Greg. He has red hair and is always cracking jokes. He even makes jokes when our social studies teacher calls on him to give a serious opinion in class. No one else could get away with that, but somehow he does. Maybe because Paisley laughs really loud whenever he says something funny. And because she laughs, we all laugh too. Our teacher knows he can't shut us all down, so he just puts half a smile on his face and waits till we get quiet.

It's not like we all take the same classes, though. Paisley is the only one in my French class. None of my besties are in my computer science class. That's because I got put in the advanced section. I didn't ask for it; I'd rather not be alone, but I tested out of the class they're all taking. It wasn't hard to do, because I used to hang out with my older brother while he was working on his Python homework. He would quiz me. He was trying to prove how much smarter he is. So of course then I had to prove him wrong.

The advanced section is almost all boys. I don't like any of them. I usually lean forward at my desk so my hair falls like a curtain across my face. Makes me feel like I'm safe in myself even when my besties aren't nearby.

When I said we each have a boy we like, that wasn't completely true. I don't have a Dirk or Josh or Zachariah or Greg. When we all talk about boys, I mainly talk about their boys.

But then there's Ricardo.

He's one boy we all like. He's got that extra special rizz none of the other boys have. We spend a lot of time talking about why that could be. Scarlett thinks it's because he's older. Maybe she's hoping Josh will be like Ricardo in a couple years.

I don't agree it's about his age. He may be in eighth grade, but so are a ton of other boys, and we aren't crushing on any of them.

Tia thinks it's his cuteness. She points out the muscles he got from being on the swim team. And the dimple when he smiles. He's cuter than Zachariah. She'll admit that.

Whatever is special about Ricardo is a big deal for me, because he's the reason I'm not interested in other boys. In my book, none of them measure up.

When we discussed all that at the sleepover, I said, "I think what makes Ricardo special is his confidence."

Tia wanted to know how I could say he's confident if I've never talked to him.

Which of course I haven't. So I had to come up with something. "He seems confident," I said, "because he's not always hanging out with his buddies." I explained that when we see him at the mall, he's usually by himself, doing his own thing. Like earlier, in the bookstore. He was reading the jacket of a book. Not like a boy reading a book is automatic cute. But when he heard us giggling, he looked up and flashed his dimple.

Everyone agreed that was cute. But they didn't see how it was a sign of confidence.

"Besides," Paisley said, "the five of us always do everything together. Are you saying we're not confident?"

I had to think about that. Because I do think we're confident. Some of us more than others. Even if I'm probably one of the others.

"He's still cute when he's with other boys," Tia threw in. "Maybe more cute."

Riley said that was true but she also understood what I was getting at. "Because he's usually by himself, we can see how he relates to people who aren't his guys."

"Right," I said. "That's what I meant. Because he's confident, he doesn't just stick with his guys and ignore everyone else. He pays attention to people. He's actually nice to them. Even people he doesn't know."

"Even little sixth-grade noobies," Scarlett said.

"Even *you*!" Paisley said.

Of course I knew what she was referring to. It happened a few days ago, when the five of us were walking out of school together at the end of the day. Ricardo was standing next to the flag pole. Like maybe waiting for someone.

As we walked by, he said, "Hi, Li."

We barely made it to the other side of the street, out of earshot, before they were whooping and pointing at me. Jumping all over me.

"Oh my god, Li!"

"Did you hear that?!"

"He likes you!"

You better believe we talked about it for hours. For days. We're still talking about it: How did he know my name? And why did he just say *my* name? Is it possible he likes me?

When Paisley brought it up again at the sleepover, I wanted to protest that it didn't mean anything. It was one hi. And he didn't say hi when we saw him at the bookstore. But she wasn't totally wrong. He did single me out. They all saw it. I couldn't deny that.

They jumped out of their sleeping bags and started teasing me, pulling on my hair. Making me blush. And then laughing at me for blushing.

They each swore they would get him to say hi to them too. Like it was a competition. Like I'd already won, but they wanted to take my win away.

Tia proposed we go back to the bookstore.

"You think he'd be there again?" Riley wanted to know.

"Okay, maybe he wouldn't look at books two days in a row," Tia said. "Let's just go to the mall as we planned. After we check out those press-on nails, we can go to the sports store. Or the electronics store."

"Or that video game place," Scarlett said.

"Or the food court," Paisley said.

They were piling on. Within minutes, they'd formed a plan. We will stop at the beauty shop, then go to the ice cream counter in the food court, where we can get milkshakes and keep an eye out for Ricardo. If that doesn't work, we'll cruise around to some other spots where he might be.

I didn't like their plan. But I also didn't want to seem like a scaredy-cat. Anyway, they didn't leave much room for another opinion. We always do everything together, right?

This morning, as we were eating the French toast Tia's mom made, the plan was firmed up. We'd each go home and do our Sunday morning chores, then we'd meet up at the park across from the entrance to the mall.

I figured I might as well act like I was on board. A little grumpy is better than scared.

"Bet we see him," Scarlett said. Tia's mom was there, so she kept it vague.

"You'll see how nice he is," I said.

"No," Scarlett said, whipping around to me. "We'll see how nice he is to *you!*"

Really, they wouldn't let it go.

It's Sunday afternoon. I've vacuumed my room. Walked the dog. Finished the last bit of my homework. Everyone in my family is gathered in the living room to watch the big football game. Except me. My besties' families are most likely also watching. The five of us have no interest in football. It's nothing but a bunch of puffed-up guys smashing into each other. Knowing how we feel, our parents expect us to make other plans when there's a game. Whatever we do won't be at one of our houses because we can't even stand the noise of football coming from the TV in the background.

Which is why I'm glad we're going to the mall, even if I still don't love the plan. All of us live within walking distance—except Riley, whose older sister has offered to drop her off. As I walk the mile from my house to the mall, I pop in my earbuds so my favorite playlist can put a bounce in my step.

But my thoughts are bouncing too. The closer I get to the mall, the less I want to go through with this. So many things could go wrong. Like if we see Ricardo, he could ignore all of us, including me. It could become clear he's not the nice guy I think he is. That would be bad. I'd have to stop liking him so much.

What would be worse, though, is if he ignores me but says hi to Scarlett or another of my besties. Like she's cuter. Which she probably is. I would die.

The best case would be if we go to the mall and he's not there. But he is there a lot. It's where we see him most. So I can't count on that.

I wonder if he has a girlfriend, like some of the other eighth-grade boys. I've never seen him with one, though. I try to imagine what it would be like to be his girlfriend. What it would be like to hang out with him instead of my besties. That would feel weird. Of course, it isn't as if a boy saying hi once—even if he said my name—is a reason to think about being his girlfriend. We'd have to at least start talking.

Which won't happen with my besties around. There's a reason you have besties. You don't have to go anywhere alone. And wherever you go, you don't have to worry, because you know they'll be there to back you up. Now I'm realizing how that's also a problem. It will be a lot harder to talk to Ricardo if my friends are standing around. Probably impossible.

And I do want to talk to him. I just don't know if he wants to talk to me. And I'm not sure how to find out. I'd have to go to the mall by myself. Before I had besties, I used to go with one friend. Sometimes I went with my brother, if he let me. These days, I talk to my brother's buddies when they come to our house. It's easy enough. They're juniors, so to them, I'm the little kid sister. But talk to Ricardo alone? I don't know about that.

When I get to the park, my besties are sitting on a bench, waiting for me. I guess all my thoughts slowed me down, even with my bouncy playlist. They stand up as soon as they see me. They're ready for the mall.

But I'm not.

"Hey," I say, "how about we do something else today?"

Riley looks surprised. "Like what?"

"Don't you want to check out those nails?" Scarlett says. "And I thought you—"

Before she can say, "want to see Ricardo," I say, "I do want to see the nails. But we can do that another day."

"What do you have in mind?" Tia asks.

I suggest skateboarding. We could go to the skate park. Or just practice ollieing off some stairs. I point to a set of steps on the far side of the park. "Those are perfect. What do you say?"

"We don't have our boards." Paisley points out the obvious.

"Okay," I say. "Then what about swimming? We haven't done that since summer."

"Right," says Tia with a smirk. "You want to go to the pool."

Scarlett builds on that. "You wanna join the swim team?"

Now they're all laughing.

It takes me only a second to realize why.

Riley puts it into words: "You think *he* might be at the pool."

That wasn't what I was thinking. "All I'm saying," I mutter under my breath, "is nobody goes to the mall anymore. It's so yesterday."

I can see them exchanging glances. Like, *What's got into her?*

Paisley comes over and puts an arm around me, holds me up against her. Like I'm a one-year-old taking her first steps who tripped and fell. It feels comforting, so I don't pull away. "We get it, Li," she says. "We get why this is hard. And you don't have to do it if you don't want to."

The others echo that: They want me with them, but they aren't forcing me to go.

"Whatever you decide is fine," Tia says. "But we're going."

Perhaps if I had more confidence, I'd tell them to go without me. But I'm so used to us doing stuff together. So I just nod and follow them toward the mall entrance.

We had planned to go to the beauty shop first, but Riley suggests we stop at the food court for milkshakes. I think she's trying to make me feel better. It's sort of working.

I'm first in line and I order a s'mores shake. Riley gets rhubarb and strawberry. The others all get chocolate. Even though the court is crowded, we find a free booth and sit down.

My back is to the main walkway, but the others are actively scanning the throng.

"Hey, is—" Tia exclaims.

Paisley and Riley crane their necks.

Scarlett jumps up to get a better view. "*That* guy?"

I bend forward so no one—and especially not *that* guy—can see my face. I fix my gaze on my shake. I don't care if they've spotted Ricardo; I'm not looking. Not even peeking through the strands of my hair. He'll have to waltz over to our table, stand in front of us, give me a dimpled smile, and say hi. Otherwise I don't care about anything except the toasted marshmallows floating in my whipped cream.

"Nah," Riley says. "Doesn't even look like him."

As Scarlett returns to her shake, Tia points out that Ricardo wears black a lot, which makes him hard to spot in a crowd. Riley counters that black can look cute on a guy. They argue over that until Scarlett says, "Even if black isn't always cute, it's sexy."

To which everyone giggles up a storm.

We move on to discuss Ricardo's haircut and why it makes him look so handsome. No argument there. Except Tia thinks he shouldn't wear quite so much product. I'm about to say it's perfect as it is, but I'm afraid she'll give me a hard time about being too biased.

Suddenly we hear a loud popping sound.

"Whoa!" Paisley says. "What was that?"

Everyone freezes. Looks around. Listens.

It was just one pop. Like a single firecracker.

"Was it a gunshot?" I ask.

"Maybe a transformer blew," Riley says.

"Or some kid popped one of those balloons in front of the party supply store," Tia says.

No one thinks it was a gunshot.

But I'm not so certain. "Really," I say, "we should get out of here."

"You haven't finished your shake," Scarlett says. Like that matters.

I stand up, shake in hand. Heart pounding. "Let's get out of here."

"Come on, Li," Tia says, tugging at my arm, pulling me back onto the bench beside her.

"We get what you're doing," Scarlett teases.

"No excuses, girl!" Riley says.

I know what they're thinking: I'm making up an excuse to leave because I'm still worried about seeing Ricardo. But that's the furthest thing from my mind.

There's another series of loud pops. Much louder. Definitely not balloons.

People around us are getting up.

Paisley grabs my arm. "What should we do?"

"Get down!" Tia shrieks.

But it's too late.

Milkshakes are spraying in all directions as she falls.

And I fall on her.

Moira

I am Moira and I am a statistic. I was forty-five when I was shot. I was living in Washington, DC, with my husband, Richard, and our two teenagers. I was a clinical neurosurgeon at Georgetown University Medical Center, conducting research on restoration of the blood–brain barrier. My pronouns were she/her. I am survived by my husband and son.

"In uber, eta 45 min"
    I read Jessica's text and reply, "cu soon"

Jess is my youngest cousin and the one I feel closest to. We both attended Johns Hopkins, and she followed in my footsteps after I went into medicine. That bonded us. We took different paths—she's a family physician in Kentucky, I'm a neurosurgeon here in DC—but we stay in touch, mainly through lengthy texts and late-night phone calls.

She hung in there with me when I was weighing whether to accept the tempting and lucrative proposal from an industry partner seeking to commercialize my research on the blood–brain barrier in the form of a cutting-edge intraoperative technology. Tempting as that was, Jess helped me see it could turn into a conflict-of-interest scenario that compromised my academic freedom. Or worse. So I walked away.

More recently, I've been the one offering support as she struggles in her career. I hate seeing her become a shadow of the trailblazing physician I know her to be. I can't imagine practicing medicine in a state that has effectively turned back the clock on women's health care by half a century. I was shocked when she told me about the exodus of doctors—not just those quitting from pandemic burnout and the general failings of the medical system, but those fleeing because of repressive restrictions on women's health care. "I'd understand," I said, "if you decide to leave too."

But she didn't. "Quitting isn't an option," she said when I pressed her. "Who would I be as a doctor if I abandoned my patients? People need to know that quality medical care is available."

She goes through life as a doctor. It's what she does. I'm the same way. Wherever we go—not just in a hospital, but on an airplane or to a school or a theater or any public place—we want to bring a sense of safety. People may not know I'm a doctor, but if the need arises, I want to be able to say, "There's a doctor in the house. You'll be okay."

I told Jess I was proud of her—admired her—for staying, for standing up for women's fundamental rights. For upholding her Hippocratic oath even under the most noxious conditions.

In truth, though, I suspected she was making a mistake, a big one, by remaining in a job that had become untenable, especially since she wasn't in a position to fix the larger issues. However, given how resolute she sounded, I worried that if I pressed too hard, I'd come across as judgmental and she'd feel I had let her down. Or she'd see me as an outsider incapable of relating to her predicament. Either way, what we needed was an uninterrupted discussion in which she could provide the full story and we could objectively assess next steps. But we never seemed to find it. The more stressed she became, the less available she was, until we were communicating exclusively via texts. Short, choppy texts, written at odd moments while multitasking.

The other day, she sent me one that said, "patient labs ↑ start ABX."

I fired back, "???"

She quipped, "sorry, my coffee-to-patient ratio is off the charts today"

I replied with a laughing emoji and advised reducing her caffeine dosage, unless she planned to move her clinic into Starbucks. I also suggested she clear her schedule and fly to DC for the weekend so we could have some much-overdue in-person cousin time.

Since her kids are away at summer camp, and her husband, Eric, is—as she put it—old enough to fend for himself for a couple days, she agreed. Her mileage ticket took her into Dulles, and she planned to Uber to our house.

In fact, rush-hour traffic turns out to be worse than predicted, and her forty-five-minute ride stretches into more than an hour. As soon as I see her Uber pull into our driveway, I run outside.

"Sorry I'm late," she says as we embrace.

"No worries!" I stand back and regard her with a smile. "This is your time to unplug and relax."

I expect a smile in return, but all I see is my smile reflected in her sunglasses. So I grab her carry-on and head into the house.

She follows. "I'm glad I took time off," she says, pushing her glasses to the top of her head so she can see in the dim hallway, "but I'm not sure about fully unplugging. This case I'm dealing with—I haven't told you about it yet—is a monster."

I don't like the sound of that. This weekend is supposed to allow her the headspace to take a fresh look at things. "You aren't on call, are you?" I say.

"If I were"—she stifles a *humph*—"I wouldn't have gotten on a plane."

"For sure," I say. "But you have your team. They're covering, right?"

"Yes and no," she equivocates. "The issues we're facing have ramifications way beyond this case. They only said I could take time off after I promised to be available if they need me."

"Okay," I say. "We'll talk about all that. In the meantime . . . I hope you're up for pizza."

Our family has a Friday evening tradition: a pizza picnic. It's the one time of the week we all block out on our full-to-overflowing calendars so we can spend it together. If the weather is warm, we pick up pizza and take it to the park; if it's cold or rainy or otherwise inclement, we have our pizza delivered and eat it on the faux-sheepskin rug by the electric fireplace in the den. This is a balmy summer evening, so there's no question we're going picnic style.

As Jess steps out of her travel shoes and into a pair of mint-green thong sandals I'm guessing she picked up at a dollar store—but that look elegant enough on her dainty feet for a night at the opera— Richard rolls in. He drops his briefcase by the door and gives each of us a hug. His job in the Congressional Budget Office keeps him cranking seven days a week, but he manages to get away early on Fridays. Now he does a few hip shakes and shoulder shimmies to show how he's rebooting himself for the picnic.

"Where are the kids?" he wants to know.

Just as I'm explaining they're in their rooms doing teenage stuff, they come bounding down the stairs, crying, "Pizza, pizza, pizza!"

"Crispy crust!" says Rachel.

"Pepperoni!" shouts Sam, registering at double her decibels.

"How about . . . both?" Their dad is a born mediator, which works well for him in the budget office, not always so well at home.

After clarifying that Jess is still a vegetarian, I place an order for an extra-large New York–style veggie pizza, with side orders of pepperoni for Sam and garlic for Richard (which by extension, means garlic for me). Everyone will feel satiated on my watch.

Then I fetch the picnic basket I put together while waiting for Jess, with corn chips and turtle brownies and plates and everything else we need. Plus the cooler, filled with sodas and beer.

"Where to?" Richard asks.

Again we have choices: Hains Point, Meridian Hill, the National Mall, Garfield Park. The kids typically thrash this out between themselves. One or the other always comes out on top, sometimes for multiple weeks in a row if neither Richard nor I invoke basic standards of fairness. Now, however, I stop the process before they can rev it up. "We have a guest," I remind them. "How about we ask if she has a preference?"

Polite humans that they've been raised to be, they respectfully concur. I even detect a hint of embarrassment as Rachel realizes she missed a fine point of etiquette. Her social cognizance is maturing nicely with her years. I'll take some credit for that.

Jess does have a preference: the National Mall.

In medical school, she says, when she could find the time, she took the train to DC and walked from Union Station to the mall, then wandered around exploring the landmarks. I sense a touch of nostalgia, which could be helpful if it revives her initial passion for medicine. Or prompts her to move her practice to DC.

Richard chimes in to say he wants to see the street musicians who often perform at the mall.

With all that settled, we climb into our minivan—I sit in back with Jess, though I know we won't really be able to talk yet—and head to the pizza parlor. After picking up our order, we're on to the mall.

When we're only a few blocks away, Jess's phone rings. She glances at it, then shoots me an *I have to take this* look.

We all shut up—not so we can eavesdrop, but so she can hear the caller over our boisterous chatter.

"I can't talk now," she says, her voice hushed. After a few monosyllabic replies, she hangs up and apologizes to us, saying she'll need to return that call when we get to the mall but doesn't expect it to take long.

Much to Richard's chagrin, no musicians are in the vicinity when we arrive at our favorite grassy spot near the Washington Monument. We spread out the patchwork bedspread we use for a picnic blanket and hope someone will show up to perform while we're eating. As we bring over the pizza and everything we'll need from the van and unpack it, Jess wanders a short distance away to make her call. She paces back and forth as she talks. Looks intense.

The kids know better than to come off as pesty or demanding. But I also know they don't like cold pizza, so after what feels like a reasonable delay, I invite everyone to start eating. Jess, I say, will understand.

And she does. "Glad you started without me," she says as she kicks off her sandals and drops onto the blanket. "I'd feel like a jerk if my emergency messed up pizza night."

We chat about nothing in particular until the others have finished eating. Only after Richard and the kids have dashed off to toss the Frisbee and work up an appetite for dessert do we finally have a moment alone.

We exchange glances, each waiting for the other to speak first.

"So?" I say.

"You think I should quit?" she asks.

While I do think she should quit, that's her decision to make, so I turn the question back on her: "Can you really keep this up? Do you even still want to?"

"That's what I came here to discuss," she says, looking askance at me. "I thought you were proud of me."

"Of course I'm proud of you," I say quickly, then add, "I'd also be proud if you decided you needed to leave, and you left."

Jess repeats what she's told me before—she's committed to being there for her patients yet unable to deliver the care they need. I feel her frustration as she toys with a chunk of crust left on her plate. "Nothing in my training," she says, "prepared me for the cases we're seeing now. I'm sorry I haven't had a chance to give you details."

"That's okay," I say. "Tell me now."

"All right, consider this," she says, shoving aside her plate and shifting into clinical mode. "Female in her twenties, no significant past medical history, presents with an infected left foot, initially treated for a gunshot wound in the ER."

"Who shot her?" I can't resist butting in.

"Her boyfriend."

"Domestic violence?"

"Yes, both emotional and physical abuse. I took a holistic approach, addressed all aspects of her care. Like I always do. When she said she'd left the boyfriend and couldn't do anything more to protect herself, I told her she wasn't powerless. He could still be held accountable. Obviously I didn't give any legal advice. I just said I wanted to be sure she received the services that are rightfully hers as a gunshot victim."

"Did she get the help?"

"I thought she did," she says in a tone that suggests otherwise. "She filed a police report, which they should have done in the ER. The judge slapped a restraining order on the boyfriend."

"That's what you'd want," I say. "Right?"

"Right. Except when the case went to trial, she lost."

"You mean she was lying, and he didn't really shoot her?"

"He never denied shooting her." She pauses, as if she can't believe what she's about to say. "He claimed he shot her in self-defense."

"Self-defense?" I can't believe that either.

"He said she wanted an abortion—"

"So she was pregnant?"

"First trimester. He testified they argued about it and he shot her in self-defense to stop her from harming his unborn child." Jess explains the woman wanted to terminate her pregnancy because the father was abusive and she didn't have the means to support a child on her own. Without the funds to travel out of state, abortion wasn't an option. Even if she raised the money, she would have been late term by then.

I try to make sense of this. "So the man was acquitted on the grounds that he prevented an abortion? No matter if shooting the woman could have killed her—and the baby?"

"I know," she says, "it's outrageous. Absolutely unbelievable! Her belief in the right to make her own choices about her body created a bias against her that was hard to overcome in court. The public defender didn't help with that."

"Did she have the baby?" I'm almost afraid to ask.

"She's carrying it to term. Both are healthy," she says. "At least for now..."

The skepticism I hear as her voice trails off tells me she's aware of the elevated suicide risk for pregnant people suffering from anxiety or depression—and that's without the added complication of being shot and losing a court case. Jess knows that despite her holistic approach and any referrals she may make, this patient's prognosis is poor.

It's like Jess is describing life on an alien planet where society doesn't operate according to laws as we know them. A planet where doctors can knowingly cause a patient's death instead of preventing it. Not only is she in an untenable position, she's living a nightmare. If I were in her shoes, I would leave. No, I would already have left.

Continuing to hold myself in check won't help, so I say, "Can I tell you what I really think?"

"Of course," she says. "Always."

I look her in the eye, then spit it out: "It's your decision to make, but in all honesty, the way I see it, you have to stop trying to be the savior. The personal cost to you is too high. I think you should leave."

I expect her to argue back, to reframe "leave" as "quit" and insist on her commitment to following her ethical standards, regardless of the cost. But she doesn't do that. She simply says, "It's more complicated than you think."

I ask her to explain.

"You know that monster case I took the call about? It's on the verge of blowing up."

I assume this is another abortion case, also headed for court. Presumably this one will implicate her directly. "You mean you could be *forced* to leave your job?"

"If it goes to court, I could be charged."

"For what?"

"For saving a woman's life," she says, her voice soaked in sarcasm. This patient, she explains, a married mother of two, pregnant with her third child, came to the clinic presenting with excessive bleeding. Jess referred her to an ob-gyn, who subsequently admitted her to the hospital. "None of the doctors who examined her consider the fetus viable," she says. "The presence of minimal, erratic cardiac activity can't make an unviable fetus viable."

"Yet they refused to operate?"

"So far. They won't do anything except keep her for observation."

"To observe what?" It's a rhetorical question.

"Exactly," she says. "Waiting and watching normally means we're still weighing treatment options. These docs are waiting because they want to protect their own skins. None of them—and I know them well enough to say this—believe it's a sin to provide treatment that will save a woman's life. But they're afraid the hospital will hit them with a fine. Or file murder charges, and they'll go to jail for performing an illegal abortion."

"Sounds like that's essentially any abortion at this point."

"State law technically allows for exceptions when the mother's life is at risk," she says. "But how that plays out depends on how hard-line the local officials choose to be. In this case, they're as hard-line as you can get."

"Enough to go after you?"

"More than enough in this environment. As the doctor who has the patient's full medical history and made the referral, and who's stayed in the loop to maintain continuity of care, I could be held liable without being the primary decision-maker."

"Okay," I say. "I see how that makes it hard to extricate yourself."

Jess explains that's why she said it's complicated. This patient is in the hospital as we speak. "There are a number of possible outcomes," she says. "Either she gets treatment or she doesn't; either the hospital takes legal action or they—" She stops and redirects herself. "Really, the only thing on my mind is getting this patient the medical care she needs. And fast—"

Before she can complete the thought, her phone rings. She picks it up, nodding at me to indicate it's her team again.

As she takes the call, I pop another beer from the cooler, lean back on my elbows, and watch Sam sprint across the field to catch the air-bounce Richard just threw. As he dives and misses, Rachel comes from behind to grab the Frisbee a fraction of a second before it hits the ground. She wheels around and releases it with a snap of her wrist, sending it soaring toward Richard. Looks like they've worked up an appetite and then some.

On the grass to my right, two street musicians are getting ready to perform. One is softly tapping a tambourine; the other is tuning a guitar. An empty guitar case sits open for tips.

I feel grateful to be living in this city, picnicking in the shadow of the Washington Monument, free to pursue my career as a doctor, with my integrity intact. I'm confident my patients will receive the care they need . . . even while I know the health-care system needs a major overhaul.

I'm prepared for Jess's call to last as long as the first one, but she puts the phone down after a few minutes. As she turns to me, I see a mixture of bewilderment and distress and disbelief on her face.

"Bad news?" I say.

"The patient is . . . gone."

"I'm sorry," I say. "That isn't the outcome anyone wanted." I'm about to remind her it's not her fault, there is nothing she could have done to prevent this, but she cuts me off.

"Not *gone* like you're thinking. She didn't die. Her husband removed her from the hospital. She didn't even sign a DAMA."

"Oh my god!" I say.

She explains that the couple lost all trust in the medical system. "We as doctors failed them," she says. "*I* failed them. Taking matters into their own hands has put her life at even greater risk. She must be aware that if she miscarries at home, she and her husband could be prosecuted for murder."

I ask Jess what her next step is at this point.

"Our team is touching base again in an hour," she says. "I may have to take an early flight back."

Much as I don't want her to leave, I tell her I understand.

"It's ironic," she says. "This patient's noncompliant discharge could end up taking the burden off the doctors if the hospital no longer has a reason to pursue charges against us."

"You're in a no-win situation."

She doesn't need me to spell that out; we both know this case has only amplified the impossibility of continuing to practice in a context where her own health and safety are at risk, yet without benefit to her patients.

"Moira, I know how much you'd like to see me pack my bags," she says. "That may not happen as soon as you'd like, but it could very well be how all this unfolds." She goes on to say that she and Eric have talked about relocating to the DC area. His work is flexible, and he's on board for making the transition if she lands a job offer here. If, God forbid, she were to be implicated in a lengthy court case, she would fly back to Kentucky to testify. She doesn't say what she'd do if faced with a guilty verdict. I guess she'll cross that bridge if and when she has to. Which is hopefully never.

As we're talking, the musicians who have been quietly strumming stand up and launch into classic Bob Dylan. As they belt out "Like a Rolling Stone," a crowd gathers.

Richard and the kids come running, and I break out the brownies.

Jess smiles at me as she bobs her head in rhythm with the beat. It's understood we can't talk more, and she may be leaving in the morning. But that's okay.

Richard grabs a brownie and jumps to his feet. He starts with a few hip and shoulder shakes, but within seconds he's reached full-tilt boogie, his mouth full of fudgy caramel, his arms waving, gesturing for me to dance with him.

I wave back that I'll join him in a minute.

And I have every intention of following through on that, even though my dance moves are nothing to brag about. However, looking away from the musicians and the growing crowd and glancing to my left, I see a couple arguing. The man is tugging on the arm of the woman, who seems to be trying to break away. A second man is tailing the couple. I can't tell if both men are pursuing the woman or if the second man is pursuing the first man. They're headed our way, picking up speed as they move across the lawn.

No one in the crowd has noticed them, because everyone is facing the musicians, engrossed in the music.

Rachel doesn't notice either. She has risen to her knees and is cradling the tin of brownies, taunting her brother. He's lying on the blanket in front of me, demanding she give him a second even if she hasn't finished her first. Past experience tells me where this is headed.

Before I can intervene, out of the corner of my eye, I see the second man pull out a handgun.

He aims at the woman. But we are in his direct line of fire.

As he shoots, I lunge at Rachel. Throw her to the ground. Fall across her body.

But she's already been hit.

As have I.

I can't feel my body, but I know Rachel isn't moving underneath me.

I can't detect her breath.

Or mine.

More shots ring out.

Everything has gone pitch-dark. From somewhere far, far, far away, I hear a voice say, "Is anyone here a doctor?"

Nixon

I am Nixon and I am a statistic. I was eighteen when I was shot. I was living in Redmond, Oregon. My pronouns were he/him. I am survived by my parents, two older brothers, and a half sister.

I've always had an interest in guns. I grew up around them. My dad owns guns. My grandfather owns guns. My uncles own them. You get the picture. Guns are a normal part of life around here.

To be clear, I'm not obsessed with guns, like some people are. One kid I know at school—all he ever wants to talk about is firearms. He doodles them in his notebook. Has pictures of them on his phone. Every post he makes on his socials has something to do with shooting or guns. I'm nothing like that.

If I'm going to obsess over something, it would be baseball. I can watch baseball morning, noon, and night and never get tired of it. I follow my favorite teams, know all the game scores and player stats. I even have a baseball card collection that I started after my uncle gave me a box of Kellogg 3D cards he fished out of cereal boxes as a kid. I've got almost three thousand cards now.

But all that's for fun. Guns are for serious shit. They're for protecting people and keeping law and order. As my dad says, guns are what make a man a man. Whenever anyone questions our right to own as many guns as we want, he points out that the only person who can stop a bad guy with a gun is a good guy with a gun. The way I think of it, I want to become that good guy.

I'm looking forward to getting my first piece. I turned eighteen last month, so I can legally purchase a rifle. I might do that. Or I might wait till I'm old enough to get a handgun. I'm pretty sure I'm not gonna get a lot of guns, though. Probably just one for now. Later I might want more.

One reason I haven't rushed out to get a gun is I'm still on the fence about college. Sounds like owning a gun would be too much of a hassle there with all the rules and restrictions. I can get into our local community college because my grades aren't terrible, and they accept all applicants. I'm just not sure I want to go.

For one thing, I'd have to get a job to pay the tuition. And if I'm working full time, I probably won't want to be bothered with taking classes. That would be like having two jobs but getting paid for only one.

My folks aren't pushing me to go. Mom went for a year and dropped out. From what she said, the whole experience is overrated. She does tend to have strong opinions about stuff. And she's usually right. Like when she told me not to register the dirt bike I bought online. If I'd registered it like I thought I had to, I would have ended up paying a bunch of unnecessary taxes. Who needs that.

The other thing is that a degree isn't required for what I want to do. I know what that is: something sports related. Not as an athlete, though. I can be perfectly honest and say that, though I'm on the high school varsity baseball team, I'm not the most physically fit guy, not a five-tool player. That's why I'm the catcher. I've got a good arm. Plus a good eye. And I'm a great team player. None of that means I'd want to put in all the work it would take to maintain the body of a professional athlete. Nope.

I used to think about being a fitness coach. Then I wouldn't have to do all the hard work myself. I'd just be taking others through their workouts. Motivating them.

In fact, I'm a fantastic motivational speaker.

When I was ten, our church held a contest for best inspirational speaker. My topic was "God Wants You to Obey Your Parents," and

I won first prize in the youth category. Not that I excelled at obeying my parents. More like the opposite. But I could say things that got folks fired up. I talked pretty fast and they couldn't catch every word, but it went over big.

My parents still tease me about obeying them. Like when I asked to borrow the car last Saturday night, and my dad jangled his keys in front of me and said, "Nixon, you may take the car, but God wants you home by midnight."

We both laughed, because we knew why he was saying that. And the truth is, I've turned into quite an obedient son. Kind of like I motivated myself.

These days, I'm thinking about becoming a sports broadcaster. That's something I can do without college. And it ties in sports. I think I'd be good at it.

Today is our first home game of the season.

We're playing one of the best Portland-area teams. They slaughtered us 11–1 in the final game last season. Honestly, it got demoralizing. If I ever work as a play-by-play announcer, I'll do my best to champion the underdog in situations like that.

Now, I put on my mask, tighten my shin guards, grab my mitt, high-five my guys, and walk out to the catcher's position.

Our starting pitcher is on the mound with the ball. The first batter is in the batter's box, adjusting his grip on the bat. I'm crouching, mitt on my left hand, two in the pink, as I like it. The umpire is ready to call play.

Suddenly a boy darts out of the visiting team's dugout and onto the field.

"This isn't happening!" he shouts.

His coach jumps up to stop him. But then he sees what all of us are seeing: The boy is holding a rifle. The coach stops in his tracks.

My first thought is *Damn, I wish I'd already bought that gun. I need it now to take care of this creep. To be the good guy with a gun.*

But I don't have one.

And since we're in a school setting, most likely no one else does either.

So I spring into action the only way I know how: talk this boy out of shooting.

He's wearing the team's red-and-white uniform, standing just inside the baseline, not more than twenty feet from me, facing the pitcher. Doesn't look like he weighs over a hundred pounds.

"Hey!" I exclaim as I take a few steps toward him.

The force of my voice stops everyone. On a dime. Including the boy. I feel the crowd's eyes lasering in on me. They're counting on me. I'm a senior. I'm a motivational speaker. I can handle this until the police get here. I'm sure multiple people have already texted 911.

"Hey," I say again, my voice lower.

He swivels ninety degrees. His rifle is raised, and now it's aimed at me. He doesn't say anything.

Since I've started this, it's on me to do the talking. "So," I say, like this is a normal interaction between two guys on a baseball field, "you're on the team?"

He still doesn't say anything.

I know everyone behind me is watching, even if they can't hear what I'm saying. The important thing is to keep talking, to engage this boy in a normal, easygoing conversation. "You like baseball?" I say. Without waiting for a reply—because I don't think one is coming, and I need to hold him here—I add, "I've been playing since grammar school."

His body is motionless, but his eyes are darting side to side, making sure no one is moving.

They're not.

"Your team's the best," I continue. "You guys always beat us."

I add a couple more things about baseball, but he's still not responding. Obviously the police aren't close by. It could take them longer to get here than I thought. I can feel my mouth drying out, my pulse racing. That is a real rifle I'm staring at. Looks like a Remington 700. Probably his dad's hunting rifle. I have no reason to think it's not loaded. That he won't shoot. I just know I'm not about to become anyone's sacrificial lamb. To make sure that doesn't happen, I've got to make this boy feel we're connecting. Baseball isn't working, so I shift topics. It's a risk, but I take it.

"You like guns?" I say.

"Course I like guns!" he snarls.

I mentally pump my fist. Doesn't matter if he sounds angry, at least I'm getting a response. "Me too," I say. "Don't have one yet. But I'm buying one real soon."

"Good for you," he says.

He's still being snarky, but he's finally connecting with me. I can feel it. It was a stroke of genius to realize we can bond over guns, something we both have an interest in. "I'm thinking of getting a rifle," I say. "Maybe like yours."

Of course I'm hoping he'll drop the gun. Hoping he'll walk over and thank me. Snap out of it. End this shit. It'll be all over the news tonight: "Redmond senior hero talks gunman down." But that's just in my imagination right now.

I can feel the attention of everyone spread out on the field and in the stands, all frozen in place, zeroed in on us. I feel their faith in me. I'm all they've got. I have to come through for them. If it's the last thing I do.

I recall what my dad always says: Guns don't kill people; people kill people. Which means this boy's gun isn't the problem. I don't have to be afraid of it. I don't have to worry about getting shot. It's the boy who's the problem. I don't mean he's a bad person; he's just mixed up. Maybe very mixed up, but deep down, I'm sure he's a good kid. He's like me; we both care about guns. Which gives us a basis to connect. I have to stay with that.

"You know," I say, "you don't really want to shoot me, do you?"

He doesn't move, just stares at me through the scope on his rifle. "Maybe I do."

Of course that's not the response I want. But I also don't want to grovel. It's hard not to plead for your life when you're staring down the barrel of a gun. I remind myself: The gun isn't what's wrong here. Like my dad says.

"When I get a gun," I say, "I'm going hunting. There are lots of great places near here. Have you been?"

"Maybe I have," he says. "So what?"

The way he says it, I have the sense he hasn't been hunting. Isn't even interested in hunting. I'm starting to sweat. The fingers in my mitt are shaking. We've only been out here a few minutes, but it feels like an hour. Where the heck are the police? I'll have to dig deep and find a way to do what I always do to inspire people. Time to call on God.

"You know," I say, "God loves you."

"Right," he says.

"God loves all His children," I say. "But I don't think God wants you to shoot me or anyone here."

He angles his face slightly away from his gun so he can spit hard on the ground. "How do *you* know what God wants?" He says it like he's spitting at me.

But I have an answer for him. It's something I can get fired up about. Even now, in this crazy moment, I can connect with him heart to heart because we're both children of God. "I know what God wants," I say, "because God has a purpose for each and every one of us. You're a child of God. Your life is precious. In your darkest moment, His light will guide you. He will save you. I promise!"

"Speak for yourself," he mutters.

He may not be hearing me yet, but I'm on a roll. I know I'm speaking truth, and I've seen that truth move so many people. I'm certain it can move this boy too. "We're all children of God," I say. "We are here to obey His word. Of course we also obey our parents. That's part of His command." I stop for a second, drop my mitt, and clasp my hands before me, as I would in prayer. "We're all sinners, but we can become better."

I feel as if we're out here alone, just the two of us in a bubble, talking man to man, with no one else watching.

"You're my brother," I say. "Can we pray together?"

He tips his rifle slightly downward so I'm no longer directly in his crosshairs.

My muscles relax a notch. He may not be ready for prayer, but he's listening. I'm getting through to him. Like I knew I could. "Please," I say, in a voice that sounds as close as it can get to begging without losing my dignity, "trust me. I understand you. I can help you."

His rifle moves a hair's breadth lower.

"I support your rights and freedoms," I say. "You don't have to be afraid of losing your freedom, of losing your gun. I'll stand by you. We'll all stand by you." I know I'm going out on a limb saying this, but he's got to know we will support him. If he feels supported, he'll be able to do the right thing. "You don't have to be afraid of anyone."

As I say that, I take half a step toward him, start to extend a hand.

Instantly he jerks his rifle back into position and barks, "Who says I'm afraid?"

"That's not what I meant," I say quickly. I thought we were connecting, but I guess it was only for a second. As soon as I took one step toward him, he took what feels like a dozen steps away from me. Snapped himself back into whatever has this crazy hold on him.

"You think I'm afraid, don't you?" Now he's talking back at me.

For the first time, I'm flustered. This is unraveling, and I don't know how to fix it. "No, no," I say. "I don't think that."

"Yes you do," he says. "You think I'm afraid to shoot!"

"No," I say again. "I think you don't *want* to shoot."

"You and your God," he sneers. "You've got no idea what I want."

He pauses, and this time I'm the one silent. The one who doesn't know what to say. All I see is his gun pointing at me. The gun that's going to kill me. A piece of metal I can't speak to, let alone inspire. It's not people who kill, I realize; it's people with guns who kill. So obvious! Why didn't I think of that before? Someone needed to stop this boy from getting a gun in the first place. That was how to stop him from shooting me.

"I'll show you," he continues. "I'm not afraid to shoot you!"

As he says that, I hear sirens and a commotion behind the bleachers. It's the police. Finally.

He hears them too.

So does everybody else.

There is no more time for words.

I see his finger move to disengage the manual safety on his rifle.

In the split second it takes for him to shoot me, I call out to God.

Owen

I am Owen and I am a statistic. I was twenty-one when I was shot. I was living with my partner, Denise, in Minneapolis, Minnesota, and working as a tech writer. My pronouns were he/him. I am survived by my parents, my sister, and the woman I fully anticipated would become my wife and the mother of my children.

My life changed in one split second. And I wasn't even there when it happened.

A year ago, my girlfriend, Denise, and I were seniors at the University of Minnesota. Since we were already spending as many of our waking moments together as we possibly could—as well as some of our not-so-awake moments—we decided to move out of student housing and get our own place. We found a third-floor studio in Dinkytown, within walking distance of school. The refrigerator lacked a freezer, only two burners on the gas stove worked, and the sofa's fake leather was so slippery you were in danger of sliding off if you didn't keep both feet firmly planted on the floor. But hey, we had both a bed and a sofa, and we could afford the rent as long as we didn't splurge on too many meals out. Which wasn't a problem since it was a luxury just to cozy up over simple dinners at our own place.

Both of us took our studies seriously. For me, it was English. For Denise, it was a double major in political science and history. The idea was to graduate and then start making plans for the rest of our lives. Together.

I had a part-time job tutoring high school students. I felt satisfaction each time I saw a properly placed comma, a corrected parallelism.

When a tutee showed me a paper that had earned an A-plus, I felt like I'd accomplished something myself. But I wanted to do more. I envisioned awakening entire classrooms to the power of foreshadowing, narrative hook, suspense, simile, metaphor. Inspiring students to find their own voices, share their stories with the world. I would be on a mission to stave off the death of literary fiction. One essay at a time.

I considered other career options as well. I could be a journalist reporting on the local literary scene. Or perhaps go further afield as a travel writer. Knowing my ancestors had fled the famines in Ireland, I wanted to do more than analyze the writings of Oscar Wilde and James Joyce. I dreamed of exploring my Celtic roots in person, writing about what I discovered. Of course, being a travel writer could be hard for anyone who intends to start a family with their significant other. As I do.

Denise and I valued commitment, but we weren't talking marriage. Not yet anyway. We thought we'd live together and see where it took us. She didn't want to plan a family until she was fully established in her career. I understood that. Even if I promised to shoulder an equal share of childcare, the system was rigged such that she would end up with the greater burden. She hoped to get into law school at Yale or the University of Chicago, with UMN as her backup. I wanted to support her success in any way I could.

Cuddled up on the sofa, holding each other so tight we couldn't slide off, we discussed what we'd do if she got into Yale. It had a 5 percent acceptance rate, but that didn't stop us from being optimistic. I said I'd apply for a teaching gig in the New Haven public schools. If I worked full time, we could afford a one-bedroom apartment with fully functional appliances. We talked about getting around on bicycles, at least until Denise was also bringing in some income. I really hoped she'd get into Yale.

Then one afternoon, while I was hammering out a paper for my postcolonial lit seminar, she came home early.

Usually she went to the law school library after her classes so she could study without anything or anyone—like me—distracting her, and rolled in just in time for us to share a late dinner.

When I heard the door crack open, I looked up from my computer. "Surprise, surprise!"

"A pleasant surprise, I hope," she said.

"When am I not pleased to see you?" I countered. Which was of course true, even if it had suddenly become harder to finish my paper.

She bent over to kiss me, then nuzzled the nape of my neck. She'd finished her studying, she explained, and felt über-prepared for her exam, so she was taking the night off. Then she plopped down on the sofa and scrolled through messages on her phone, while I went back to my paper.

A few minutes later, she looked up. "Hey, you!" she said. "Let's go to a movie."

That was out of the blue. We hadn't been to a theater in months. When we did manage to squeeze in a movie, like most students, our go-to was streaming. I told her I liked the idea, loved her spontaneity, and the movie she'd picked sounded intriguing, but I was up against a deadline. "You can still go," I said. "Tell me all about it when you get home."

"Oh, c'mon!" she said. "Don't be a poop . . ."

But then she realized how stressed I was over my paper. She wiped the makings of a pout off her face and said she'd ask a friend to go with her.

Which she did. The friend said yes, and off they went. She even resisted suggesting I'd regret staying home when I heard their rave reviews.

I returned to my paper.

After a couple of hours, I was making headway but getting hungry. I found a can of New England clam chowder in the cupboard and threw together a salad. I took everything back to my computer.

I know, eating at my keyboard is a terrible habit, but I wanted to get the paper done so Denise and I could have some QTT when she got home.

Refueled, I plowed ahead with the paper.

When I finally looked up, it was after nine o'clock. That gave me pause. It must have been a very long movie. Or maybe Denise and her friend had gone out for a bite afterward. Except she would have texted me about that.

So I texted her.

No answer.

I keep news alerts turned off on my phone. I don't like being bothered by that sort of stuff, especially when I'm studying. I figure whatever news is really important will be there when I choose to catch up with it later. Besides, most news is so repetitive. I did an experiment for one of my classes in which I listened to the news every day for a week, then changed it up and listened on only one day the following week. I wrote a paper in which my thesis was that people watch the news too much. I got a C minus. Which probably explains why Denise majored in political science and I did not.

In any case, when she didn't text back, I got nervous.

I went online to check the news. Immediately I saw the national headline: "Multiple Fatalities in Minneapolis Shooting." In a movie theater. In the theater Denise went to.

I freaked!

I tried calling her.

It went to voicemail.

I tried calling her sister, who lives in Saint Paul.

She didn't pick up.

Fortunately, at that point, a call came through from Denise.

She was okay.

"My God, Denise!" was all I could say. I breathed the deepest sigh of relief I've ever breathed in my life.

She asked if I could come to the emergency response area near the theater, where she and her friend had been taken, along with other survivors, as officials tried to account for everyone and provide medical assistance. They'd been under lockdown, but she was now free to go.

No, she said before I had a chance to ask, she didn't need medical care.

Only later, much later, did I realize my life had changed in a split second. It would never be the same.

Over the next several months, Denise went through the therapy program available to survivors. Though she insisted she was fine and eager to refocus on her studies, I convinced her not to quit prematurely. I didn't want her to have a setback that could have been prevented had she seen the program through.

Honestly, I felt she handled everything a lot better than I would have had I been in that theater. Seven people killed, twenty-six injured. And she witnessed it all.

The weird thing was that I didn't see any of that firsthand, yet I was the one having nightmares. I would dream I was in a theater, watching a movie. I was always sitting in a center seat in a middle row. Suddenly an actor on the screen pulled out a gun. I thought at first it was part of the movie. But then he would wheel around and shoot into the audience. Real bullets. I always woke up in a sweat, pinching myself to make sure I was still alive. Shocked that an attack could blow up my reality, and from such an unexpected direction.

At one point during Denise's therapy, she was advised to attend a movie if she felt ready. The idea was to gradually increase exposure to anxiety-producing situations that resembled the initial trauma. She had already shown her tolerance to mentally picturing that she was in a movie theater; the next step was to do an exposure in the flesh. Kind of like the advice I'd heard for people after a car accident: Get back in the car soon so you don't develop a fear of driving. I think they call it vehophobia.

Denise was supposed to have a friend come with her for support, so of course she asked me.

I said, "Whatever you need, I'll be there."

She said, "Let's do it."

Neither of us had been to a theater since the shooting. We chose a weekend matinee to minimize any associations that might arise at an evening show. Of course it wasn't the same theater; that wouldn't have been possible since it was still closed. Frankly I thought they should never reopen it. I, for one, wouldn't want to go there. Instead we chose a classy place with heated recliner seats and picked a romcom that wouldn't trigger anxiety. It was on the other side of town, so we had to drive there and pay for parking. But the extra expense was worth it: I wanted Denise to be comfortable and relaxed in every way. I was sure she would ace this.

We arrived early and found seats in a row toward the back, near the door.

"In case you want to leave," I said.

"I won't want to leave," she said. "Stop being such a worrywart."

"I'm not a worrywart," I said. "I'm just loving on my girlfriend."

When the movie started, we were holding hands and clucking at each other over the corny dialogue in the romantic scenes. Everything was going well.

Then, about halfway through, with no advance warning, I couldn't breathe. I literally couldn't draw air into my lungs.

My heart was racing.

I thought I was about to black out.

After what felt like forever—but was probably only a few seconds—my breath started again.

Still, nothing felt normal. It was a struggle just to sit there.

I didn't want Denise to know anything was wrong. This was her time to heal, and I was there to support her. The last thing I wanted was to take away from that in any way. So I quietly withdrew my hand on the pretext of scratching my nose. But really I was just trying to breathe. I kept thinking all the air had somehow been sucked out of the theater.

Then it got worse.

I began to fear I would forget who I was. Like I was only hanging on to Owen by the slimmest of threads, and that thread was about to snap. I had briefly experienced something similar when I took hallucinogens with friends during our first year on campus. My brain short-circuited, and I wasn't sure who I was. This was even scarier. It felt like a medical emergency. Like the grip of death.

By then I wanted Denise to know.

But I was unable to speak. I couldn't even whisper a word. It was as if the thoughts in my mind could no longer find a way to reach my tongue.

I didn't know what to do, so I bolted.

I ran through the lobby and out the front door. It was a chilly but bright afternoon. I stood on the sidewalk gulping air.

Denise wasn't far behind.

"What's the matter?" she said.

I shook my head. I still couldn't speak.

She looked worried. "Are you okay?"

She reached for my hand, but I didn't want to be touched. That's how intense my panic was.

She pulled out her phone, and I realized she was about to call 911.

I shook my head forcefully to let her know that wasn't what I needed.

We stood there, on the edge of the sidewalk, people rushing past us on their way home or headed to their evening activities. Slowly I calmed down. My breathing returned to normal and I could speak again.

I told Denise I didn't know what had come over me. "I couldn't breathe, I couldn't speak," I said. "I thought I was going to die."

"We need to get you checked out," she said.

I didn't dispute that. "I hope I'm too young for a heart attack," I said.

"Probably," she said. "But we need to make sure."

She did her best to keep things light, to relax me, as we walked to the car. She even made a crack about how she should have gone into premed instead of law, and I was able to give her half a smile.

By the time we got to the ER, I was feeling reasonably normal. Just super shaken up.

I described everything to the doctor, and he examined me and made a diagnosis: panic attack. The fact that I'd never had one before didn't matter.

My life had changed again. In another split second. It was irrevocably altered that night when shots rang out as Denise sat in the movie theater. And it changed again when I panicked at another theater.

Over the following weeks, I had more attacks. One on a bus. One at a restaurant. One at the student union. None of them were as overpowering as the first, but they were debilitating because I never knew when one would occur.

I quit my tutoring job because I was afraid of being in the enclosed space of a school or coffee shop or bus or anywhere I might not be able to easily escape. I could walk from our apartment to the university, but I was too anxious. I skipped as many classes as I could without flunking out.

More and more, I just stayed home. I told Denise I'd never go to the movies again. I don't think she believed I'd stick to that, but she didn't press me. She asked a friend to go to a movie with her to complete her therapy exposure. Which she aced. No surprise there.

She convinced me to try therapy myself. I was reluctant because

I thought I'd have to dig up all sorts of unpleasant memories I didn't know existed. But it turned out to be nothing like that. My therapist quickly helped me see that my panic attacks tied back to the night Denise was at the mass shooting. She was a primary victim, but as her partner, I was a secondary victim.

I didn't understand why my symptoms were worse than hers.

The therapist didn't have an answer for that. Other than that each person has their unique response to trauma.

I thought that perhaps because I loved Denise so much, I took on her experience and felt it as if it were my own. Ultimately, though, it didn't need an explanation; what mattered was that I could heal. I could get my life back.

It has taken me many months to do that. Even so, my life isn't back to where it was before the shooting. This is our new normal.

Denise was accepted by all the law schools where she applied, including Yale. The letter from Yale arrived a couple of weeks after my first panic attack. I wasn't in a space where I could move to New Haven and get a teaching job. I told Denise that wasn't a reason for her to miss out on her dreams. I suggested we try a long-distance relationship for a while, but she wasn't having it. She reminded me that, just as I'd been there for her, now she would do the same for me. And she meant it.

My grades took a dip, but I was able to graduate. I didn't even consider attending the graduation ceremony.

I had to completely reassess my career path. Teaching and travel writing—anything that involves being with too many people—was out. Hopefully I can get back to those goals in the future, but in the meantime I'm focusing on freelance writing projects I can do from home. It didn't take long to land a lucrative contract writing user manuals for a technology firm. It's not literary criticism or creative writing, but my salary allowed us to upgrade to a two-bedroom apartment. And buy a gorgeous soft-but-not-slippery sofa.

Every week I see progress.

Recently my therapist suggested I might be ready to go to a movie. I agreed.

Denise came with me to the same theater where I had the panic attack. I felt a little uncomfortable ahead of time, but nothing I couldn't tolerate. I resisted sitting near an exit, because my therapist had told me sitting near an exit might make me feel safer in the moment but would send the wrong message to my nervous system. This so-called safety behavior would signal that a threat did exist and I wasn't really safe, and thus reinforce my anxiety.

After we took our seats in the theater, I felt more at ease. I knew there was no actual threat. Everything went well during the movie, and we celebrated afterward with pad kee mao at a family-owned Thai restaurant near our apartment.

I'm confident now I can handle being in crowded spaces without having a panic attack.

At the same time, I'm aware of my vulnerability and everyone's vulnerability. And I've gotten in touch with my anger over the shooting. Over all the mass shootings. All of them.

With Denise's love and my therapist's support, I know I will continue to gain strength. It will be a slow process, but I will get there.

This afternoon, as I'm sitting at my desk in our second bedroom, which I turned into an office, working on a user manual for a documentation platform, I get a text from Ivan.

"Owen, been a while," he says. "all good?"

While I was having panic attacks, I stopped hanging out with friends. Only my closest buddies knew what was going on. Everyone else probably assumed I'd fallen into the abyss of senior year and would resurface at some point. Ivan was one of those. We met in our Shakespeare seminar first year and played a lot of tennis on the Fifth Street courts.

I text back: "dude, we gotta catch up"

"how about now?"

That wasn't what I had in mind. But I'm not up against a deadline with the manual, and Denise won't be home till after her Wednesday evening seminar. Actually, it could be the ideal time.

I text back: "sure"

He texts to suggest we see a movie, then go to a café to chat.

I missed all the movies released so far this year, so I tell him I'm up for that.

He texts back to meet at the theater in an hour.

When I see the link in his text, I do a double take. It's the theater where the shooting occurred.

"that place is open?" I text.

"reopened"

"really?"

"yup, recently," he replies.

"didn't know"

He texts back that they wanted to resume business but without agitating the public, so there was no publicity.

I have to think about this. Yes, I feel comfortable going to a movie, and I'm not worried about a panic attack. But *there*? I remember hoping they would never reopen. Part of me still feels that way. I try to picture myself walking in, taking a seat, kicking back and watching the screen. I'm not sure I could manage it.

I take so long to respond that he texts back: "we still on?"

"don't know about that theater" I say.

The reply he sends is so long I have to keep scrolling to read it all. The gist is that he knows how horrific the shooting was, what a tragedy it was for our city, but he also thinks it's essential for the community to move on, to heal, to get back to normality. Going to a different theater or seeing another movie would, he says, only empower those who want to destabilize society.

Obviously he doesn't know—or forgot—Denise was there. I'm not about to mention that in a text. Suddenly I'm clear: This is a bad idea.

I text back: "dude, maybe another time"

I expect him to say no problem and leave it at that. But he doesn't. He pushes back hard, says we should not make fear-based decisions; we're better than that.

I have to remind myself that, even if his text comes across as accusatory, he doesn't know what I've been through. He is probably reflecting his own sentiments, his own intention not to act out of fear. So I rein in my gut reaction and give it another thought.

Over the next ninety seconds—while Ivan is undoubtedly staring at his phone, wondering if he just pissed me off—I run through a therapy session in my mind. I remind myself that panic arises when I let myself predict a catastrophic outcome when there is no actual reason to expect it will occur. On the other hand, panic doesn't arise when I refuse to believe my negative predictions. I have tested this over and over in restaurants and stores and crowded places and on buses and even in a movie theater. What I feared would happen didn't happen.

In fact, Ivan is right: I have no reason to fear a shooting in this theater just because one occurred there before. For me to not go today would be to lapse into what my therapist calls avoidance behavior. Or—forget the psychobabble—to fall for old-fashioned superstition.

I smile to myself as I realize I should arguably feel *more* safe in this theater. What are the odds of another shooting in the same place? Besides, they must have boosted security. It's probably like a fortress now.

Without further thought, I text back, "see you in an hour"

After I text Denise to tell her what I'm doing, and she texts back a thumbs-up, I shut down the document on my screen, throw on a jacket, and I'm out the door.

When I get to the theater, I don't see any extra security. I guess whatever they've added isn't very visible.

Ivan is already in the lobby buying snacks. He hands me a pack of Milk Duds, along with an *I-bet-you-still-like-these* look, and pockets a couple more for himself.

Inside the auditorium, he heads for empty center seats in a row halfway down the aisle. Seats that might as well be marked with a neon red bull's-eye.

Anxiety prickles through me, head to toe, as if my blood just turned into seltzer water.

But then I remind myself: I didn't do the avoidance behavior of not going to the movie, and now I'm not going to do the safety behavior of sitting by an exit. Yes, sitting there might feel more comfortable in the moment, but it will make me more anxious the next time. The anxiety I'm feeling now is normal. I can handle it. With these thoughts, the anxiety dissipates.

We take our seats, the lights dim, and the previews begin.

The first is for a movie billed as a cross between *Star Trek* and *Hamlet*. A space explorer finds himself betrayed by the AI system he depends on, yet revenge is not a simple matter. I don't want to miss that one. From Ivan's snorts, I suspect he won't go with me. I bet Denise will.

With my steady income, I'll be able to treat her to more movies and dinners out. I might even find the right occasion to, as they say, pop the question. Not at a movie of course, but maybe at the upscale Irish pub where we love the Guinness braised short ribs. I can imagine her surprise when I pull a little velvet box from my jacket pocket and say, "Denise . . . "

It will be one of those split seconds in which life changes.

Having daydreamed through the next two previews, I snap to attention as the feature begins. I crack open my Milk Duds and watch two men jog side by side on a country road at dusk. Though they don't speak, the rivalry between them is palpable.

Just as I'm wondering which of the two I'll end up rooting for, the movie cuts out. The theater is plunged into darkness.

A hundred people let out a collective groan.

"Hope they fix it fast," Ivan mutters.

"That's for sure," I say.

Then I see a light move down by the screen.

Before I can tell Ivan it looks like a technician is already on the job, earsplitting shots ring out.

An acrid stench fills the theater. Burns my nose.

In the dim, smoky light, I see Ivan slumped in his seat.

More shots follow.

I duck.

But it doesn't matter. Already my body has slumped beside his.

A strange calm descends, as if none of this is really happening, as if I'm not really here.

As if I have already forgotten who I am.

Prema

I am Prema and I am a statistic. I was twenty-nine when I was shot. I was living in Teaneck, New Jersey, working for an information technology company and about to marry my fiancé, David. My pronouns were she/her. I am survived by my brother and two sets of grandparents.

I'm getting married.

Well, *we* are getting married. Prema and Dave. Dave and Prema.

For a while, whether we would go through with our wedding was in question. Not a question in my mind or his mind, but a question in what felt like a widening circle of minds. Starting with my mother.

As we sit alone together in her bedroom now, in the late afternoon on the eve of my wedding, and I watch her painstakingly apply henna designs to the palms of my hands and my forearms, before moving on to my ankles, I recall how the storm of doubt and disapproval arose.

First, though, I should clarify that neither Dave nor I is what you would call a religious person. We do see ourselves as spiritual, but we don't attend services or belong to any religious organizations. Neither of us prays—except maybe in a dire emergency—or does personal religious practices or has an altar or anything like that. I'm not a fan of rituals, at least not in my daily life. I don't like having to do the same thing over and over. Or if it's something I want to do over and over—like have a cup of coffee first thing in the morning while I check emails—I prefer to just enjoy the coffee and read the emails, without making it into a ritual. Dave is the same way. Of course, we realize it would be hard to get married in the eyes of our family and friends if we refused to engage in the ritual of a wedding.

As spiritual people, we view life as more than mere physical or material existence. I believe everything in the universe—people included, but not just people—is made of energy. It's more than a belief: When I get quiet enough, I can sense that energy all around me. Admittedly, I'm not very quiet most of the time.

I also like to think we get more than one lifetime. That's a belief I picked up from my family. Dave teases me about what he imagines I'll become in my next life. Lately, it's the librarian of lost socks. Each time I reacquaint him with a sock he has misplaced, he jokes that our marriage will serve as a great training ground for my next lifetime. He says he's open to reincarnation in theory but challenges me to offer solid proof. I've promised he'll be the first to hear about it when I find that proof.

Dave and I also cherish our families' religious heritage and culture—Jewish and Hindu, respectively. We enjoy sharing with each other what we know about their customs, and highlighting the similarities. Like when I said I wanted to have *mehndi* at my wedding, and he said henna was used in some Jewish weddings. He saw it at a wedding he attended in Israel. I told him I had no idea.

I also had no idea Mom would question our decision to get married.

When Dave and I sat down with her and my father to share our news, the two of us had been a couple for almost five years. Neither of my parents had ever discouraged or disapproved of our relationship.

Yet in that moment, Mom responded with a scowl.

Like most parents, she did her fair share of scowling, but it was usually over stuff like the milk carton left open in the refrigerator when we were teenagers or the puddle in front of the bathroom sink. Even some big stuff, like when I quit my job as a human resource manager and went into customer service at an IT company. She had a point when it came to the pay cut I took, but her judgment about the direction I was taking on my career path was flat-out wrong. My new job is way better. Plus I would never have met Dave if I'd stayed at the old one.

Mom didn't say why she wasn't thrilled about our engagement. I guess she expected me to read the scowl. All she said was, "Are you sure?"

We said we were sure.

She glanced at my father, sitting beside her on the settee.

He didn't say anything, just picked up the TV remote and flipped it casually end to end in his hand, as if it were an hourglass and he wanted to make sure we didn't run out of time.

After an awkward silence, she turned back to us. I could see from the softening in her eyes that she wasn't going to fight me on this. I'm her only daughter, so this is her only chance to plan a wedding. Besides, I know that, deep down, she wants me to have the wedding I want, with the person I've chosen, even if that's not what she would choose for me. Even if she sometimes questions my ability to make smart choices for myself.

"Okay then," she said. "How do you intend to do this?"

We gave her the simple answer: a fusion wedding.

She was on board, so we began the planning process.

Our intention was to honor both our families by incorporating the traditions of each. It didn't take long, however, to see there was nothing simple about a fusion wedding. The first time we sat down with Mom, she came with a list of questions that mirrored our own: Did we want two separate ceremonies, or did we want to combine our traditions in one ceremony? If we had two, would we need two venues? Which would come first? And would our guests view whichever came first as more important?

Dave and I also had some questions we didn't want to mention to Mom. We worried about what might go wrong at a fusion wedding held in an area known for conflict between religious groups, where the line between extremism and mainstream religion wasn't always clear. Where tensions could erupt into violence, even if no one believed that would happen. What venue, we wondered, would accept an interfaith couple without stipulations? Would any guests bring anti-Semitism or anti-Hindu sentiments to our wedding?

Initially we were inclined to go with separate ceremonies. That might lower the risk of offending anyone. But then we saw how complex the logistics would be and how much would have to be duplicated: flowers, seating, parking, security, fees. Not to mention that our guests—including those from out of town who didn't have cars—would have to travel between the venues.

After much discussion, we settled on consecutive ceremonies—first Hindu and then Jewish—at the same venue on the same day. It would be on us to communicate to our guests that the order of the ceremonies did not imply importance.

Before we could arrange a venue, we needed a date.

Mom said it couldn't be just any day; we had to consult a Vedic astrologer who could provide the most auspicious time.

I objected. I didn't want to risk the astrologer declaring that according to the stars, Dave and I weren't a perfect match. I'd heard of that happening. A cousin's engagement was canceled after an astrologer's matching found she was so incompatible with her boyfriend that even the usual pujas couldn't save them.

Mom said she would only ask for the auspicious date. Nothing else.

I was still against it. Knowing her, she wouldn't be able to resist getting the full astrological reading. If it was anything short of perfect, whatever doubts she was still harboring would come roaring back.

When I told Dave about my worries, he pointed out that, having promised to only ask for the date, she couldn't tell us about anything more without breaking her promise. Even if she knew.

"Let's just do it," he said. "It will make her feel better."

I liked that he was looking out for Mom. So I agreed.

Our planning process was a fusion dance in and of itself. Though we tried to achieve a balance, that wasn't always easy. For example, Hindu weddings are typically long, which meant our first ceremony might seem like the main event. We didn't see a way to avoid that. Guests would have to appreciate the length as a cultural element. Nor could we avoid the potential for boredom that comes with a long ceremony. Our Indian guests would be used to long weddings; the others would hopefully feel more comfortable when they realized they weren't expected to stay glued to their seats the entire time.

The further we got into our preparations, the more parallels we uncovered. Some allowed us to reduce redundancy. In a Hindu wedding, for instance, the couple sit in a *mandap*, while in a Jewish wedding, they are in a chuppah. The two canopy structures are essentially the same, so we were able to build one that served for both ceremonies.

Other parallels added richness. In a Hindu wedding, the couple circumambulate the sacred fire seven times and exchange seven vows. In a Jewish wedding, the couple walk around each other seven times, and the cantor offers seven blessings. We liked the idea of including both rituals, with their similarity unifying our ceremony.

Other rituals were a perfect complement. For example, in a Hindu wedding, the groom ties a *mangalsutra* around the bride's neck to signify their union. I wanted us to include that, even if I wouldn't necessarily wear the necklace every day afterward, as is traditional. We both wanted to exchange rings—which we could do as part of the second ceremony.

Finding a location was tricky. It would be difficult to have a fusion wedding within the temple of one of the traditions. However, after some research, we found a Hindu temple that had as part of its property a community center that, unlike most similar venues, was willing to rent space to nonmembers. It was perfect for our purposes, and its garden was included in the rental.

It was all coming together.

Once we had the date and location, the next task was to let everyone know. We started with the guests who were farthest away: my father's parents, living in Gujarat, India.

My father reached out to make sure they could make the trip.

They said no, they wouldn't come.

I was crushed. I couldn't imagine my wedding without Dadaji. It didn't matter that I'd heard the stories, seen the reports, knew that only 2 percent of marriages in India are interfaith. Women who chose husbands not of their faith placed their lives in danger. Some were killed. It was hard to believe but true.

Somehow I had emotionally insulated myself from all this, as if it could only occur in a distant corner of the globe and would never touch me or my family. As if it were unrelated to the religious tensions in Teaneck we worried might spill into our fusion wedding.

Besides, I reasoned, Dadaji loved me. For my sake, he would brush aside politics and dogma, overlook his objections. Wouldn't he?

I cried on Mom's shoulder when I realized he wouldn't budge.

Most of her family live in California. Since they're used to American ways, she expected all of them to come. She joked it would be hard to keep the guest list under three hundred unless some turned down the invitation.

Dave said he wasn't inviting his entire extended family, so that would help.

The two of them joked about it, but I wasn't laughing. I was stuck on what it meant that my grandparents were refusing to come to our wedding.

I told Mom I didn't understand how they could be so harsh.

She resisted telling me to ask my father for an explanation; she knew it would be easier for me to hear it from her: "They don't like the kind of wedding you're planning."

I countered by saying how popular fusion weddings have become. Dave and I had gone to two just in the past year.

"In America," she said.

Which of course was true.

The last time I'd been to India was before college. I had fond memories of my grandparents' sprawling villa in Ahmedabad. More recently, they'd made annual trips to this country. I always thought they enjoyed Disney World and the other places they wanted to see. They had come for my brother's wedding only a couple years ago. What was different now?

"Do they really expect me to change my wedding to please them?" I said.

The way Mom bobbled her head told me what should have been obvious: There was nothing I could change about my wedding that would persuade them to come. The problem wasn't the wedding; it was the man I had chosen to marry.

"But Dadaji isn't close-minded," I argued. "He loves me, I know it. And he gets along fine with Dave. Surely he can give us the benefit of the doubt?"

Mom bobbled her head again. "He likes David, he just doesn't think your marriage will work out."

"He won't give it a chance to work out," I said bitterly.

Mom didn't dispute that. Some things weren't open to negotiation. I understood then that her initial hesitance about my wedding was simply her wish to shield me from a reality I would eventually run up against.

She and Dad told anyone who inquired that my grandparents were too old to make the trip. But everyone knew they had visited last year. And when they visit next year, no one will be fooled.

Dave still thinks Dadaji will come anyway and surprise us.

I tell him please not to give me false hope.

Now Mom is putting the final touches on my ankles. She has been working quietly, giving me space to reflect on my wedding and everything that has led up to it.

Every step of the way, we have sought to find a balance between modern and traditional, between Hindu and Jewish, between man and woman, between Prema and Dave.

We decided to throw bachelor and bachelorette parties but to keep them small, with only our closest friends. I had the option of making mine a mehndi party. I liked that idea, until I realized it would mean only the women were adorned with henna. If we were keeping things balanced and going modern, Dave and the male guests shouldn't be left out.

Seeing my dilemma, Mom offered to do the henna herself. She used to paint my hands when I was young, so I knew she could do it. Her only stipulation was that it not be a party, with many people watching and wanting their hands done too. I guess she's a bit shy about her skills.

We've been sitting here for almost five hours as she did her magic on my hands and feet. Now she takes a mixture of lemon and sugar and dabs it on the drying henna.

"See how dark it is!" she exclaims. "They say this means your husband will always adore you."

I hardly slept last night. I was terrified I'd roll over and mess up the henna. Okay, that's a bit of an exaggeration. In truth, I couldn't sleep because I was too excited. Dave and I are getting married. For real! We weathered the storm and didn't let others' doubts or opposition deter us, and it's happening.

I was up early, which was good because getting dressed and putting on my makeup and jewelry took even longer than I had imagined.

With consecutive ceremonies, we didn't have to buy two sets of outfits and won't have to change midway through, as some couples with fusion weddings do. We put a lot of thought into what's appropriate for both ceremonies. Mom wanted me to wear red, the usual color for a Hindu wedding, but that didn't fit with the second ceremony. Nor did a sari. After viewing many options, Dave and I decided on a white-and-gold skirt and blouse for me and an ivory sherwani with matching shawl for him. When I remarked on how heavy the skirt is, Mom chuckled and said I didn't know what I was talking about: The red skirt she wore for her wedding weighed thirty pounds.

Really, though, mine is the perfect double-duty dress. And it has double dupattas. The thinner one will work perfectly as my veil in the second ceremony. In keeping with our intent to be equalitarian, Dave will put the veil on my head and I will put a kippah on his.

Now I stand next to the windows at the back of the community center, awaiting the moment my uncle will lead me to the mandap. A call came through on his phone, which he'd forgotten to silence, and he wandered off to take it. So I'm by myself as I look out across the garden.

It's such a serene setting.

If anyone at the center harbors objections to our interfaith wedding, they have at least given us peace and privacy to follow what is in our hearts.

The mandap's delicate white canopy is offset by vines thick with roses cascading down all four posts. Mom was pleased with our choice of roses. If I wouldn't wear red, she said, at least we'll be surrounded by red. And it will smell divine.

I know I'm not supposed to peek. But I can't resist.

As I do, Dave makes his entrance. With his shoulder-length golden curls and sleek sherwani, he's so handsome. Anyone who thinks he isn't the husband for me or that our marriage won't work out doesn't know me. Doesn't know us.

I have to turn away, so strong is the urge to rush out to him. What were we thinking? We need to go through every part of this together!

But then I remind myself that both our traditions consider it inauspicious for the bride and groom to see each other before the ceremony. Dave told me some Jewish couples don't see each other for a full seven days beforehand. I'm glad we didn't attempt that.

When I look again, my mother has led him to his chair in the mandap. She is touching him on his forehead in the space between his eyes, blessing him with a tilak, a small vermilion mark. Accepting him as her son-in-law. Then she steps back and places a garland around his neck.

I open the door—careful to stay in the shadows, out of view—so I can hear the priest chant the opening Ganesh mantras. I know Dave is listening too. Even though we can't see each other, we're united through the powerful sounds.

The mantras carry me, like a river flowing through my life and back to my childhood, back to the holy days when we sat on the hand-knotted carpet and listened as Dadaji chanted. Back even to ancient memories from a far-distant century. I see one and then another shadowy scene in which only the syllables of the mantra being repeated over and over are clear. Perhaps, it occurs to me, this is what reincarnation means: memories from another time that seem as real as the present moment. I make a mental note to tell Dave. I'll see if he accepts it as proof.

My father has joined my mother and they're sitting before Dave, washing his feet. Though I can't see very much from this distance, tears flood my eyes at the sight of my parents on the ground, honoring my almost-husband. I didn't think I'd get this emotional. At least not before I enter the mandap.

Now my brother and cousins are hanging the *antarpat*, the curtain that will separate Dave and me until the mantras that unite our lives have been spoken. They reposition Dave's chair so he is facing the curtain, then place an empty chair on the other side for me.

My mother was so proud when she showed me the special cloth that had been used at weddings in her family and been passed down over generations. She spread it out on her living room carpet so I could admire the detailed, colorful hand embroidery. So I could take my place within our family's history.

As I stared at it, all I could see was the huge red swastika at the center. "I'm sorry," I said. "We're not using this."

My father snapped at me to stop being Hinduphobic.

"Dad," I said, bristling at his use of such a politically loaded term, "this is my wedding."

He explained that the swastika is an ancient sacred symbol that signifies auspiciousness. I should want that at my wedding. He wasn't bothered about how a swastika might make Dave or his family or guests feel. "If anyone objects," he said, "tell them it has nothing to do with the Nazi symbol. Say it predates the Nazis by millennia, and you are reclaiming it."

I was adamant: "We're not using an antarpat with a swastika. We have to get a new cloth."

The curtain they are hanging now is raw unbleached muslin. No hand-crafted embroidery. No family history. Perhaps no extra auspiciousness. But I know it won't hurt or offend anyone.

I take my uncle's arm, and we step into the bright sunshine. Heads turn as I glide across the expanse of lawn, moving slowly, majestically, in my heavy skirt. I wish Dave could see me.

As we pass the first row of guests, the rabbi smiles up at me, clearly pleased with our ceremony thus far.

I step into the mandap and take my seat in the empty chair, thankful for the maternal hands that reach out from behind me to adjust my skirt so it doesn't bunch up.

Dave is inches away, on the other side of the muslin wall. So close yet so far. If this ritual is meant to make us feel we exist in separate worlds, it has succeeded. Enough! I'm ready for the curtain to come down, for us to inhabit the same world in every way possible. A wave of impatience sweeps over me. *The problem with rituals*, I think, *is they take too long.*

But I have to be patient.

I close my eyes, force myself to focus as the priest chants the Vedic mantras. These words, I remind myself, are invoking the deities of my tradition, purifying the atmosphere, uniting our families, creating the foundation for our marriage. When the auspicious moment arrives, the curtain will be removed and Dave and I will look into each other's eyes—for the first time as husband and wife. We will exchange garlands, my dupatta will be tied to the end of his shawl, and we will walk together around the sacred fire. Seven times.

Suddenly I hear a popping sound coming from the community center. Drowning out the mantras.

I know I shouldn't let anything break my concentration, but the sound is alarming. I turn from the curtain and look over my shoulder.

Some guests are looking too.

A man emerges from the center. He has a gun.

My mother jumps up behind me. *"Bandook hai!"* she screams.

The curtain blocks Dave's view. I know his eyes are closed; he's focused on the mantras. Because he doesn't understand my mother's Hindi, he doesn't realize there's a gun. He has no idea of the danger.

Ritual or no ritual, I spring to my feet.

Rip down the curtain.

As shots ring out, I collapse into his arms.

Quinn

I am Quinn and I am a statistic. I was fifty-three when I was shot. I was living in Hickory, North Carolina, working at a local bank and looking forward to early retirement. My pronouns were she/her. I am survived by my daughter.

My boss doesn't like me. He knows as well that I don't like him. It's a mutual dislike fest, and it's been that way for quite a while.

It started after my old boss—a basically decent, if tedious, fellow who kept everything professional—retired, and Ken stepped in. He didn't just step in, though; he intentionally transferred from another branch so he could leapfrog over our assistant branch manager and claim the top position. All of us, the assistant manager included, had assumed she was a shoo-in for the job. Ken made life so unpleasant for her that she was out within six months.

He would do the same to me if he could. If I let him.

What does he dislike so much about me? I could write a poem—like the one we studied in high school—that starts with "let me count the ways . . ." But honestly, he has enough dislike for a full-length novel. I'm not about to write a poem, and definitely not a novel, so I'll put it like this: He is two decades younger than me. And that's a huge problem for him.

After I turned fifty, I looked around the bank one day and realized I was the oldest person here. I doubt any of the tellers are over thirty. Certainly no one is close to hitting the half-century mark.

Virtually all the tellers are women. No surprise there.

None have their own desks. Which means they're on their feet pretty much the whole day. You don't have to be an ergonomics expert to see all the cases of back pain waiting to happen. The only reason I'm still here is that my prior boss promoted me before he left. Now I spend most of my day training new tellers and serving as a personal banker. And I make more money.

I also have a desk. Not that I stay seated all day; I move around when I'm working with the tellers. I've been doing a lot of training lately. That's because we have a high turnover rate, at least double the industry average. I'm not sure where they all go when they leave, but I will say job dissatisfaction here is at an all-time high. The boss I hate is hated by everyone else as well.

If I intended to look for another job, I probably would have done so when Ken took the reins and morale plummeted. But I didn't, and then inertia set in. Lately I console myself by considering my options for early retirement. As a single mom who's now an empty nester, the prospect of an open-ended expanse of time is appealing.

I do enjoy the young tellers, though. They come in fresh and eager, and look to me as a mentor. I'm almost like a second mom to some.

Like with Leslie now. We're a couple weeks into her training, and already I can tell you a lot more than just that she has stellar math and computer skills. I know the audiobook she listened to when she fell asleep last night, the food allergies her cat has developed, and how much rum punch she plans to imbibe on her twenty-first birthday next month. I know where she hides the spare key for her bicycle lock. She knows a few things about me too.

Most of the tellers need a fair amount of practice to communicate well with customers. Leslie is a natural at it. From day one. She always displays that little extra flash of friendliness that doesn't take away from her efficiency but lets customers know they're cared for and makes the transaction go more smoothly. She should do well here, at least for as long as she remains.

But now as I return from my coffee break, I notice something is wrong. I mean personally wrong with Leslie. She has a tissue wrapped around one index finger and is dabbing under her lash line, careful not to ruin her makeup. Looks like she's been crying.

I slide behind the counter and tell her to take five. I'll cover for her.

When she comes back, I ask how she's doing.

"Okay," she says.

"I guess okay's okay," I say, unconvinced. Clearly something triggered her while I was getting coffee. Neither of us mentions her tears, but I suggest grabbing lunch at the end of her shift.

We go to the Japanese place a couple blocks from the bank, and both order glass-noodle soup.

As we wait for our food, I say, "You don't have to say anything if you're uncomfortable, but I'm here to listen if you care to share what's on your mind."

"It's *him*," she says.

Of course she means Ken.

Between mouthfuls of soup, she unloads the full story. He came over to talk with her when she was alone at the counter, asked her to go out with him for a drink after work. "I told him I'm having dinner with my boyfriend," she says.

This is the first I've heard about a boyfriend. Which surprises me, considering how open she's been with me.

Before I can ask, she clarifies: "Was it bad to lie about having a boyfriend?"

"Depends," I say. "Did it work?"

"I don't think so." She explains he didn't consider the boyfriend an obstacle. Or care that she's underage. He proposed happy hour at the Ol' Hickory, so she'll have plenty of time to change before dinner. "He didn't give me an out," she says. "I know he'll keep bugging me if I don't go."

"Did he threaten you?"

"That's the thing," she says. "He didn't make actual threats."

"But you feel harassed?"

She nods emphatically and confirms that he says and does so many little things to throw her off-balance. Always when no one else is around. Like when his finger skimmed her wrist the other day when she was counting twenties and he whispered, "Nice tattoo. Don't let your ink rub off on those bills." And then he forced her to look at a silly video on his phone, so she lost count. Which made him laugh. She tears up as she's speaking.

"I didn't mention it to you before because I didn't want to complain," she says. "Do you think I'm making too much of this? Am I being paranoid?"

"Not at all," I say. "This is what he does. It's harassment, plain and simple."

"How do I stop him?" she asks. "When I go back, he'll keep pushing. If I say I don't drink, he'll make some crude remark about how virgin drinks turn him on. I know he will. I could say I'm meeting my boyfriend straight after work. But he'll ask again tomorrow."

"You're in a tough spot," I say. Legally, I explain, his behavior goes against industry standards at the federal level, but our workplace is known for its poor enforcement. Ken takes advantage of that. "If you challenge him," I say, "he will retaliate. If you go along with his demands, he'll give you perks on the job. Or at least promise those perks."

"That's disgusting," she says. "You aren't suggesting I go out with him, are you?"

"Of course not. I'm describing the reality."

"Which is that I can't possibly go out with him. No way in hell!" She sounds desperate. "He's a total creep. And he's much too old."

I tell her I agree. She isn't the only one who is disgusted. Lots of people have had a hard time with him. "That's why," I add, "so many employees don't last long at this branch."

"Guys too?" she wants to know.

I explain there was a guy named West who had worked his way up to assistant bank manager. A handsome fellow with classic hunter eyes and hollow checks, he never expressed much emotion, but he also wasn't shy about his career ambitions. Ken took his drive as a personal threat.

Recently—not long before Leslie started at the bank—the two of them got into a shouting match in the break room. West insisted he'd been promised a raise. Ken denied it. Their argument grew so loud everyone in the lobby could hear it. Which gave Ken an excuse to fire him on the spot.

"Do you think West had a legit concern?" she asks. "Was he telling the truth?"

I tell her I don't know for sure, but it wouldn't surprise me if Ken baited him into the fight by making a vague promise he didn't intend to keep, knowing West would blow up when he realized he'd been had.

"Really, Quinn," she says, shaking her head, "with everything you've told me, why are *you* still there?"

I don't have an answer for that. Except that Ken hasn't tried to bait me into leaving, most likely because he sees me as an old employee who isn't motivated to move further up the ladder, so he'd rather keep me around than risk hiring some young upstart who might dethrone him. "An upstart," I say, "like you, Leslie."

She knows I mean that as a compliment. But it doesn't offer much reassurance. Or any real solution.

"I'm sure I'm not the only one besides West who has ambition," she says. "But are you saying he forces the other tellers to go on dates? Are they sleeping with him?"

"I don't know," I say quickly. "From what I've heard, he doesn't necessarily take it that far. He pushes things to the limit but knows there are limits. Like I said, a lot of tellers leave. The ones who stay tend to give him a wide berth."

"Gosh," she says. "Maybe I should quit now."

"That's up to you," I say. "But I think you have a lot of talent and I hope you stay. Or at least that when you do leave, it's on your own terms and at the time of your choosing."

"Fair enough," she says. "So what should I do now?"

I admit there aren't a lot of great options. "Since you're certain about not going out for drinks, I'll do everything in my power to support you. And if he retaliates, I will support you then as well."

"How do I file a complaint against him?" she asks.

I explain the process for reporting workplace harassment. "You should definitely file," I say, "but I wouldn't hold high hopes for the results, based on what I've seen."

As we walk back to work, we come up with a plan. Afternoons midweek are typically slow, and I would normally leave Leslie alone at the counter so I could get work done at my desk. Instead, I will stay with her. In case anyone asks, our excuse will be that I'm reviewing safety protocols with her.

"He won't dare ask me about drinks if you're there," she says. "I'll be safe. When I leave, I'll go straight home and not answer my phone. If he asks again tomorrow, which I bet he will, I'll be clear: I'm not going out with him. And I'll file that complaint. One way or the other, he'll get the message."

Back at the bank, we put our plan into action. I sit on the stool behind Leslie at the counter. It is in fact a slow afternoon, and the two other tellers are able to handle most of the customers who come in, leaving Leslie and me free to focus on reviewing the safety protocols. She raises a lot of astute questions, so it's not a waste of time.

After about an hour, I glance up just as a man is entering the lobby.

He is wearing a black ski mask.

Instantly my training kicks into gear. I quietly tell Leslie to step aside and let me handle this.

She muffles a gasp as she sees the man.

The other tellers are with customers, so he walks straight up to me.

All the protocols are running through my mind as I stand calmly and regard him. Maintain eye contact. Give him what he asks for. Don't play the hero. This is the first time in all these years that I've faced an actual robber.

And then I realize it's West.

I can't see his full face, but I recognize his icy blue hunter eyes. Brows low over his eyelids.

I don't let on that I recognize him.

He doesn't say anything, just pushes a paper toward me.

I read: "$3000 no alarm or I shoot"

I nod to acknowledge I understand his request and will comply. He knows the silent alarm is to my left, under the counter, so I keep my hands away from it. But he also knows other tellers can activate the security system, even as they—and their customers—appear to stand frozen in place.

While I am gathering the cash, he puts another slip of paper in front of me.

This one is all caps: "GET UR BOSS"

He figures Ken is in the vault, and he knows I can send him an instant text alert. I nod again and send the message, telling him to come out front.

Hopefully Ken pulls the alarm as soon as he sees my alert. Which means there isn't much time before the police arrive, and West knows that. Hopefully the two of them can exchange a few angry words; if the officers get here in time, they can arrest West, and everyone gets out of here safe and sound.

Ken steps out of the vault behind me just as I hand West the envelope with cash.

I expect West to wave it in his face and say something to the effect of "That raise you promised me? See, I got it anyway!"

Seems like a really bad idea for him to stick around and reveal his identity, giving the police more time to get here. But he's probably more focused on vengeance than on thinking things through.

They stand confronting each other.

I can't tell if Ken realizes it's West.

West doesn't do what I expected. He doesn't wave the envelope. He doesn't reveal his identity. He doesn't speak a word—not to Ken or anyone else.

He simply whips out a gun.

And shoots Ken.

As people duck, he backs toward the exit and shoots randomly into the lobby.

I hear Leslie scream.

And I—

Rob

I am Rob and I am a statistic. I was seventeen when I was shot. I was living in Mandeville, Louisiana, and was a senior in high school. My ideal job was working with animals. I had my whole life ahead of me. My pronouns were he/him. I am survived by my parents.

Mr. Chesbury's apron belly jiggles in rhythm with his arm whenever he writes on the board during civics class. His red-and-white-striped tie goes along for the ride.

He isn't a particularly large man or anything like that. But I guess he likes his beer. He's probably the me that I'll be in a few decades.

Someone always titters.

When one kid titters, a few more can't help themselves. I mean, once it has been pointed out to you, you can't not see it. You can't even not watch for it.

Mr. Cheesy—and no, we don't call him that to his face—figures they're laughing at some mistake he made. So he stands back and stares at the board and searches for it. Of course he can't find anything. Because he's done nothing wrong. Eventually he figures that out, grumbles to himself, and goes back to writing whatever he was writing.

I sit in the back row and watch this and all the other dramas unfold. I don't bother to titter. It's not that funny really. I also don't participate in class discussions unless I'm forced to.

Civics isn't my favorite subject. Not even close.

I'd much rather be in biology. I pay attention in that class. If you ask me, birds and animals are a whole lot better than humans.

Humans have messed up this world. I think we could say it's beyond redemption at this point.

From what I've read, large areas of this city will be under water by the time I'm Mr. Cheesy's age. Downing too many beers will be the least of my concerns. Most people aren't worried, though. They seem to believe adding a few levees will take care of any future flooding. But what if they're wrong? What if they're underestimating the seriousness of the problem?

You'd think these would be fitting questions for a civics class—not the scientific facts, but our social responsibility for fixing things. Yet Mr. Cheesy hasn't included any of them in our lessons, and we're more than halfway through the semester. I don't know what he's waiting for.

Some days, I watch his red-and-white tie flap around and try to guess what makes Cheesy tick. I bet he liked teaching when he started out. He might even have been a good teacher. At some point, he probably got tired of his students' tittering. In fact, he looks pretty tired most days. Like he's powering off one coffee for every three beers.

I can't imagine being a teacher who has to work day in and day out to get students like us to care about stuff like civics education. The only thing worse would be to be a politician who has to argue with other human beings about what to do so we don't all end up under water.

This is why I want to work with plants or animals. Maybe be a landscape architect. Which is basically a better-paid version of what my dad does. He's a gardener. If I get ambitious, I might become a vet. Obviously I'm thinking veterinarian, not veteran. It would be awesome to spend my days with animals and get paid for it.

But all that assumes I will still be alive to have a career.

We've been studying the Constitution. Cheesy thinks having and abiding by the Constitution guarantees a future for us all.

Right now he is giving a lecture on civic duty. It is our civic duty, he says, to defend the principles enshrined in the Constitution, including those protected by the Bill of Rights. As citizens, it is our duty to participate fully in the democratic process—to vote in elections, serve on juries, stay informed about issues that affect our lives. Blah, blah, blah.

I'm not saying it's really blah-blah-blah. That's just how he makes it sound.

Ethan, sitting next to me in the back row, has his own ideas about civic duty. He can't resist whispering them to Bella, who's sitting in front of me.

"Hey!" he hisses at her.

Without turning around, she tells him to shush.

But he's just getting started. "Come on, babe!" he says. "Lemme do my civic duty. You know, Rocky Hollow. You and me. After school."

His whisper is loud enough for the whole back row to hear him. As seniors, we've all been to Rocky Hollow. Some of us more often than others. It's off the rail trail, safely beyond the reach of the path lights. Most popular make-out spot in town.

Mr. Cheesy picks up on the commotion, even if he can't hear the details. "Quiet in back!" he barks.

That shuts Ethan up. For a few minutes.

Then I notice him scribbling on a piece of paper. When he's sure Cheesy isn't looking, he hands it to me and gestures to pass it on.

I take a peek, though I'm pretty sure I know what it says. And I'm right. He's asking if anyone has any edibles on them. I refold the paper and pass it to my right.

For the next five minutes, I track it as it makes its way along the back row and then up the side aisle. Everyone opens, reads, and passes it on. Until it gets to Wendell. After he opens the note, he bends over and fishes for something in his backpack, locates it, and places it in the paper, which he refolds and sends back along the same track.

When it reaches me, I hand the edible to Ethan.

He winks at me and pops it in his mouth.

I refocus on Mr. Cheesy just as he is wrapping up his lecture. He says if we want to live in a democracy, we need to fully participate as citizens. Each and every one of us has to do our civic duty. Because democracy isn't guaranteed.

Which sounds reasonable.

My only question is, why do I somehow get the feeling Cheesy doesn't actually believe what he says?

Last week he had us write essays on the value of democracy.

Some kids complained we did that back in middle school.

"In that case," he said, "this should be a piece of cake."

It wasn't easy, though. He made us read our essays aloud in front of the class and then defend our ideas. Participation wasn't optional.

Wendell read his essay first. Its thesis was that democracy makes us weak. He also said we need strong, patriotic people—not immigrants—leading our country.

That upset Bella. She said her parents are more patriotic than many people who've lived here their whole lives.

Another kid jumped in and said that immigrants take away other people's jobs.

All of which made Mr. Cheesy cross his arms over his belly and frown. "If you look back far enough," he said, "most of you will find you have ancestors who were immigrants." Then he slapped an assignment on us for extra credit: pick a famous immigrant and write about how they contributed to this country.

I'm definitely not doing any work for extra credit. In biology, maybe. No way for civics.

Not that I don't appreciate some of the stuff Mr. Cheesy says. I do. Like about the value of democracy. He harps on that a lot, and some of the time it sounds like he believes what he's saying.

I get the point he's making now—that democracy is what allows us to practice our civic duty in the first place. If we lived under a dictatorship, our rights as citizens would be limited. We'd have to be loyal to the dictator in our every word and deed. If we spoke out of turn, we'd be thrown behind bars. Jeez, probably half this class would be headed for jail.

Mr. Cheesy said the other day that immigrants come to this country because they don't have rights elsewhere. Wendell took that to mean Cheesy is soft on immigrants.

To me, it's more like he's soft on humans.

I mean, he's not asking the hard questions. Like about how humans should respond to dramatic increases in sea level. Or why humans are constantly killing each other. Really, how come people have so much hate? It's like an epidemic. Or even how—beyond lecturing to a class like ours—you can convince someone to do their civic duty.

My dad didn't vote in the last election. He said it took too long. Some people had to wait in line for six hours. Cheesy would say he doesn't take his civic duty seriously. I'll be able to register to vote on my next birthday. I'll probably do it. But if I have to wait in a long line, that will suck.

Everyone in the back row is on their phone. Cheesy never cracks down, so why not? Except Ethan. He just tossed a paper airplane at Bella. That edible is bringing out his immature side.

I expect Cheesy to read the room and realize he needs to start engaging us.

Right on cue, he turns to Rita, who's in the front row, and says, "Remind us, what part of the Constitution describes our freedoms?"

She knows the answer: the Bill of Rights.

He builds on that. "Let's review. What are some freedoms we enjoy in this country?"

When no one answers—we've covered this topic so many times already, and the fatigue is real—he calls on Ethan. That's no surprise, since he is slouched over, doodling on the cover of his civics text.

Ethan sits about six inches taller. "Can you repeat the question, sir?"

"What freedoms do we enjoy in this country?"

Ethan thinks for a second. "To eat what we want!" He grins, satisfied he has toed the line between smart and smart-ass, then retreats the full six inches.

Mr. Cheesy isn't satisfied. "That's a freedom you have at home," he says. I guess he doesn't realize Ethan has it in his classroom too. Along with the freedom to scroll. Now Cheesy's off and running on a tangent, lecturing about our right to food. It's recognized by the United Nations but not at the federal level in this country.

Perhaps it's off topic, but I want to hear more about why that is. Humans have to eat. We're like animals in that respect. I might have to break my rule about not speaking in this class.

Before I get it together to raise my arm, Mr. Cheesy shifts back to his original question: "What freedoms do we enjoy in this country?"

Rita calls out, "Freedom of speech."

Someone else says, "The freedom to own a gun!"

Mr. Cheesy writes their answers on the board—his belly and tie jiggling, to the sound of a few titters. Then he turns around and surveys the room. His eyes land on Wendell, who is fixed on his phone. Clearly not listening. "Wendell," he says, "what freedoms do we enjoy?"

It should be amusing to watch him grasping for an answer to a question he didn't hear. But instead, he says without hesitation, "The Second Amendment!"

Cheesy points to the board. "Already have that."

Wendell covers by saying it's the most important freedom. Like it should be written down twice.

Cheesy wants to know why.

Wendell doesn't look like he's thought that through, but he has to come up with something. Fast. "If you die because you don't have a gun to defend yourself," he says, "none of your other freedoms will matter."

Bella doesn't wait to be called on. "Guns are the *reason* I don't feel free!"

Everyone spins around to look at her.

"Bella?" Cheesy calls on her, as if she raised her hand.

"Everywhere I go, I worry about getting shot. About my family getting shot. That's not freedom," she says. "That's the opposite of freedom."

Cheesy frowns. "So you want to take everybody's guns away?"

There is a chorus of boos.

"I just want commonsense laws . . ." Bella is sitting in front of me, so I can't see her face. But she sounds scared. She says kids shouldn't have guns. Then she rattles off things that could help, like banning assault weapons and high-capacity magazines.

Ethan chimes in to support her. "When my dad hunts ducks, the law limits him to three rounds."

Bella glances over her shoulder at him. "There's no limit if you hunt humans. That's insane."

"What's insane," Wendell says, jumping to his feet, "is passing laws that limit our freedom to defend ourselves."

"That's tyranny!" the kid next to him says.

"Just kill me now," says another.

No one could call this class boring. But what's happening doesn't feel right either. Wendell is glaring at Bella, his arms crossed in defiance. Like he's about to walk over and slug her. I've never seen him so riled up.

"I'm not against self-defense," she says. "I want to stop mass shootings. They aren't self-defense. They're murder."

"Are you kidding me?" Wendell shouts. "Since when did any law stop a murder?"

"Maybe not every murder," Bella argues back. "But laws that make it harder to get guns will stop some murders."

"Stopping even one shooting would be worth it," Rita says. "It's common sense, like Bella said."

"Hell no," Wendell spits out. "These are my rights you're talking about."

Things are getting out of hand.

Mr. Cheesy raises his voice, trying to reestablish order. "Why do you think the founders put the Second Amendment in the Constitution?"

But nobody's listening.

"You can't just shoot people," I say. "Or animals."

Mr. Cheesy pounds a fist on his desk. He's never done that before. "The purpose of laws—"

"No way!" Wendell screams, pointing at Cheesy. "You can't take my rights away!"

I look at Ethan, and his whole face says, *Yikes!*

He's probably thinking, like I am, that Mr. Cheesy has had enough. We're about to watch him grab Wendell by the collar and march him to the principal's office. Like you'd do with a seventh grader. But hey, Wendell has done this to himself.

Mr. Cheesy takes a step toward him.

As he does, Wendell bends over and reaches into his pack. My first thought is he wants to make sure his edibles are hidden. Like that's the worst of his worries.

Instead he pulls out a gun.

It's orange plastic.

A couple of kids snicker. *What's he doing with a toy gun?*

But it's not a toy.

It's a ghost gun.

He raises it. Shoots Mr. Cheesy in the chest.

Before any of us can react to protect ourselves, to stop him, he shoots Bella. Shoots Ethan.

Shoots me.

Sage

I am Sage and I am a statistic. I was sixty-three when I was shot. I was living in Paradise, Nevada, working in the women's clothing section of a department store on the Strip. My pronouns were she/her. I am survived by my husband, Nick, and our two grown children, Abby and Bobby.

Every day I take the bus to the department store where I work, on the Strip in downtown Vegas. In the evening, I make the same commute in reverse, to our home in Paradise, south of the airport. Been doing it for two decades.

My son, Bobby, once calculated how much time I'd spent on buses, total. In my life thus far. I don't remember the exact number, but it was well over a year.

I told him more people should use public transportation. It's good for the planet.

Plus I feel quite blissful when I'm on a bus.

That's because I've found pleasant ways to pass the time.

One is a little game I started playing as a child. Growing up in Chicago, we took municipal buses to and from school. Since my friends all had different routes—and my house was farthest away—I had lots of time alone. To amuse myself, I would observe people and guess what their lives were like. I imagined their families, their pets, their likes and dislikes. Their deepest secrets.

After a while, I switched things up and challenged myself to only look at the backs of people's heads. It was amazing how much I could glean from so little information. A pigtail. A bald spot. Pointed ears, crooked ears, red ears. Each one had a story. I sometimes had envisioned the plot for an entire movie by the time I hopped off the #78 bus a block from my house. Not that I ever made any movies. But I did wonder whether, if I encountered any of those people again, I would recognize them from the backs of their heads.

While our kids were growing up, I didn't ride buses very often. I was a stay-at-home mom, and my universe was limited to the triangle defined by the grocery store, the elementary school, and the playground. Self-contained. Safe.

Once Abby and Bobby were in high school, though, I was itching to do more.

I hadn't worked in a while, so I wasn't sure what I wanted to do. The country was in an economic downturn, and there weren't a lot of jobs, but I found one at a department store, working as a clerk selling women's dresses. It didn't pay well, but I took it. The store closed a year later, and I was able to snag a similar job—this one right on the Strip. I've been there ever since.

My husband is a plumber, so our schedules dovetail. Now that our kids are out of the house, about to start families of their own, and our dinnertimes are more casual, Nick and I still treasure our evenings together. Tonight when I get home, I'll reheat the stroganoff I picked up at the Star Court buffet on my way to the bus stop. He will open a bottle of pinot noir. We may even light a candle.

Of course, I'd make more money working at a casino. That extra cash would come in handy, for sure. A friend who left the store to become a craps dealer earns twice what I do, if you figure in all the tips she gets. She tried to recruit me, but I said no, sorry, I feel more comfortable, more at home, in our store. All the hype and glam and glitz of Vegas really isn't my style. I see enough of it as I interact with the hordes tumbling over each other to grab our best bargains. It's all around me as I walk down the street. When I go to a restaurant. As I sit on the bus.

Now, taking the last empty seat, at the far back of the bus, and balancing my bags on my lap, I catch a whiff of stroganoff. That warm, meaty aroma tantalizing my taste buds until we reach my stop on Cactus Avenue will be nothing short of torture. So I do what I did as a child, and what I often do on my commute home: I observe the people around me.

I focus first on a woman in a seat across the aisle two rows ahead. My eye is drawn to the skin on the back of her shoulder. It's a small patch of skin, running between her neck and the strap of her green floral-print cotton sundress.

That skin is so tender.

The more I look at it, the more I melt into it. Melt into her.

I would guess she's in her thirties, but there's something younger and more vulnerable and innocent about her. Something untouched. The softness of her skin speaks to me; it tells me she lives alone, keeps her apartment immaculate, goes to bed early, makes sure to get enough rest every night. Pampers herself. I see her submerged in a steaming hot rose-petal bath, a dish of artisan deep-fried gelato waiting for her on the tub's porcelain-enameled ledge. Not that she would want anyone to know any of this.

Her soft skin also tells me she takes care of others. She has a nurturing nature.

You might wonder how I could possibly know all that from a small spot of skin. Especially from this far away. I can't say I really *know* it. I merely listen to what my imagination tells me. Right now it says this woman works as a nanny. I see a little boy in her arms, his hand grasping at the soft skin on her neck.

I feel her sadness too, like a deep, invisible imprint on her sensitive skin. She's single because someone she waited for didn't wait for her.

As I train my eye on her, I can see that story unfold.

As a schoolgirl, she is peering through a chain-link fence, watching another girl ride on the handlebars of a friend's bike as the two of them circle the playground. She longs to befriend that bold girl, yet she's too shy to ever reach out.

I see her admiring the same girl a few years later. Now the girl is wearing a leather jacket and parking her naked bike in the school lot. This girl has never been interested in her, so she still watches the girl silently from afar. Leaves a bouquet of daisies on the seat of her cycle. Writes a poem and sticks it through the slats of her gym locker. Never reveals who she is.

But somehow the girl finds out.

As I stare at the patch of skin on her shoulder, I see the two girls talking in a school hallway. It feels intense and I want to listen, but our bus is pulling into a stop. The woman stands up. The soft skin on her shoulder constricts as she raises her arm to grab the hanging strap. When the bus stops, she walks off.

The door closes on her story.

I still have a long way to go before I'll be home, so I look around and refocus on a man sitting a row behind the seat vacated by the woman I was observing. My eye is drawn to his steel-toe cowboy boot, sticking almost midway into the aisle. Its heel is on the floor, the toe pointed up, almost as if this man is trying to trip somebody.

If boots had lungs, his would be screaming.

I want to recoil from him, but I remind myself I'm just an observer.

And I'm a bit curious. So I fix my gaze on his boot's silver buckle, below the frayed bottom edge of his jeans. Immediately I feel how angry this man is.

If you were to ask why he's angry, I would probably speculate that he lost big bucks at a casino or perhaps that his boss owes him past wages. But no, the silver buckle tells me a different story. He's angry because his girlfriend has been pilfering money out of his wallet. He had suspected it for a while, and late last night he went to her apartment to confront her.

I watch as he lets himself in using the key she keeps under the doormat, tiptoes through the darkened living room, and bursts into her bedroom.

She wakes up with a shriek when he flips on the light.

He strides to the side of the bed and stands over her. "I know what you're doing," he says. "Don't deny it!"

"I have no idea what you're talking about," she says, clutching the sheet, trying to cover her naked body.

"You've been stealing!" he says.

She denies it.

"You're lying!"

She denies that too.

He kicks the side of the bed with his steel-toe boots. "You lost my money playing the slots. Over a thousand dollars. Admit it."

"I didn't. That's bull!"

He kicks the bed again. Harder. "I can prove it."

She backs up into the pillows. "No you can't."

"Damn straight I can, you bitch!" he says as he lunges at her.

I see his fingers close around her neck. She twists and thrashes, but his anger is like an iron blanket smothering her.

It's so vivid, I can't bear to observe any more.

This is not a story I want to know.

So I shift my gaze to the young man who has just taken the seat in front of me. I can only see the back of his head. But that's all I need to know he's young, a college student. Definitely not violent or abusive in any way.

His blond hair sits like a cloud above his neck. As I rest my eyes on a curly strand behind his ear, I hear soothing music. Although he's studying science—I think engineering—I sense how much he loves to create music.

I see him talking with his mother in her kitchen before he leaves for campus.

When she admonishes him to work harder, he bends to kiss her forehead and reminds her he was valedictorian in high school. "You have nothing to worry about," he says.

He's composing a new song now. I can hear it. It's relaxing R&B, with mellow sustained chords, layered with soft electronic piano. The vocals are velvety, soulful. I only wish I could pick out the words.

I see a setup with drums and keyboards in the basement of his parents' house. He practices his new song there whenever he can find a free moment. Friends drop by to jam with him. It's a small, private world. For a full-time student, that makes sense. But I feel his longing to create music that will reach more people. He dreams of performing for a real audience. Perhaps at a club on the Strip.

Though he spoke with confidence to his mother, I feel his doubts. I want to reassure him, tell him his dreams will come true.

Of course I can't do that. Never in all my years of observing people on buses have I revealed what I saw or heard.

Except one time.

The bus was crowded that day, standing room only. I was seated, and a little girl, maybe four years old, was wedged between the grown-ups, directly in front of me, one elbow touching my knee. She was sobbing. Her mother's full attention was on her phone.

Of course I focused on the child. It was easy because she was at eye level.

I saw her getting ready to leave the house with her mother. "Hurry up," the mother said, looming large in the doorway. "We'll be late."

"But Rolfo!" the girl wailed. "I need Rolfo!"

I assumed she meant a dog.

"Go get it," her mother said. "Be quick."

When she said "it," I figured Rolfo must be a stuffie, not a dog.

The girl ran back into the house and looked all around.

She took so long, her mother came after her. She'd used up what little patience she had to begin with.

"I can't find Rolfo," the girl cried.

"Come on," the mother said. "Forget about it. We're not reading on the bus anyway."

Rolfo, I realized, was a book.

Standing close to me on the bus, the girl was still crying. I imagined myself going into her house and searching for her book. I was pretty sure I saw it under her bed, covered by her pink panda flannel pajamas.

I leaned over and whispered, "Rolfo's under your bed."

She heard me.

I don't think her mother did. But she didn't want a stranger saying anything to her child. They must have reached their stop just then, because she yanked the child away and shoved her toward the door.

I always wondered if she found the book.

Now I want to help this young man sitting in front of me. But how? I can't just tap him on the shoulder and announce that his music will one day reach its audience. I'm not psychic. Nor do I want him to think I'm psychic. I'm someone who observes, not meddles or intervenes. I remind myself that one time with Rolfo was an exception.

Or maybe there are times when it's right to intervene.

As I'm debating this, the bus pulls into a stop.

The cowboy boots get up and walk off. Really, the bus feels safer without that man on board.

A couple more stops and I'll be home. I inhale a quick sniff of the stroganoff. Enough to remind me of what I will share with Nick. Very soon.

More people get on the bus, but I don't pay attention. I want to make the most of these last minutes. I close my eyes and drop back into my game. No one can say I'm not good at this.

As if gazing into a crystal ball, I focus my inner eye on the curl behind the young musician's ear, try to find the words to his song.

Immediately I hear "letters of the lost."

I don't know what that means. Could these be his lyrics? I think maybe so.

As if in confirmation, more come through: "Letters of the lost, of hope and regret / I write to remember, rhyme to forget."

I smile to myself. Those are strong words, filled with passion, with mystery. Words that make you think. My eyes still closed, I whisper aloud: "Letters of the lost, of hope and regret / I write to remember, rhyme to forget."

I doubt he can hear me; there's too much noise as the bus roars away from another stop.

But I want him to hear. So I whisper louder. "Letters of the lost—"

As I do, my inner eye explodes.

I'm flooded with light. Even with my physical eyes closed, I can see every detail of everything around me. The worn canvas shopping bag with the stroganoff on my lap. The young man's hair curling behind his ear. And beyond him, a tall man standing beside the driver.

The man's eyes lock with mine. They are hard, impenetrable, cruel. Evil. The eyes of a killer. I am certain he intends harm.

If there were ever a moment for intervention, this is it.

My eyes pop open.

A tall man is indeed standing by the driver. Staring at me. I am certain his are the eyes of a killer. I must warn everyone! But how? What can I possibly say or do to stop him from doing what I know he's about to do?

Before I can figure that out, he unleashes a litany of hate. A volley of heinous verbal bullets.

As shocked passengers stop conversations midsentence and pivot toward him, he pulls a handgun from his jacket pocket. Brandishes it in the air.

The driver slams on the brakes.

The bus lurches.

Bodies fly forward in their seats.

The man rushes the aisle, spraying bullets.

One strikes me.

I double over. The pain is so intense that I vomit.

Tex

I am Tex and I am a statistic. I was thirty-one when I was shot. I was living in Sandpoint, Idaho. That is already way more than you need to know about me. I am survived by no one.

Okay, I'll tell you straight up—this is one story you won't want to read. I'm serious. You can stop right now. Just skip me. The whole world has been treating me that way for thirty-plus years anyway. You don't have to do any different.

But hey, if you insist on sticking around, I'll be brief. No need to waste your time.

I've been living up here in Sandpoint since I dropped out of college. They said I flunked out, but that's a lie. I was the one who was done with them. Don't know why I ever went down to Moscow in the first place. Let alone stuck around for two years. A bunch of sickos there.

I came back and got me a cabin in the woods. You might say it's a wreck of a place, but it suits me. Cheap rent, and it's five miles to the nearest neighbor. Cliff, who owns the gas station in town, gave me a part-time job that pays enough to cover my basic necessities. Plus freebies when my truck needs repairs. Which is often.

I really thought I could make it here. I was all for a life in the woods, hunting, fishing, swimming in the lake. I appreciated that people around here leave you alone, let you do your own thing. Lots of preppers and survivalists have moved into the area in recent years. You know, like-minded folk.

But then *they*—you know who I'm talking about—go and mess it all up.

They want you to believe all the wildfires around here are because of the climate changing. What a crock! I've done enough research to know it's the government that's setting fires. They're literally smoking us out.

Except for the years I spent in Moscow, I've lived in this area my whole life, and I can tell you this isn't normal smoke. It's way thicker, and there's way more of it, for more days. I guarantee you they're putting something toxic in it, something to destroy your lungs. It's getting harder and harder to breathe.

I know why they're doing this. They want to force everyone to move to big cities. They want us out of areas where we can live free, and into crowded places where they can control us. When I'm in my cabin, no one can put a chip in me.

If I have to leave because I can't live here, then they've won.

You might say, well, there's smoke in cities too.

If that's your argument, you've missed the point. You aren't as smart as they are. I mean, you gotta think like them.

Let me help you.

First of all, all this smoke is a temporary condition. A smoke screen. Literally. They use directed-energy weapons with high-energy lasers and other high-powered electromagnetics to start fires and burn down homes and places of business. These high-tech fires burn items of all colors except blue. That should tell you something.

Once everyone has relocated to cities, they will stop setting fires. The toxic smoke will have served its purpose. Actually, if they'd managed to use vaccinations to put chips in enough people, they wouldn't have needed this wildfire tactic. But too many of us got wise to their plan. We subverted it. So they had to ramp up to the next level: wildfires.

They can produce microchips as small as two nanometers. Do you realize how small that is, and how easy it is to inject into people?

When they get those chips into you, they can control your body, your mind, and everything about you.

I'd rather die.

Seriously.

My life belongs to me. And I control when I end it.

That's nobody's business but mine.

I've known about everything I'm telling you for some time. Like I said, been doing my research. And I said I'd keep this brief. I'm not trying to make friends, and I don't give a fuck what you think of me. All this is happening because they want to kill off dudes like me, want to replace us with all the degenerates.

I hate all their guts.

I wasn't planning to let them win. But with all the fires this year, it's clear they have already won. They won because I no longer want to live in this world. I'd rather be dead than live in some city and be chipped.

If I'm going to kill myself, I might as well take as many of them with me as possible.

Last week I quit my job at the gas station. Told Cliff I'd be taking a trip. He probably has no idea what I'm up to. Or maybe he does.

Once when we were talking, he told me guns are like sex. Said a man who doesn't understand that isn't a real man. I don't really care what he knows, though. I'll never see him again.

I walked away from the station yesterday evening with a short-barrel rifle I'd seen lying around in the back room. Cliff had gone home in his old pickup, so I tested the rifle on the back tires of his new SUV. Did the job. As he'll figure out on Monday morning.

With that gun tucked into an old compact rifle bag, plus a couple pistols, I'm as ready as I'll ever be.

I actually own four rifles, six pistols, a couple ghost guns, a homemade silencer, and about a thousand rounds of ammunition. I was planning to bring all of it with me. But at the last minute, I decided to leave it in the cabin. When they discover it, they'll realize dudes like me mean business.

The drive to Moscow takes me about two hours.

I arrive just as the homecoming week Sunday afternoon kickoff is getting underway. Because I planned everything in advance, I know where the crowds are. And I know exactly where to station myself: on the roof of the tallest residence hall. I still remember the secret way we students got up there.

With no feelings and nothing left to lose, it'll be like living a video game for real. No fear, just cold-blooded killer. *Bang, bang, bang!*

When they do the final count, they'll see that hundreds were shot. I'm telling you, nobody is better than me. Nobody! I'll make big headlines today, even if I never see them.

It's a point of honor not to let anyone take me down. I intend to do that myself. The ultimate act of control. Sure as hell not going to make myself the target of any manhunt.

But I didn't calculate quite right.

As soon as I get up on the roof, take out my rifle, and let loose on the crowd below, the police have the building surrounded. I expected that. I also figured three minutes minimum for them to get up here. Time for me to do plenty of damage. What I failed to notice was that the guys I snuck past in the eleventh-floor lounge were campus security officers. They burst onto the roof within a matter of seconds.

Before I can do it myself, they take me out.

The bastards.

Unity

I am Unity and I am a statistic. I was nineteen when I was shot. I was living in Nashville, Tennessee, where I was attending community college and rocking out with friends. My pronouns were she/her. I am survived by my parents, my two sisters, and my homie Jax.

When Jax announced he had a surprise for me, I knew it would be totally dope.

And it was. Tickets to the Luna Starr concert.

I mean, a chance to see Luna in person! And he didn't get the cheap tickets either. How could I be so blessed?

You might assume someone who's grown up in Nashville has gone to a million concerts and seen every megastar who passed through town. Not necessarily. Especially not a college student living at home. Like *moi*.

I'm always looping Luna's latest song, so Jax knew how hyped I'd be about these tickets. It's also no secret I don't have extra cash lying around.

I've known Jax since high school. He was a grade ahead, so I was a bit in awe of him and kept my distance. But after I enrolled at the community college, where he was already a sophomore, we connected in a bigger way. Not bigger like he's my boyfriend. More like my homie. Or the older brother I never had.

At the beginning of the year, he had a steady girlfriend, so there was no thought of the two of us getting together. Then he and Mona split up. Even so, not much has changed between us. His bear hugs are still just friendly bear hugs, and when we meet for coffee or go jogging at Richland Creek, it doesn't feel like we're on a date. I'm not looking at this concert as a date either. But maybe he is. Maybe that's why he wowed me with these tickets. I'd be lying if I said the thought hasn't crossed my mind.

I told him that after I cash my paycheck and buy my textbooks for next semester, I'll reimburse him. He insisted he doesn't need a penny from me. It didn't sound like your typical friend-zone response.

Now I'm on the front porch of my parents' house, waiting for him to pick me up. I've got on my—what else?—oversized Luna T-shirt with the exploding stars. I styled it with a pair of faded denim shorts, star-patterned black fishnet tights, and my faux-leather jacket. My hair is claw-clipped at the top of my head so my neck stays cool and no strands get in my eyes while I'm dancing. My running belt and comfy black running shoes will give me the freedom to dance without losing stuff or having my toes crushed. And believe me, I will be dancing! I bust out a few moves now just to get in the mood.

As I'm pogoing across the porch, Jax drives up in his old Corolla. He and his brother co-own the car, which has been on the planet as long as I have. He gets out when he sees me, scoots around to the passenger side, and holds the door open. He's never done that before. Again, not exactly friend-zone behavior.

As we drive off, he explains that we might meet up with some friends and all go into the arena together. "If," he adds, "you're okay with that."

I ask who all will be there.

He throws out names: "Jose, Louisa, Yusuf, Vaughn, Mona, Kirby, Clyde."

I pick up on Mona, though he slipped her name into the middle. "How do you feel about seeing her?"

He shrugs. "Even if we aren't together, we have common friends. I want things to stay copacetic."

I tell him he has a good attitude.

"I try," he says. "Besides, I think she and Vaughn are an item now."

"Ouch."

"Not ouch," he says, reaching to give my thigh a soft pat. "It just shows both Mona and I have moved on."

I'm about to let this—and the pat—slide. But if he's saying he wants to move on with *me*, we'd better talk. The last thing I need is to find myself in a situationship I didn't sign on to. However, I don't want to get all heavy on him. So I call up my best teaser voice: "Is this a date?"

He laughs. "Want it to be?"

"Maybe," I say. "And you?"

"Same."

It's kind of cute, us being coy with each other. "I'll have to think about it," I say.

He laughs again. "Fair enough. Let's both think about it."

I consider for a moment. "Can I give you my verdict at the end of the evening?"

"Fine with me," he says. "As long as we're doing this together."

I like how we're mutually acknowledging our choice point, yet without pressure to choose, and no correct choice. We don't have to become a couple. Maybe we'll get there, maybe we won't. Jax is my homie regardless.

Happy about how we're vibing, I launch into my favorite new Luna Starr song. The one that starts with "reigniting our spark / on a night bleak and dark."

He tells me I sound awesome.

"Thanks," I say. "At least I know the words."

"What do you mean?" he says. "You have an amazing voice."

"I'm a better dancer."

Everybody knows I love to dance. And I'm good at it.

I started in grade school when my mom enrolled me in ballet and gymnastics. I loved being pretty and graceful as well as strong and dynamic. Tutus in all colors hung in my closet. My grand pas de chats turned heads. Whenever anyone asked what I wanted to be when I grew up, I said a ballet dancer.

In high school, I performed Odette in *Swan Lake*, tangoed in the dance club, and choreographed the dance team's halftime show routines.

Then I had a major growth spurt, and my trainer said I couldn't audition for a role in *The Nutcracker* because I was five foot ten.

I was gutted. It's not like I could control my height.

My trainer tried to soften the blow. Many dance companies, she said, use dancers taller or shorter than the average. Still, my height would limit me.

After I added another inch, I quit.

I don't mean I stopped dancing. Far from it. Whenever I hear music that grabs me, I bust into dance. I dance to rock. To classical. To hip-hop. Breakdance. You name it. Often I dance to my own inner music. I even dance to silence.

When I saw our tickets were general admission in the pit, the first thing I thought of was the thrill of dancing to Luna's music live. Hopefully we won't be too squished.

We park in the garage down the street and find our friends waiting outside.

There's an awkward moment—in my mind anyway—as Mona rushes to hug Jax.

He responds by also hugging Vaughn, then slings an arm around my shoulder and pulls me tight against him as we all head toward the entrance. I guess he wants Mona to think we're an item. Like her and Vaughn.

Though we're early, it takes what feels like forever to make our way through the ticket line and security checks. I'm not complaining—of course we want to do whatever it takes to keep everyone safe. The opening act has started by the time we secure places as close to the stage as possible. I'm already so warm I shed my jacket and tie it around my waist, over my running belt.

When Luna comes on, we all jump in unison—thousands of bodies propelled by the beat of the bass and drums, as spotlights flash and pulsate across the stage and out into the arena. As if that's not enough, a transparent LED screen display sends us hurtling through outer space.

Luna emerges from an ever-expanding galaxy, stars exploding in all directions. It's epic!

My pulse is racing. I'm screaming at the top of my lungs.

It's too crowded to dance freely, but I don't care. Just being here is enough. I'm feeling the crowd, feeling the music. Having the time of my life. As I dance with Jax, our bodies move in sync not just with each other but with everyone else.

Then something I never dreamed possible happens.

As Luna finishes one song, her dancers retreat to the back and she steps to the front edge of the stage. She waves her arms toward the crowd, beckoning for some of us in the pit to come up and dance with her on stage.

"Go, Unity!" Mona screams.

"You've got this," Jose says.

"Girl, you're the best!" Vaughn says.

"For real?" I say.

"For real!" they cry.

Brushing aside the thought that Mona will twerk and grind all over Jax as soon as I'm out of sight, I untie my jacket from my waist and thrust it and my running belt at him.

He takes them, steals a quick kiss, then nudges me forward.

The next thing I know, my friends are linking arms and escorting me through the crowd, as people clear an aisle to let me pass. Strangers hoist me onto the stage.

When I pull myself to my feet, I'm standing beside Luna. I knew she was tall, but now that we're side by side and I'm matching her inch to inch, I feel like I've met my twin.

She must feel it too, because she winks at me.

The crowd erupts as she throws back her head and howls. She claps her hands and stomps her white over-the-knee stiletto boots, making the silver-beaded fringes of her bodysuit flash like masses of tiny stars.

The crowd roars louder.

The musicians strike the chords to her next song.

Of course I know the words: "Reigniting our spark . . ."

Luna motions for us to dance with her.

And we do. This isn't the moment to be shy. We sway. We shake. We shimmy. We hop and jump, twirl and twist and spin.

I quickly see that while the others may be boogying like there's no tomorrow, none are dancers like I am. They don't have the moves. They don't have the style or versatility or vision.

This is the chance of a lifetime. It doesn't matter that I'm wearing a T-shirt, shorts, and running shoes and not a sequined outfit. A sea of people may be watching, but I can't see them anyway because of the lights. And I can't worry about what they might think. This is my moment to let loose.

As the music pours through me, fueling me, I pirouette, leap, and soar. I rise in the highest firebird I've ever done, my legs in full split, my head arching back to touch my thighs. Seemingly suspended in air, carried by the music.

When she sees me, Luna applauds without breaking the flow of the music.

It's like we're doing a duet—her song, my dance.

So this is what it's like to be on the big stage, to give my body to a cosmic performance. To dance like I'm a planet circling a star. To be born myself as a star at the center of the universe. I never thought I'd experience anything so awesome. Even if this is only a once-in-a-lifetime thing, it's all I could ever have wished for.

Suddenly I hear a commotion.

My first thought is a fight in the crowd or a security breach.

Two bodyguards grab Luna and whisk her off the stage. The musicians drop their guitars and dash after her.

As shots ring out, I cower with the other dancers.

There is nowhere to hide.

One flies off the edge of the stage.

Another crumples.

The spotlights are blinding as I try to scramble down. To reach my friends.

To save myself.

I never see the man who shoots me.

Victor

I am Victor and I am a statistic. I was fifty-eight when I was shot. I was living in San Francisco, California, and working as a psychotherapist. My office was on the nineteenth floor of a high-rise near the corner of Pine and Market. My pronouns were he/him. I am survived by my mother and brother.

A thirty-year-old investment broker with an ex-boyfriend who doesn't have a steady income of his own, Evelyn initially came to therapy because of their constant fighting. They had conflicting views on just about everything. Commitment topped the list. She desperately wanted it, he was ambivalent about it. His actions demonstrate just that: He moved in with her, then he moved out, and now he wants to return.

"How do you feel about taking him back?" I ask as we near the end of our session.

She pulls a tissue from the box I keep on the coffee table as she considers this. She blows her nose, then says, "I don't know."

Having listened to her recount how upset she is with her ex's attempts to reunite, I expected her to push back against my question, to say she's had enough of his manipulations and is ready to draw some boundaries. Apparently not. Even if she will eventually move in that direction, she's not there yet. She's still too torn. Too confused. The rapid tap-tap of her foot against the leg of the table tells me she is also angry and resentful, even if she doesn't realize it.

To encourage greater self-awareness, I say, "I can see you're unsure about what you want. How does it feel to be unsure?"

"Not good," she says a bit too quickly. "I thought you'd, you know, help me straighten all this out."

I register a hint of rebuke—at me, not the ex-boyfriend—but decide to overlook it. For the moment. Which isn't to say I discount the value of a therapeutic alliance; my clients need to feel they're engaged in a working partnership with me.

I gaze past her as I weigh the best use of our remaining moments. On a clear day, the floor-to-ceiling windows offer a view of San Francisco Bay. You can see the towers of the bridge and beyond. But we don't get much sun at this time of year, and I'm staring at a thick marine layer that isn't about to lift. Kind of like the fog in Evelyn's mind. I hope to lighten it, even if only a bit, before she leaves.

Over the past year, she has explored the trauma of her parents' divorce when she was a child, and how that has played out with her boyfriend. She eventually realized their problems weren't entirely one-sided: She had her own reasons to fear commitment. In fact, her desperation to commit was masking that fear. She was terrified of recreating the dysfunctional family dynamics she knows so well. I suggested couples therapy, but I don't treat couples and she didn't want to start over. Besides, their fighting had diminished and she felt they could work things out together.

I asked if she was ready to terminate.

She said yes.

Right after that, and without warning, her boyfriend moved out. She spiraled. Instead of terminating, she scheduled two sessions per week so we could revisit the issues around trust and abandonment that she has struggled with in relationships as an adult.

Now I refocus my gaze on her and summarize what she said today: Her ex was calling and texting, asking to see her. The hurt from their breakup was still fresh, so she didn't respond.

"I couldn't keep ignoring him," she says, as if that is self-evident.

Which it isn't. "You didn't *feel* you should ignore him," I say.

"I had to see him," she asserts. "At least once."

I continue my summary. "So you invited him for coffee. But you were disturbed because he was nice to you. You said it would have been easier if he was belligerent. Like he was when he walked out."

"He was so sweet," she says.

"That confused you."

"It did. He said he'd been practicing mindfulness and he's a different person now. But I remember when he met a shaman and took ayahuasca. He said he was a different person then too, and look at how that turned out."

"He left you after that."

"He did."

"And made hurtful comments."

She winces at the memory, then recovers quickly. "Yes. But when he came over this week, he apologized for all that, admitted he was wrong. He wants to make it up to me."

I sense she is trying to get me to reassure her, to—as she put it—straighten things out for her. Of course that's not how therapy works. She has to find her own clarity. She should know that by now. "Tell me," I say, "how do you feel in this moment as you're thinking about his apology?"

"I feel hopeful," she says. "We were so happy when we met. I'd give anything to get that back."

Her foot tapping on the coffee table leg belies her words. I suspect she is afraid of her own anger. She is likely furious at not feeling free of the trauma from her family of origin, even after a year of therapy. So I say, "You'd like him back, yet you're not sure how you feel about seeing him again."

Her eyes pop, as if seeing her emotional bind for the first time. "Right," she says. "I thought I was done with him. But now he's acting like the man I fell in love with. I don't know if I can trust him."

"That has to feel scary," I say.

She glances at the tissue box. "Suppose I let him back in, and he disappoints me again?"

"That's a risk you may or may not want to take."

"Exactly," she says.

I bring it full circle: "That's why you said you don't know how you feel about seeing him again."

"You get it," she says. Her tapping foot comes to a sudden rest on the carpet. "I want him back if he has really changed. But first I need to know without a doubt that he's for real."

"How do you think you might find that out?" I ask.

"I don't know," she says, then laughs. "I guess I say 'I don't know' a lot."

"Which is fine," I say. "It may cause some anxiety, but it's okay to feel you don't know something."

"As long as I can figure it out over time."

"Of course," I say. "And speaking of time, our time is just about up for today."

She looks startled, as clients often do when they've been deeply absorbed in a session.

To help the transition into their daily activities, I offer to end each session with a brief guided meditation. I take clients to their happy place, so they will be equipped to deal with whatever stressors and curve balls the world throws at them after they leave the safe space of my office. Not everybody likes it, but most do. Evelyn always asks for it.

She does so now. "I really need it," she says.

I begin by guiding her to sit comfortably, to close her eyes and scan her body. "Notice any tension," I say, "and breathe into those places . . . Long, slow breath . . . Let yourself just breathe."

I pause and observe both her expression and her posture. In the space of a mere minute, she has sloughed off multiple years. This meditation is so effective.

"Now, Evelyn, visualize yourself in your special place, your happy place." I pause to let her get there. She has done this so many times, I'm sure she is already visualizing the tropical beach she once told me is her go-to happy place.

Then I croon more directions to help her settle in: "Forget about everything else in the world. None of it is important. Just focus on your happy place . . . Look around your inner world. What do you see? What do you hear? How does it smell? Take it all in and let yourself be refreshed . . . Just sink into your happy place."

I pause again to let her bathe in the experience. If truth be told, this is my favorite part of each therapy hour. It's the one time I feel certain I am helping my clients, giving them something of lasting and lifesaving value. I believe it could literally save their lives.

I reinforce that for her: "It's very simple. You have control over your own state of mind. No matter what happens in the world, Evelyn, no matter how terrible or disturbing, you are protected and safe in your happy place. Nothing can touch you. Nothing and no one can harm you."

I give her another minute, then bring her out: "Remember your happy place. Remember its positive vibration. Remember how you feel. Keep what you have found with you . . . When you are ready, you can return to this room. As I count down, you can open your eyes."

I count slowly from ten to one.

At one, she opens her eyes. She is smiling and relaxed.

"Thank you, Doctor," she says. "I feel so much better. These sessions are the best lunch hours of my week."

I give a humble nod to acknowledge her compliment. "So I'll see you on Thursday?"

"Yes, I'm looking forward to it."

She stands up, puts on her jacket, picks up her bag, and walks to the door.

Yes, she will need numerous sessions to explore her feelings enough to recognize the bind she's in and come to a resolution, but I believe she will get there. I think she will conclude she has been in an unhealthy relationship and will choose to aim for something more fulfilling. I could be wrong, and she could make a different decision, but that's what my training tells me.

I usually schedule ten minutes between clients. Either I take a bathroom break or I do some deep breathing on my own. Sometimes I look over my notes.

My next client is Warren Samuels, another psychotherapist. I always want to be on top of my game with him, so I pull up my notes and start studying them.

Our sessions revolve around his resistance. Whenever we get close to one of his core issues, he retreats. He'll say, "I'm not getting much out of therapy; it's a waste of time." Or "I don't really need therapy." Sometimes we spend the whole session talking about the value of a therapist being in therapy. He always agrees it's valuable. Just maybe not for him. However, he doesn't quit. He hasn't even threatened to quit. He just resists. I've pointed out on numerous occasions that this is how he keeps himself stuck. And he always agrees.

As I think about creative ways to get him past this blockage, I glance at the time.

One o'clock.

He should be here. Not only has he never missed a session, he's never been late. Never. This is odd. Unless, it occurs to me, he's finally acting out his resistance. In which case, we'll have plenty to talk about when he does get here.

By now he's ten minutes late, so I text: "Will I see you today?"

Immediately he texts back: "The building is on lockdown. Thought you knew. Are you okay?"

Lockdown?!

I'm about to text back for clarification when I notice only one bar on my phone. I've lost Internet connection. The Wi-Fi rarely fails in this building, but when it does, you're pretty much incommunicado because cell reception is so poor. What an inconvenient time for a service interruption. Or, it occurs to me, it could be caused by whatever is causing the lockdown.

Seeking clues, I look out the window. The street is cordoned off and empty of people. Multiple police vehicles block the nearest intersection. Something is going on. I have no idea what.

Out of habit, I turn to the computer on my desk to search for answers, but of course it's useless without Wi-Fi. Back on my phone, I try to pull up a news site. All I get is a "no service" error message. My signal is too weak.

I place a call to a friend. It doesn't go through.

I wonder if I should try to call Evelyn. Maybe confirm that she made it back to work okay. Except, if I manage to reach her, she might consider it unprofessional for me to check up on her. She wouldn't be wrong.

I'm starting to panic.

Could there be an active shooter in the building?

Or a hostage situation, maybe on the ground floor?

If we're having some kind of emergency, everyone should have gotten an alert. Or maybe I did get an alert but it didn't come through on my phone because of the bad reception. For that matter, the building has a public address system for emergencies. I know because they test it periodically. Always happens when I'm in session, and the poor client jumps. It's annoying.

Why have I heard nothing? When this is over, I'll have to raise a stink about that.

Nor does being on the nineteenth floor make this easier. I'm not about to risk getting on an elevator. I suppose I could take the stairs. It's a long way down. Images of people stuck in the stairwells on 9/11 come to mind, but I brush them away. This is nothing like that.

In this kind of unclear lockdown situation, the best would be to shelter in place. I'm sure that's what the alert said. It would also say to stay put until an all-clear notice has been sent. That must be what everyone else on the nineteenth floor is doing.

So I lock the door.

Normally, the shoji screen carefully angled to cover the pane of glass alongside the door takes care of privacy. Clients sitting on the sofa aren't visible to anyone walking by in the hall. But if a shooter wanted to get in, that screen would be useless. They could smash the glass with one blow and gain entrance.

The door to my office may be locked, but I feel very unsafe.

The enhanced soundproofing in this building isn't helping either. I appreciate the quiet while seeing clients, but now the acoustic insulation means I can't hear anything that could clue me into what's happening downstairs. Or for that matter, on this floor.

All I can do is sit tight and wait this out.

I should have gone to the bathroom during my break. The urge to urinate is intense, but I don't dare walk across the hallway and relieve myself.

I sit on the sofa—hidden by the shoji screen, even if it offers little protection—and take deep breaths. Try to relax.

Yet panic is building. I recognize the signs: racing heartbeat, cold sweat, clenching in my chest, the nervous tic on my right nostril. I don't know why I'm reacting like this when all I need to do is patiently shelter in place for a little while, and everything will be fine.

Then it occurs to me: I already have the perfect tool!

As I always tell clients, "All you need is your happy place." It takes care of any situation. Whether you're stressed out or things aren't going your way or you're on a long and boring airplane flight—just go to your happy place. Take refuge in your own inner world. Even if you're stuck in traffic and can't close your eyes, you can still recall your happy place.

What I need to do now is obvious.

I close my eyes and whisper, "Relax, Victor. Scan your body for any tension..." I feel constriction in my neck and shoulders. I breathe into it, and it loosens a bit. But then I feel a tight knot in my stomach. I'm trying to breathe into that when I hear a loud boom. Loud enough to penetrate the soundproofing. It's hard to tell where it came from.

I get up and look out the window.

A man is crouched on a low roof on the other side of the street. He quickly moves out of view, and I'm left wondering: *Was that law enforcement? Or a sniper?*

It's not just the glass by my door, I realize. I also have to stay clear of the windows.

Instead of going back to the sofa, I sit on the floor in the far corner of the room, pull my knees up to my chest, wrap my arms around them. Tuck in my head. Make myself as hidden as I can be.

I squeeze my eyes closed and try again: "Relax... breathe into the tension."

What was that sound?

My eyes fly open.

I guess I'll have to do this with eyes open. It may be harder, but I can still go to my happy place.

"You can do this, Victor," I whisper. "Visualize yourself in your special place, your happy place." For me, it's tubing on the Russian River on a warm summer day. Whenever I do this meditation, I picture myself sprawled out on my tube, beer in hand, floating down the river, not a care in the world. No life jacket or sunscreen needed in my happy place.

But it's not working now. I can't get there.

Maybe the problem is my open eyes. So I force them shut. "Come on, Victor," I say. "You have control over your state of mind. No matter what happens in the world, no matter how terrible or disturbing, you are protected and safe in your happy place. Nothing can touch your inner world. Nothing and no one can hurt you."

Not only does that not work, it increases my panic. *Who am I trying to fool?* I can't make my body any smaller, any less visible. Someone *can* hurt me. I'm *not* safe.

All my training has left me unequipped for this.

Instead of visualizing myself on the Russian River, I imagine shooters roaming the floors of this building. I imagine hostages held in a downstairs office. I imagine a shooter headed for the nineteenth floor.

My mind is spinning out of control, catastrophizing like the world is coming to an end. I'll have to schedule an urgent session with my own therapist. Hopefully she can make time for me tomorrow. In the meantime, I need to get out of this building so I can cancel my remaining clients for the day, go home, fire up the Jacuzzi. Find my happy place. For real.

But first things first: the bathroom. My heart is pounding as I unlock the door and peer into the hallway. No one in either direction. *Where is everyone?*

I make a beeline to the bathroom. No one here either.

After I do my business, I feel halfway normal again. I consider going back to my office and waiting to get an all clear in some form. But I don't want to be stuck in here, huddled in the corner, trying to find my happy place, and failing again. So I decide to make a run for it, down the back stairwell.

At the far end of the corridor, I open the fire door and listen.

Nothing.

I sprint down a few flights. Still nothing and no one. My heart is racing, but I tell myself this won't take long. I'll be out within minutes.

About halfway down, I hear shouting.

I can't go back up now.

I pick up speed, double-stepping till I reach the first floor.

The shouts are louder now.

I stop at the fire door leading into the lobby. Look through the thin pane of glass.

I see multiple bodies on the floor. A standoff between police and men armed with assault rifles.

Before I can duck, one of the men spots me.

I'm in his line of fire.

The glass explodes in my face.

Its shards shatter my world.

Wanda

I am Wanda. I'm a number. I was four when I was shot. I was living in Fargo. That's in North Dakota. I went to South Dakota one time and saw some big stone men on a mountain. I was living with Mommy and Penny and Marigold. Sometimes I stayed at Daddy's house. I am survived by Mommy and Penny and Gramps and Granny.

I like to tell stories.

I tell them to my mommy. I tell them to my daddy. They write my stories down for me. Mommy said someday, if I want, all of them can become a book.

Sometimes I tell my stories to my sister too.

Her name is Penelope. That sounds too weird to say, so I call her Penny. She doesn't like it. She wants a grown-up name. She's in third grade. I asked if she could write down my stories. She said she could, but it would take too long.

All my stories have a happy end.

Gramps and Granny say I'm blessed because I can tell stories.

When I have a new story, I always tell it to Marigold first.

Everyone says Marigold is just a doll. But that's not true. She's my friend. She is as real as friends are real.

Some days she's also my pretend sister. I don't mean my pretend friend. She's my real friend and my pretend sister. Penny doesn't know that. I don't think she would like it.

Penny calls her a rag doll. That's not very nice. Mommy uses rags on the bathroom floor. When I got sick, she used a rag to clean it up. Then she had to throw the rag away and get a new one. Rags are yucky dirty.

Marigold is in my stories. She does all kinds of fun things I want to do but can't do. Not yet.

Like she has a special kind of bike. It can fly when she wants it to. Here is one story.

Marigold is riding her bike. She looks up and sees a big blue fish. It is wearing blue flippers and it is swimming in the sky.

She says, "Mommy, can I swim with that fish?"

Her mommy says, "No, Marigold, you have to go into the house and eat your lunch."

Marigold doesn't want to do that. She gets on her special bike and she flies into the sky. She flies in the clouds. She puts on her flippers and swims with the big blue fish.

She is happy. And she doesn't need any lunch.

The end.

When I told this story to Marigold, she liked it. Then I told it to Mommy, and she said she would write it down so nobody will ever forget it.

I see Mommy every day. She takes me to preschool and she picks me up afterward. I told her I wanted to bring Marigold to school. I said please.

She wouldn't let me.

I got upset. I screamed loud.

The next day, I heard Mommy ask the teacher, "Is it okay if Wanda brings a lovey?"

The teacher said kids can bring a toy. One toy. She said I have to leave my toy in my cubby.

I asked Marigold if she wanted to go to school with me.

She said yes.

But when I took her the next day, she didn't like staying in the cubby. So now I don't bring her anymore.

I don't see Daddy every day. He lives in another house. I don't think he likes us very much anymore. Sometimes he comes to our house for dinner, and sometimes I go to his house to play. There aren't many toys at his house, so I always bring Marigold.

I got to sleep at his house last night. Just Daddy and me. And Marigold, of course.

He told me there's a parade downtown today. It's called Memorial Day. I'm happy he is taking me with him. And he isn't taking Penny.

I thought we would have breakfast first, but he only made coffee. He said we had to hurry because the parade was about to start, and we could eat there.

He said there's always a good crowd on Memorial Day.

We are in the crowd now. I know it's a good crowd, because people look happy. They look like good people. Good people go to parades. Like Daddy said.

We are standing on the sidewalk. I can hear the marching band, but I can't see it. I try jumping, but I still can't see it. Too many tall people.

So Daddy lifts me onto his shoulders. He holds my feet so I won't fall.

I hold on tight to Marigold. If I don't fall, she won't fall.

Now I can see everything. The drums. The tubas. The pom-poms. The girls waving big flags. They make their flags spin like helicopters. Like they can fly.

I'm going to write a story about the girls waving flags. Marigold will be in it.

Now I see a big float. It is a castle. A queen is sitting on the throne. She has a crown of flowers. There are flowers all over the float. I look at her and she waves at me!

Two girls next to the queen are twirling batons. They're pretty. I wish Penny could see them.

Actually, no, I don't wish that.

Penny has a baton. She wears her pink skirt and does a routine. When she joined the club at school, she had to get a bigger baton. Mommy said I can get a baton too. But I have to wait till my birthday.

The next float doesn't have any flowers. No queen. No girls with batons. It has soldiers with guns. They're waving flags. American flags. They look like good men. I think so anyway.

A man walking with the float is giving out little flags.

I reach out and he gives me a flag.

One of my arms is around Daddy's neck. The other is around Marigold. I can hold the flag with that hand and also make sure Marigold doesn't slip.

Now there are just some people marching. They're not much fun to watch. I wave my flag at them to make it more fun.

It's sunny, and I'm getting hot. Too hot.

I ask Daddy if we can go home.

"Now?" he says. "Wanda, the parade isn't over. Don't you want to see the clowns? And the jugglers?"

I tell him I want to see them, but I'm hot. And I'm hungry.

"How about this," he says. "After we see the clowns, I'll get you an ice cream cone."

I do a bounce on his shoulders to show how much I like that. I can't wait to get ice cream. I hope they have strawberry. I hope it is in a waffle cone and it's cold.

Now I hear firecrackers.

Our neighbors set off firecrackers on summer nights. They sound scary, but it's fun scary. Like when you crawl onto your mommy's lap and she says, "It's okay, dear. It's just the neighbors having a fun time."

I know the neighbors are good people.

I ask Daddy if we can see the fireworks.

"I don't see why not," he says. "I'll check the schedule. Mommy can take you."

Then I hear another firecracker. This one is louder.

"Can we see them now?" I ask.

"No!" He sounds angry. "That's not fireworks!"

"It's firecrackers, Daddy," I say. "Firecrackers and ice cream! Firecrackers and ice cream!"

Now he's really angry. I don't know why.

There's an even louder firecracker. It feels like it went off in my ear. It hurts.

Daddy yanks me down from his shoulders. Marigold flies out of my arms. He holds me to his chest as he runs through the crowd. Other people are running too.

"Stop!" I cry. "I lost Marigold!"

But he's not listening.

I've lost my flag too, but I don't care. I just need to find Marigold. "Let me go!" I scream as I kick to get free.

He's screaming too.

A firecracker hits him in the head.

It hits me too.

Now I can't see Daddy.

I'm flying in a black cloud.

Those weren't good firecrackers. That wasn't a good parade. Those weren't good people.

I don't want this story.

I would never write it. Not ever.

It doesn't have a happy end.

Xander

I am Xander and I am a statistic. I was forty-nine when I was shot. I was living in Green Ridge, Missouri, with my wife, Nadia, and two of our children, Uma and Rami. Our third and oldest child, Kamal, was in his first year at Boston College. My pronouns were he/him. I am survived by my parents, and my sister and brother-in-law and their two children.

We have so much to be thankful for.

Nadia places the gravy boat next to the halal turkey and takes her seat at the foot of the dining room table.

I look across at her and smile.

Around the table are our three children, my mother- and father-in-law, Nadia's sister, my brother and his wife and two children, my aunt and uncle, Nadia's cousin and her husband, and our next-door neighbors and their son. Nineteen of us at a table meant for sixteen. No one minds squeezing in—as they all talk at once, catching up on the news since we were last together.

Nadia waves her hands to signal it's time to begin our feast.

There is a hush as everyone turns to her.

"Xander?" she says.

I look around the table and thank everyone for coming. While I'm aware some Muslims consider it haram to celebrate Thanksgiving, I'm of the school that believes it's fine to mark this secular occasion much as we do the Fourth of July or Labor Day. I propose we now take a moment of silence so each of us in this mixed-faith group—my uncle and our neighbors are Christian—can say our own prayer. Wherever I may be, I always offer *dua* silently to myself before I eat. I'm grateful every day of the year, and take every chance I can to express it. With my campaign schedule, I missed lots of family dinners in recent months. Now that the election is over, I'm looking forward to being at home more.

The turkey was carved in the kitchen, so all the food is ready to be served. And everyone is ready to start eating. But I'm moved to share more gratitude.

"Do you think we could hold off for a few minutes?" I ask.

"Da-a-a-d . . ." eight-year-old Rami moans.

Nadia peers at him sternly over the rim of her glasses, and he quiets down. Instead he throws shade by fixedly eyeing the mashed potatoes.

"Before we eat this delicious meal," I say, "I'd like each of us to voice our gratitude. Would that be okay?"

Everybody is willing.

"Who wants to go first?"

"You go," Nadia says.

"Well," I say, "of all the many, many things I'm grateful for, what stands out is the result of the election. I went into it as a long-shot candidate, an outlier in a small conservative town that has never had a Muslim mayor. To say the odds were against me would be an understatement. But here I am!"

Everyone claps and cheers.

"You rock, Dad!" Uma says.

"I'm especially grateful," I continue, "for the volunteers who went door-to-door to speak with their neighbors and persuade them to take a chance on me. And of course I'm deeply beholden to everyone who voted for me."

I pause for a second. I don't want to monopolize the conversation, but I have a bit more to say. "I'm also grateful to all the women who backed me knowing I will support the issues that matter to them. I'm ready to stand by everything I said and get to work in January." I look around at all the happy faces—even Rami's—then add, "But I'd better shut up before you think I'm launching into another campaign speech."

Nadia smiles. "There are so many things I could say, but I'll just second what you said: I'm grateful for everyone who voted for you. They could have made other choices, but they didn't. What I want to add is my thanks to *you* for stepping out and taking a risk for the sake of our community. The easiest thing would have been to keep your day job and stay out of the limelight."

She's right about that. I took a big risk. Unfortunately I wasn't able to do it without making enemies. After I took positions that were popular with most voters but alienated certain fringe groups, I received death threats. Some said, "We're coming after your ass." One said, "We'll get you at your home." That freaked Nadia out. Understandably so. She even asked me to consider withdrawing from the race.

But I couldn't do that. I told her this was the political climate we are living in, and to withdraw would be to hand my opponents a victory. Ultimately, she respected my decision.

I tell her now that I'm thankful for her continued support.

Then I turn to my son. "Rami, what are you most grateful for?"

"The *food*!" he says without hesitation, as if it would be incomprehensible to be thankful for anything else. "Especially the pecan pie."

The grown-ups chuckle.

"Same here, Rami!" his grandfather says.

They air-five each other across the table.

"*Alhamdulillah!*" Grandpa says, half rising from his seat as he gestures to everything on the table: the turkey, the stuffing, the mashed potatoes, the salad, the cranberries, the bean casserole. "What am I thankful for? Right now, it's the blessed sense of smell. Without it, I'd never appreciate the aroma of this food. And in a few minutes, I will be equally thankful for the human sense of taste." He lowers himself back into his seat, then adds, "Wonderful as the food is, my gratitude would be incomplete if I didn't express it to the cook who prepared it for us."

Nadia, who was that cook, humbly deflects the praise.

Grandpa turns to his wife, seated by his side, and lays a hand on hers.

Nana picks up his cue. "Let's see. I always say I'm equally grateful to the wonders and gifts we receive in this life and to its tribulations." She pauses, as if hoping that is a sufficient sharing. But we're all looking at her, so she continues. "If I have to single out one thing I'm especially thankful for, it would be my hip surgery. As you know, I was reluctant to do it. But Nadia kept pushing me, saying how happy I'd be if I could get around again."

"Without all that agony," Nadia throws in.

"You were so right!" she continues. "I have to say I'm thankful for this body of mine, and also for the surgeon who did his magic. I never imagined I'd be moving around again, almost like a teenager, sitting through dinner pain free."

"Maybe you can shoot some hoops with me after dinner," Uma teases.

Nana's eyes widen. She's more likely to watch Uma than make shots herself, but she plays along. "You'd better watch out. I have a mean floater game."

Uma laughs. "Okay, my turn," she says. "Obviously I'm grateful to have made the basketball team. But here's the thing: I'm most grateful for our coach. I used to think it was just about each of us playing well enough to win the game. Now I understand how the coach makes us all better. Without her, we couldn't win a championship."

I sense everyone is getting antsy about the food growing cold, so I suggest just summarizing what we're grateful for, and we can discuss it more while we eat.

Kamal says he's grateful he made it home for Thanksgiving in spite of the storms that canceled half the flights out of Boston.

Nadia's sister says our gratitude is incomplete without an acknowledgment of the Indigenous people who lived on these lands before any settlers came along.

Our neighbor says he is grateful he was able to buy the house next door, and especially grateful both our places were spared when a wildfire tore through the area this summer.

As his wife is about to share, there's a loud knock at the door.

We all stop talking.

Exchange glances around the table.

"Are you expecting someone?" Nadia asks.

"No," I say. It's Thanksgiving. People are at home with their families. I can't think of anyone who would stop by now.

"Whoever it is, we have plenty of food," Nana says.

"Yes," Nadia echoes. "And plenty of room. We can pull up another chair and all squeeze in a bit more."

There is another knock. Louder.

She looks at me. "Will you answer it?"

"Of course," I say, standing up and laying my napkin on my chair. "Let me see who it is."

As I walk through the living room to the front door, the knocking escalates. Now the person is pounding on the door.

It doesn't sound like someone with good intentions. As a small-town mayor with no security detail, I'll have to handle them with caution. I put my hand on the knob and open the door a few inches.

A man in a bulky gray trench coat is standing in front of me.

I've never seen him before. Not that that's unusual since I've become a public figure.

"Hello?" I say.

He glares at me, his eyes narrowed, his jaw jutting forward.

Over his shoulder, I see an old pickup idling in the driveway. A man in the driver's seat. Waiting. In a flash, I read the scene. It's his getaway car.

Instinctively, I step back to shut the door.

He is faster.

He pulls a sawed-off rifle from under his coat.

Shoots me point-blank.

As I grab my chest and my body crumples to the ground, he steps over me and runs into the dining room.

Yael

I am Yael and I am a statistic. I was twenty-five when I was shot. I was living in Chicago, Illinois, with my grandmother and working in a bagel shop. My pronouns were she/her. I am survived by my bubbe, my parents, and my sister and brother-in-law.

After my grandmother was widowed, she invited me to come live with her in Chicago. At least for a while, she said. It was entirely my choice, no pressure. She wouldn't give it a second thought if I said no.

I took a while to mull it over.

I'd lived in New York City all my life, and the mere thought of moving from Brooklyn to Chicago made me feel homesick. The Midwest was foreign territory. Except for a few second cousins, I didn't know anyone there besides my bubbe. She and I had always been close. When I was a kid and she and my grandfather still lived in Brooklyn, I often stopped by their house after school. There'd always be a treat waiting, something warm and sweet. Like her fresh-baked rugelach.

Now that she was living alone, I knew she needed me. Her health was good, so this wasn't about becoming her caregiver. It was a chance to move out of my parents' basement, where I'd been hunkered down, to explore the wider world, find a cool job, and stay with Bubbe for as long as I wanted. Besides, she wasn't getting any younger, and this would give us precious time we otherwise might never have.

So I said yes.

The timing was right since I'd just graduated. Being a humanities major meant all sorts of doors were supposed to open, but I had yet to decide which I wanted to walk through. Chicago seemed like a good place to hang while I figure all that out.

When I got here, however, I was hit with homesickness.

I was okay when I woke up to the sun peeking through the blinds of my second-story bedroom. I was okay as I shuffled to the bathroom, took a shower, and slipped into my sweats. I was more than okay when I went downstairs and had bagels and schmear and black tea with Bubbe, and when we took turns reading each other snippets from the New York newspapers. But as soon as I walked out the front door, it hit me. I couldn't escape the reality: I was in a strange city. An alien city.

Sometimes the feeling was so intense it paralyzed me. I would turn around and go back into the house, stay there for the rest of the day holed up in my bedroom, only emerging when Bubbe coaxed me to come help her roll out dough for a fresh batch of rugelach.

Most people probably wouldn't react so strongly to the differences between cities, but I noticed every little detail. Each time I walked by a greystone, I missed all the brownstones. I missed all the different accents of people as we passed on the street. I missed the pervasive smell of freshly baked goods. Maybe it shouldn't have mattered, but it did.

Homesickness rolled over me in waves. Unable to stop it, I debated whether I should return to Brooklyn. It was tempting, but I didn't want to leave Bubbe. I had the nagging feeling that if I left, I would never see her again. So I choked back my homesickness and stayed.

She suggested a job might help me acclimate.

Turned out she was right.

I signed up with a temp agency and almost immediately started getting assignments. I cycled through inventory specialist, office assistant, events coordinator, dog walker, and social media manager. Some were part-time jobs, so I held down two at once. I enjoyed the variety, enjoyed meeting new people.

My homesickness didn't go away entirely, but it faded. Little things helped. Like hopping on FaceTime with family or friends in New York when I needed a pick-me-up. Or waking up extra early and jogging down to the bagel shop before work to pick up egg-everything bagels for Bubbe and me.

One morning I walked into the shop and noticed a sign in the window that said HIRING.

Wow, I thought, *I could* live *in a bagel shop!*

Sarah interviewed me on the spot, and I walked out with a dozen free bagels and a job.

I've been working there for the past two years, and I love it. I don't care that I'm not using my humanities degree; what matters is that I feel at home. In fact, my homesickness is completely gone.

Like me, Sarah is from New York. Wanting to bring a piece of home with her, she opened a bagel shop. Her husband is a lawyer at a private equity firm downtown but often stops by on weekends to help out.

I started with cashiering, but now I'm part of the core team. We are three full-time—me and two others—and three part-time people. A diverse bunch. It might surprise you, but most on the team aren't Jewish. Amira is Muslim. Hugo is Catholic from Ecuador. None of us have any issues with our differences; rather, we appreciate them.

Whenever someone comes into the shop and inquires about politics, Sarah says, "We're a bagel place. We're not a political place or a religious place; we're a bagel place."

And that's how we operate. Some team members are interested in politics and some aren't, but nobody brings that to work. What we're focused on is perfecting the flavor of each schmear and producing bagels with the right amount of chewiness.

Personally I wouldn't mind if Sarah made a public statement, for example, expressing support for religious freedom and denouncing hate speech. But if that's not how she wants to run her business, that's her decision. If I open my own bagel shop one day, I might do things differently.

I get up before the crack of dawn most mornings so I can be at the shop in time for the early shift, which starts at 3:00 a.m. I blow Bubbe a kiss as I tiptoe past her room on my way out. She doesn't mind because she knows I'll be home early. We only have breakfast together on days when I'm not working, but we always share dinner.

The shop is close enough for me to walk to work. In winter, the frigid air sweeping off Lake Michigan smacks me awake as I turn onto Grand Avenue. The streets are usually deserted at this hour, but I keep a bottle of pepper spray in my purse just in case. I've never needed it.

This morning, though, spring is in the air and I'm smiling as I speedwalk to work. I never eat before leaving home for the early shift, because I know a day-old egg-everything bagel with my name on it awaits. When I get there, I'll remove the trays of bagels that have been retarding in the fridge overnight, turn on the oven, and heat up water in the large kettle. While I wait for the water to boil and for Sarah and the rest of the team to arrive, I'll slather honey walnut schmear on my day-old and bite down.

My mouth waters as I conjure up the taste of that bagel and anticipate the shop filling with the aroma of the day's first batch of bagels turning golden brown in the oven.

As I round the corner a few buildings down from the shop, I notice it's darker than usual. The streetlights are out. That's odd, especially for all of them to be out. The city usually keeps up with maintenance. I strain to see if anyone is hiding in the shadows in front of the shop. But no one is visible.

The lit screen of my phone is all I need to key in my code, open the door, and disarm the security system. But when I approach the door, I jump back in shock. It's not just a problem with the streetlights; the whole front of our store has been vandalized. Red paint is splashed across the door, anti-Semitic slurs painted on the bench in front. The words "we'll be back" are scrawled in large red letters on the window.

The bottom drops out of my stomach.

I don't know whether to go inside or turn and run. I glance around again. Still no one in sight. I'm afraid to stand outside alone, so I take the risk and unlock the door.

Inside, I'm afraid to turn on the lights.

With only the glow from my phone, I go to disarm the security system, only to discover its wires have been cut.

Heart pounding, I walk toward the back of the bakery and peer through the doors. No one is there. But the window high on the back wall has been smashed. Glass litters the counter and floor.

My hands tremble as I call Sarah.

She greets me with a cheery "Good morning, Yael. I'm on my way!"

As soon as I blurt out a single word—her name—she realizes something is wrong. Terribly wrong.

I briefly describe what I found, and she shifts into high gear, firing off questions, starting with "Are you okay?"

"Yes."

"Did you call the police?"

"No."

She tells me to sit tight. She's calling the police. I'm supposed to dial 911 if I notice anything even remotely suspicious before she gets here.

I go into the bathroom and lock the door.

I can't stop shaking.

Within minutes I hear sirens.

The police arrive before Sarah.

I'm answering their questions, explaining what little I know—which is basically nothing—when she bursts in.

She immediately sends me home in a cab, promises to call me as soon as she has any updates. In the meantime, the shop will be closed, so I should take it easy, not worry. The important thing is that I am unharmed.

When I get home, Bubbe is still asleep.

The *whoosh* as I flush the toilet is loud enough in the quiet house to wake her. She comes downstairs to see what's happening.

"Yael?" she says. "What are you doing here?"

I tell her about the vandalism, the red paint, the slurs, someone climbing through the back window.

She shakes her head. "Why am I not surprised?"

Over breakfast—which doesn't include bagels—she questions whether I can continue to work there safely.

"No way I'm quitting," I say. "If I quit, they win."

She sees my point but says she is worried about my safety. That's what grandmothers do, she insists.

We sit around for so long talking about all this that my phone rings before we've cleared the table.

It's Sarah.

She says the crew she hired has already started cleaning up. Someone is arriving soon to fix the window. And someone else to install a better security system. All the damage will be taken care of by the end of the day. The shop will open again tomorrow. "I would totally understand," she says, "if you don't feel ready or safe to come in."

I tell her I'm absolutely returning tomorrow.

"Thank you," she says, then adds, "I'm not sure everyone will be so courageous." She explains that she is making some procedural changes. For one, I won't be opening the store early by myself anymore. She will meet me there tomorrow. From now on, we will have at least two people in the store at all times.

Although I go straight to bed after dinner, I can't fall asleep. I assured both Sarah and Bubbe that I'm okay, but the truth is I'm scared to death.

A wave of homesickness drenches me. Like I haven't felt in ages. I burrow my face in my pillow so Bubbe won't hear me panic sobbing.

But then I realize this could happen in Brooklyn too. And I recall stats I learned in a sociology class: Jews are 2 percent of the US population but are on the receiving end of about 70 percent of hate crimes.

I wonder if Bubbe's fear is also keeping her awake. If her pillow is as wet as mine.

After no more than an hour of sleep, I get up, shower and dress, and hurry to the shop.

Sarah is waiting in her car outside. The streetlights—presumably broken by the same people who vandalized the shop—have been fixed, and the area is brightly lit.

She unlocks the front door, and we go in together.

A quick check shows no sign of new damage.

Sarah gives me a hug, and we get to work making bagels. As we've always done.

We bake our usual quantity, but when the shop opens at seven o'clock, there's a line around the block. Word has gotten out, and the community is here to support us.

Of course we run out of bagels and have to scramble to bake more batches. We never manage to catch up, and some people are still waiting in line when it's time to close. It's been a busy but cheerful day. Almost like a celebration. But under the surface, I know everyone is feeling the tension.

There's a lot of discussion over the next few days.

Everyone on the team decides to stay. Nobody has serious thoughts about bailing.

Sarah jokes she'll have to hire more employees and stock up on supplies to feed the masses now showing up at the store, hungering for a bagel. She laughs about it, but we know this is her dark humor speaking.

We also spend time debating what specifically might have led to the attack.

No one comes up with an explanation that makes sense. Sarah insists she didn't post or say anything that conveyed any kind of political message. She's not a political person, she says. Most of her posts are of kids eating bagels, cool latte foam art, pumpkin bagels for Halloween, heart-shaped bagels for Valentine's Day. Her most recent post showed double-crested cormorants flying low over the lake at sunrise. She scrolls through her social media accounts to see if she was hacked. Nothing.

We have to conclude the shop was attacked simply because we sell . . . bagels.

Everyone understands what that means.

It's a distressing truth, but there's nothing we can do about it. Except live with it. Hiring a full-time security guard, Sarah admits, would be ideal, but a bagel shop with a handful of employees can't be expected to carry the expense. Even with our increased sales, it's unsustainable. She points instead to all the community support we've received and says we shouldn't let a few bad actors stop us.

Gradually life goes back to something that resembles normal. The fear the attack generated subsides. We're making bagels, selling bagels, eating bagels. And becoming closer friends.

Amira and I bond over the fact that she spent most of her childhood in Queens. We're both New Yorkers who measure everything we encounter here against what we knew there. She suggests we visit the Art Institute—says I'll love it; it's second only to the Met. Fortunately they have days with free admission for residents. The problem is finding a weekday we can both take off. We're determined to make that happen.

* *

It's a Tuesday morning, unseasonably warm for mid-May, a few minutes before the shop opens. As usual, we're all scurrying around.

Amira is troubleshooting a technical issue with the point-of-sale system. Hugo is assembling ingredients to mix dough for the next batch. I'm removing some onion bagels that ended up in the rack for plain bagels. It's annoying when that happens, especially when someone complains about a couple of onion flakes on their plain bagel.

Sarah is writing our specials for the day on the board. Kombu butter schmear tops the list.

Suddenly there's a loud crash at the front window.

We all turn at once.

A young man has broken the glass and jumped inside. Several others follow. They're moving fast, taking advantage of our surprise. Our shock. Our terror.

They grab the three of us.

Spit in our faces.

We scream and scratch and claw back. The alarm is blaring. But none of it makes a difference. Within seconds, we've been overpowered.

Hugo rushes in from the kitchen. But he's no match for the two guys who throw him into a choke hold, then whip out guns and herd the four of us so we're lined up along the wall by the refrigerator.

Two attackers face us. Three more guard the broken window.

They're all young, no older than high school. Kids, really. Their eyes dart from one to the other. It's clear they have a plan and are going to execute it—before anyone responds to the alarm. Which should be any second now.

"We're here," one spits out, "to finish the job."

They take aim. Shoot down the line, starting with Sarah.

I'm on the far end.

I am last.

Zoe

I am Zoe and I am nine years old. I live in Tucson, Arizona, with my mom and dad and baby brother, Richard. I am in fourth grade. My pronouns are she/her.

Sometimes I hate school.

Today is one of those days. It doesn't matter that I like learning and get good grades; it's school that's the problem.

At dinner, after we all sit down as a family—and Richie is strapped into his high chair—Dad says grace. Then he asks me the same question he always asks: "How was school today?"

Yesterday I told him and Mom about the cave paintings we did in art class. The real ones were painted forty thousand years ago and had animals in them. So I put a rabbit and a cat and a couple of handprints in mine. Even though I used brand-new oil pastels, it still looked old. Mom made me promise to bring it home so she can hang it up.

Today was a yuck day.

The most honest answer to Dad's question would be "I hate school." But I can't say that without setting him off, so I just stare at my spaghetti. One meatball is in a pasta stranglehold. When we did monkey rolls on the mat in gym, Doug put another kid in a stranglehold, and Mr. Evans had to rescue him. I'm not going to rescue this meatball. Maybe if I keep staring at my plate, Dad will forget his question.

But he repeats it, adding my name, as if I might have thought he was speaking to someone else: "Zoe, how was school?"

I have to say something. "It was fine."

Mom frowns. I'm sure she suspects I'm doing what she calls "fudging the truth." Whenever she says that, I picture someone smearing chocolate frosting all over me with a plastic spatula. But my feeling about school right now is anything but sweet.

"Tell us more," she says. "Tell us what you did in history."

She thinks if she asks about something I like, I'll feel better and say something positive. She knows how much I love history. I love learning about how people used to live in this world when it was still young. I bet they knew some things we don't know anymore. Except in this moment, Mom couldn't be more wrong.

I tell her exactly what we did in history today: "We had an active shooter drill."

She looks surprised. "In history?"

"Uh-huh."

"Oka-a-a-y," Dad says slowly. He knows how much I dislike those drills. That bugs him. The last time after we had a drill and I told him how I felt, he called me a crybaby.

I know I'm not a crybaby, but I don't want to hear him say that again. So I keep quiet.

There's a long silence.

Richie interrupts it by throwing a handful of peas onto the floor.

Mom jumps up and runs toward the kitchen for a towel, but Dad stops her and directs her to sit back down.

Which she does.

Richie just had his first birthday, so he won't start kindergarten for years. The day he does can't come soon enough for me. When the two of us are in school, Dad can focus on him instead.

For now, it's all on me.

And Dad isn't finished. "You know, Zoe," he says, "those drills are important for your safety."

I'm just a kid, and I don't know if he's right about that. Maybe he is. All I know for sure is that drills don't make me feel any safer.

In history today, I was scared. Pee-in-my-pants scared. Afterward, when I had to wash the fake blood off my chair, I thought I was about to throw up.

I don't explain any of this to Dad, though. I just say, "I hate drills."

Mom tries to make peace. It's what she does. "Sweetie," she says, "drills don't happen very often."

As far as I'm concerned, even one a year would be too often. I explain that Mr. Evans said we're having another one after the holidays. I don't want to be part of it. "Please, Mom," I say, "will you please, please write me a note?"

Before she can say anything, Dad interrupts. He's angry now. "Your mom and I aren't writing any notes! None of the other kids are complaining. What makes you so special that *you* should be excused?"

I don't want to say I'm scared, don't want to make him angrier—maybe even lose his temper—so I hang my head and mutter something I know he can't hear.

But he can tell I'm scared. Being scared is not okay for any child of his. "Cut the garbage!" he cries. "Drills save lives. They're just simulations, a kind of—what do you call it?—make-believe."

"It doesn't feel like make-believe."

"Since when are you such a fraidy-cat?" He spits out the words. "I got you a phone, didn't I? If there is a real problem, all you have to do is call me. Really, time to toughen up, kid!"

There's no point arguing. He won't budge. Besides, I'm not hungry anymore. I push what's left of my spaghetti—which is most of it—to the side of my plate and ask if I can go do my homework.

Mom looks at me, then at Dad. When he doesn't object, she says, "Okay, sweetie, you can go to your room. But no desserts or snacks."

I only have one worksheet for math, so I finish it quickly, then curl up on my bed with a book I checked out from the library. Of course it's about history. I still like some make-believe stories, even if I'm getting a bit old for them, but I like historical books even better. The people in them seem so real. I read one about Joan of Arc. Now I'm reading about Harriet Tubman. Only her name wasn't Harriet when she was little; it was Araminta. Such a cool name. And her nickname was Minty.

I'm on the chapter where she is younger than me and has to work as a nursemaid. She sits next to the baby and rocks its cradle. If the baby wakes up and cries, Minty gets a whipping. I can't imagine having to go through that. Maybe I do need to get tougher.

Reading makes me forget about school, about active shooter drills, about arguing with Dad. About how to get Mom to write me an excuse.

I read until I get sleepy. One minute I'm following the words on the page and thinking about Minty driving oxen; the next, no one is forcing her to do slave labor, and we're somewhere playing together.

I have to pry my eyes open so I can read more.

Now she's older. She has been sent on an errand to the dry goods store. While she is there, a field hand runs in, chased by his overseer. The overseer demands Minty help tie up the man. She refuses. Instead she blocks the doorway so he can escape. She sure has guts! The overseer throws a heavy counterweight at the man to stop him. It hits Minty in the head.

I'm crying.

I put the book down and imagine I'm in the store. With Minty. I kneel beside her, wrap my arms around her. I tell her she's my best friend and I love her. My hands have a magic power. When I place them on her head, the bleeding stops. Her skull is mended. She smiles at me, and we pick each other up and run away together.

But then I think, *What if there is no such thing as make-believe? No magic power?*

Now I'm back in the store, but without Minty. The overseer is yelling at me—at *me*—to tie up the man. No one has ever glared at me with such hatred. He could kill me. All he has to do is lift his hand and beat me. Or throw that counterweight he is holding.

Would I stand up to him? Would I block his way?

I wish I could say yes.

But the truth is I wouldn't dare. I don't have the courage.

I need to read more and find out how Minty was able to be so brave.

But I check my phone and it's almost nine o'clock. Time for bed. So I stick a bookmark in the story. Then I wash my face, brush my teeth, and put on my pajamas.

Every night, I hug my parents before I go to sleep. Mom lets me go into Richie's room and blow him a kiss, as long as I don't wake him up. I want to do that now, but I'm not ready to give Dad a hug. I'd rather stay here, pretend I'm still in Minty's world and we're falling asleep next to each other.

Except I'm worried about Richie. If I don't go down and blow him a kiss, will he feel bad even though he's always asleep when I do it?

As I consider this, there's a tap on my door.

Mom pokes her head through the crack and asks, "Can I come in?"

She's already halfway across the room before I've answered.

She sits on the edge of my bed and strokes my head. "Everything okay, sweetie?" This is her way of showing me she understands why I don't want to go downstairs. She's being extra nice to make up for Dad. She never disagrees with him to his face, but later she finds a way to let me know she's on my side.

Now she says, "I thought you might be in bed already, so I came up to say goodnight."

For a second, I consider asking if she'll write me that excuse. If she's really on my side, maybe she will. Dad doesn't have to know. But then I think it might be better to wait a few days. There's still plenty of time before the next active shooter drill.

After she's tucked in my coverlet and hugged me, she goes over to my dresser. Five teddy bears are sitting on top. They used to sleep with me, arranged on my pillow like a little family. I'm going to give them to Richie soon. In the meantime, Dad jokes I'm managing a teddy bear retirement community.

Mom selects a bear in plaid overalls. "Who's this?" she asks. "I'm sorry I've forgotten their names."

"Cubby."

She brings him over.

I remind her I don't sleep with my bears anymore. Haven't in a while.

"I know," she says. "But Cubby could use some extra loving tonight."

I'm about to jump all over her for treating me like a little kid who thinks their toys need comforting. Who doesn't know the difference between make-believe and real. But then I remember this is her way of showing she cares. So I take Cubby and find a comfy spot for him on my pillow.

Mom leans down and gives me another hug. "Sweet dreams," she whispers.

As soon as I fall asleep, I'm in a dream.

I'm at school, in history class.

Mr. Evans is teaching about the Texas Revolution. Each of us has to read aloud a paragraph from our textbook.

My turn is first.

I haven't read even one complete sentence when he interrupts. "What's wrong with you?" he bellows. "Where's your gun? If you're reading about the revolution, you need a gun."

That's a shock. I mean, a *gun*? In *class*?

I look around the room. Cory doesn't have a gun. Doug doesn't have a gun. Portia doesn't have a gun. Nobody has a gun.

Abruptly the dream shifts. I'm still in history class, but now a piercing alarm is going off.

It can't be another active shooter drill! We just had one!

"They're going to kill us with these drills," Doug says.

Nobody laughs.

We stand up and start to move, slowly, grumbling and griping, as Mr. Evans herds us toward the closet. Nobody's into this. We know it's not real. It's just another stupid drill.

Plus I'm annoyed at myself. Why did I wait to ask Mom for an excuse?

Before we can all pile into the closet, there is a loud crash on the other side of the room.

We turn our heads to see what it is.

A man in military clothes has smashed a hole in the window with his gun.

This isn't a drill.

"Don't move!" he shouts.

We all freeze.

It's as if the walls are closing in and the room is shrinking. The entire room, with all of us and all our desks, is only the size of a closet now. We're huddled together in this small space.

Mr. Evans is cowering like the rest of us.

The man points his gun first at one kid, then another. He asks each one why he should spare them. He doesn't like any of their answers. So he shoots them. One after the other after the other, they all fall. Even Mr. Evans.

I'm the only one left.

As I stare up at the man, I am holding Cubby in my arms.

"Why should I save you?" he demands.

I search for an answer that would stop him from killing me. I can't think of anything clever or convincing. Really, I have no power: Either he will kill me or he won't.

"Tell me why!" he insists.

"Because I want to live."

I'm sure that's a wrong answer, but he doesn't shoot me. Instead he snatches Cubby and dangles him just out of my reach. "Why should I save your bear?" he taunts.

Then he shoots Cubby. And tosses him onto a chair.

I see red liquid dripping from the chair. It's not fake blood. It's Cubby's blood.

The man says he's out of patience. Then he asks a different question: "How old are you?"

That I can answer easily. "Nine."

He says he'll count down the years I've been alive. That's all I have left. "Nine," he says. "Eight. Seven. Six. Five."

The history of my life, I think, *is so very short.*

He continues: "Four. Three."

I feel the life draining out of me. I want to get it back. But I have no power.

"Two..."

Before he can say "One," I scream. As loud as I can.

That wakes me up.

I'm in my bed. I'm panting, shaking, clutching Cubby.

It was just a dream.

Just a dream? But it felt so real. I'm shaking like it was real. Like there was an actual mass shooting in my history class. Everyone died. And I survived.

I want to run down the hall to my parents' bedroom and tell Mom I had a scary dream. I want her to cuddle me and say, "It's okay, sweetie. It was just a dream."

I place Cubby on the pillow, push aside my quilt, and start to climb out of bed.

But then I think of Dad hearing my dream was about an active shooter drill. He wouldn't understand. No way.

I can't go to their room.

I go over to my dresser and turn on my phone. It's 2:30 a.m.

I'm still alive, I tell myself. *I'm nine years old, and I survived a school shooting.* Not like that's something to be proud of.

In the morning, I'll walk into my history class and see all my friends. And even some kids I don't like that much. They won't know that every last one of them is supposed to be dead. They won't know that only I survived. Nobody will know any of that. But I will. I'm never, ever going to forget this. I'm certain of that.

But what do I do about it?

I go back to my bed and crawl under the covers, and think.

Being a survivor makes me feel that I have to do something. I have to do it on behalf of those who didn't survive. And all those who won't survive the next shooting. And the one after that.

Earlier, it seemed so important to get Mom to write me an excuse. Now that doesn't seem so helpful. I still don't like drills. I still don't want to participate. But getting a note from Mom won't save lives.

So what can I do?

If so many survivors haven't stopped mass shootings, what could I possibly do?

I think of Minty. What would *she* do? My life is nothing like hers. I have no idea what it's really like to be a slave. But we do have one thing in common: the need for courage.

So I do what I imagine someone with courage would do.

Sitting here in my bed in the middle of the night, I start by making a list of all my friends. Because I can't do this alone.

Then I take my phone and message them, tell them we have something to talk about. Something super important. Something that can't wait. When they check their phones in the morning and see I texted at 3:00 a.m., they'll know this kid means business.

I don't know exactly what I'll say to them or what we should do. I just know it doesn't matter if no one has succeeded yet, we must do everything we possibly can to keep another kid from being shot, to stop all these deaths from happening . . .

Book Club Questions for *Shot*

1. Which person's story in *Shot* do you identify with most closely? What about it—and about you—leads you to feel this way?

2. Which story did you find most emotionally difficult to read? What about that story made it so?

3. Do you have any firsthand experience with gun violence or a mass shooting? If so, how has it affected you? If not, how have you been affected by what you have read or heard about instances of gun violence?

4. Pick one story and provide an alternative ending. At what point do you have to make a change in the story to get an outcome you would prefer? What does this exercise tell you about what is necessary to end gun violence?

5. If you were Fuji, would you have responded the way he did in the instant he saw TJ holding a gun? If not, what would you have done?

6. Ginger decided not to attend a rally due to her fear of a shooting; Owen avoided movie theaters for a similar reason. Have mass shootings influenced where you (and/or family members) go? If so, how do you handle that?

7. Rob comments on the epidemic of hate and asks why humans have so much hate. What would you say to him about that? How do you understand the relationship between hate and gun violence?

8. Do you own or plan to purchase a gun? Why or why not?

9. Which is more important to you—assuming you can't say "both" and must choose one: protecting the rights of gun owners or preventing deaths from gun violence? Why?

10. What three things would you be willing to commit to doing toward the goal of reducing gun violence?

11. Zoe doesn't want to participate in active shooter drills at school. If you were her parent, what would you say to her?

12. At the end of the book, we don't know exactly what Zoe will do with her friends. What would you advise them to do? How would you assess their chances for success?

Acknowledgments

My deepest thanks to my steadfast friend Penelope Shackelford, who followed my every step on this journey. Thank you also to Heidi Yewman and Jenny Goldsmith for offering your deep sensitivity to make this book better.

Great thanks and admiration to Brooke Warner of She Writes Press/SparkPress for her revolutionary vision and contributions to the publishing world, and to Lauren Wise, Shannon Green, and all the dedicated members of the publishing team. Many thanks also to Julia Drake of Wildbound PR for everything she does to get my books out into the world.

If you enjoyed this book, please consider leaving a review on your preferred site. New authors, indie authors, and books like *Shot* can only thrive with the support of wonderful people like you who take the time and energy to let others know about them. Feel free to spread the word in whatever way feels good to you.

About the Author

Photo credit: Jude Berman

Jude Berman grew up amid floor-to-ceiling shelves of books in many languages. In addition to a love of literature, her refugee parents instilled in her a deep appreciation for cultural diversity and social justice. Jude has a BA in art from Smith College and an EdD in cross-cultural communication from UMass Amherst. After a career in academic research, she built a freelance writing and editing business and ran two small indie presses. She lives in Berkeley, California, where she continues to work with authors and write fiction. In her free time, she volunteers for civic causes, paints with acrylic watercolors, gardens, and meditates. She blogs at https://judeberman.substack.com and https://judeberman.org.

Looking for your next great read?

We can help!

Visit www.shewritespress.com/next-read
or scan the QR code below for a list
of our recommended titles.

She Writes Press is an award-winning
independent publishing company founded to
serve women writers everywhere.